The Christmas Ghosts

of

Rothery Hall.

The Ghost from the Molly-House

Grahame Peace

The Christmas Ghost of Rothery Hall. The Ghost from the Molly-House.

CONTENTS

Christmas Wishes.

Oh, happy Christmas, full of blessings, come!
Now bid our discords cease;
Here give the weary ease;
Let the long-parted meet again in peace;
Bring back the far-away;
Grant us a holiday;
And by the hopes of Christmas-tide we pray--
Let love restore the fallen to his Home;
Whilst up and down the snowy streets the Christmas minstrels sing;
And through the frost from countless towers the bells of
Christmas ring.

Ah, Christ! and yet a happier day shall come!
Then bid our discords cease;
There give the weary ease;
Let the long-parted meet again in peace;
Bring back the far-away;
Grant us a holiday;
And by the hopes of Christmas-tide we pray--
Let love restore the fallen to his Home;
Whilst up and down the golden streets the blessed angels sing,
And evermore the heavenly chimes in heavenly cadence ring.

Juliana Horatia Ewing

PROLOGUE

My name is Jasper Claxton; I was born in 1706 in London, England. I can remember some things about my life from that time but not everything, although there are many things I don't want to remember. The past is the past, and for me, that is where it belongs. Although it can teach us many lessons, that is, of course, if we're willing to listen and learn. However, memories can feel like a burden, and I don't remember ever having any hopes, dreams, or aspirations.

I never knew my parents, and I don't know if I ever had any brothers, sisters, aunts, or uncles. I remember being one of many who were in the orphanages of the period and the cruelty, hardship, and injustices of that time. It was a world full of ignorance, difficulty, and fear. Although I know, for many, the world still is today, yet the solutions to me seem simple. Surely most people would spend their lives in joyful service, working towards building a healthy, loving world if due care and consideration, food, shelter, and a modest standard of living were provided. But I guess someone somewhere will always want the last fish in the sea.

For me, everything stopped in 1726 - I remember being cold, glacially cold; everything was so bleak and austere. The biting winter winds howled, my body was weak, my legs were frozen, I couldn't move my limbs. My breathing became shallow; I slowly closed my eyes, and the harsh world I knew faded forever into darkness.

So now I'm gone from your physical world, and although I'm in a much better place, I find I'm unable to describe it to you. I have a thousand questions I can't ever seem to answer. All I can say is I feel safe, at great peace and content, not happy or sad, and I drift between the past and your present when you call me. Although you won't know you've called me, in fact, some of you won't even remember me after I've gone, but I hope I leave you in a better place during your time in this world.

When I was born, I was put in a parish house or orphanage for the relief of the poor. This represented a vital parish building and came to serve as the focus for many parish activities beyond just the comfort of the poor. I was lucky because, for a time, I was provided with the necessary food, some primary education, rudimentary health care, and clean clothing. However, many children were brutally treated, and the death rate amongst children was high.

When I was around eight, I was apprenticed to a weaver for textile labour, working 12-hour shifts. I slept in a small barracks attached to the factory in beds just vacated by other children about to start the next shift. As an orphan, the workhouse, as they became known, was a given and never a choice for me. But in the harsh economic poverty of the time, many people were reluctant to enter workhouses and resorted instead to begging on the streets.

The early eighteenth century was an era of severe and cruel punishment; in my day, beggars were a familiar feature of most towns and cities. They would be found around shops, markets, and other busy places, which were smelly, noisy, and chaotic; all aspects of life could be seen.

Begging was a hazardous activity; vagrancy remained illegal throughout the century, and beggars were regularly whipped and imprisoned in 'Houses of Correction'. Criminals convicted of lesser crimes were fined, branded, or shamed in front of the public by being whipped or being set in the pillory (a wooden framework with holes for the head and hands, in which offenders were formerly imprisoned and exposed to public abuse and pelted with rotten eggs and vegetables).

Prostitution was another highly visible alternative to pauperdom. Many vulnerable young girls and boys were forced or tricked into prostitution through their failure or inability to secure work. In London, scores of streetwalkers openly plied their trade not only on the streets but in the capital's theatres and taverns. Dozens of infamous and dangerous bawdyhouses could be found up narrow alleyways and down side streets; sexual activity was a very public affair in the London of the 1700s.

I finally escaped the workhouse on the Lord's Day, a church Sunday in 1720. I was lucky to find work as a scullion (a menial servant) with Master Taylor at The Silver Cross Tavern in Whitehall, London, which was a prominent meeting place, a place for socialising and business where people gathered to drink alcoholic beverages and be served food. It was hard work, but it offered some occasional respite from the misery and grind of daily life.

In 1724 while working for Master Taylor, I met Mistress Margaret Clap, who ran a coffee house at her private residence in Holborn, London. She felt that I seemed 'agreeable' and offered me regular employment as a scullion along with simple board and lodgings.

I soon learned that her coffee shop served as a Molly-House for the underground homosexual community, also known as sodomites; today, you would call it the 'Gay' community. Not that it concerned me, life has a clarity when you're in danger, and I had been surrounded by thieves, criminals, ragamuffins, drifters, vagabonds, and prostitutes and seen double standards many times from those seen as paragons of virtue within the aristocracy, church, and local community.

I judged people on their character, honesty, and how they treated me and others, not on their sexual proclivities. Daily survival makes you develop a sixth sense where this is concerned; you do what you must do to survive.

I can only speak as I find, Mistress Clap or Mother Clap as she was known and her husband, Master John, showed me some basic kindness and consideration. This was the first place in my life I could ever think of as any kind of home. Mistress Clap looked after her customers; we would have thirty or forty chaps every night, but more on

Sunday nights.

*We had regular customers and paying guests who were friends of Mistress Clap. Of course, at that time, homosexual activities were illegal and heavily prosecuted and remained capital offences until 1861, when the death penalty for sodomy was repealed. Our customers lived in a dangerous underworld. Many lived in secret, not daring to talk about love and relationships; they became the ideal target for exploiters, blackmailers, and vicious entrapments. It certainly opened my eyes.

*Mistress Clap and I were always present during the Molly-House's working hours, and I would often run across the street to a local tavern, the 'Bunch o'Grapes', to buy drinks for our customers. Some thought of Mistress Clap's house as a brothel, but she intended to provide a safe meeting place where men could relax and socialise.

*On a Sunday night in February 1726, the Molly-House was raided by a squadron of police constables; we were all arrested and taken to Newgate prison. The police were unlike the police forces you think of today. In London, a system of paid watchmen operated across different parishes; they performed various duties on top of the detection and arrest of suspected criminals. The Molly-House had been under observation for some time. The surveillance was instigated by a collection of vengeful informants who led policemen into Molly-Houses, introducing each of them so that they could investigate the goings-on more thoroughly.

*Mistress Clap was eventually found guilty of keeping a disorderly house and encouraging customers to commit sodomy. We were sentenced to stand in the Smithfield Market pillory, pay a fine, and two years' imprisonment. I was terrified; I never saw Mistress Clap again.

I remember how Newgate prison was swarming with lice and vermin and full of emaciated people, all with diseases expiring on the floors in cramped loathsome cells; we were lucky to get two pennyworths of bread a day. The cruelty, stench, and decay were torments; I will never forget the awful smell. I prayed and pleaded with

God to help me, begging him for mercy, but he didn't seem to hear me.

I spent my time caring for the many sick until my demise, along with numerous others, from disease, starvation, and hypothermia that same year. The average life expectancy in the 18th century was only forty, so I guess I managed to live out half of my life, such as it was, which is more than many others did.

For a while after my death, I found myself drawn back to Mistress Clap's Molly House in Holborn, it gave me some comfort when my tears took the place of rain, and the sunshine failed me once again. I don't know how I ended up in my ghostly world and if there are others like me, or how long it will last. Could it be forever? That I cannot answer. But in my life, I've met many people with blood on their hands, people who have killed, maimed, imprisoned, and tortured their victims. I've witnessed terrible cruelty, wrongdoing, and experienced awful hardship.

I'm not a vengeful ghost, but now it's time to do the right thing. I can appear anytime, anyplace, anywhere. You see, I'm drawn to fighting injustice, and the odd troublesome spirit, of which there are many. I now travel through time and try to work for the greater good, although it's often complicated and rarely straightforward.

My ghostly past is always with me, it has a strange way of residing in the present and often catches me off guard because one day I'm in Paris in 1849, and the next I could be in Africa in 1410, but I always try to blend in. A rainy day in England can suddenly remind me of a thousand rainy days I've experienced all over the world in different periods.

Jean-Baptiste Alphonse Karr, the 19th-century French critic, journalist, and novelist, said something to me in 1849 while I was in Paris, which I have never forgotten, 'Plus ça change, plus c'est la même chose'. Meaning, 'The more it changes, the more it's the same thing.' Often translated as 'The more things change, the more they stay the same.' And I can relate to that because time travel has given me an eidetic memory and vast knowledge and an aptitude and understanding of people. I can read people, it's hard to describe, but it's often the little things that give people away, a nuance, a hesitation, a gesture. Winston Churchill said the farther backward you can look, the farther forward you can see, and I can only agree with him. However, I'd add to that and say the more you know about history, the more you know yourself.

Rictor Norton, "Mother Clap's Molly House", The Gay Subculture in Georgian England, 5th February 2005 <http://rictornorton.co.uk/eighteen/mother.htm>.

Chapter 1

Edmund Rothery stood for a long moment, slowly rubbing his temples, trying to steady himself. He had another dizzy spell; they'd started a few days ago; he wondered what could be causing them. His head throbbed as his vision swam; he felt like he was walking through a dark, spinning tunnel towards a blinding light; it was eerie. He closed his eyes and rubbed his arms vigorously, almost hugging himself in the process. It was something he did unconsciously when he felt vulnerable and needed to reassure himself.

He blinked several times, trying to focus his eyes, the dizziness passed, and he slowly gazed around him. Everything in the house looked the same, just as it always had going back to when his father was alive; the place hadn't changed in as long as Edmund could remember; he found that reassuring. Yet he couldn't shake off the unsettling feeling something was different, that something was wrong. He prided himself on preserving the house just as it had always been - in doing so, he felt he was keeping his parents' and even his grandparents' memory alive, maintaining the Rothery family history.

Edmund felt out of sorts with himself and at odds with his surroundings, distant, almost detached as if nothing was real; he shuddered as an icy chill ran through him, not that he was cold – he wondered why he didn't feel the cold, the thought flashed in and out of his mind. In fact, he felt nothing - strangely removed from his surroundings, like he was a casual observer, a fly on the wall. He gave an incongruous smile shaking his head, wondering how that could be, questioning his grasp on reality.

He sighed; it was a long weary sigh filled with conflicting emotions. He pinched himself hard, wanting to feel something because he felt peculiar - like he was having a bad dream, but it wasn't a dream. He sniffed the air deeply and loudly, wanting to capture homely smells, smells to soothe the soul. After all, it was Christmas; it had always been his favourite time of year, a time for family, peace, carols, gifts, feasting, and goodwill to all men.

As he inhaled, Edmund expected the comforting smells of Christmas; smells firmly locked in his memory, reminding him of the seasonal good cheer he'd experienced in this grand house throughout his life. The bitter holly, the refreshing scent of pine from the decorated spruce tree. The mouth-watering aromas from the food baking and cooking in the kitchen, sweet pastries, moreish buttery ginger biscuits, spiced plum pudding, succulent pies, along with meats and poultry roasting in the oven. Then there was the aromatic smell of cedarwood burning on the raging fires in the ornate fireplaces, filling the rooms not only with warmth but a welcoming amber glow. A glow guaranteed to warm the heart, bring good cheer, and make even the darkest day seem better. The radiance and warmth were like a big hug.

His mouth curled into a smile at the memory, then he sighed again, feeling deflated. He smelled nothing, at least nothing familiar; the air had a peculiar smell, earthy, but unlike anything he'd smelled before, he couldn't describe it. Edmund shook his head, feeling perplexed, unable to suppress the nagging notion that something wasn't quite right; it had been gnawing away at him for some time, but he couldn't say for how long.

What a strange year 1901 had turned out to be, a terrible year; Edmund didn't think anything could get worse after the death of Queen Victoria, but he was wrong. She passed away at Osbourne House on the Isle of Wight, surrounded by her family; she reached the grand old age of 81. It was the end of an era, plunging the country into a period of mourning. Her 63-year reign was the longest in British history; many, including Edmund, never knowing any other monarch. The British Empire now had King Edward VII, her eldest son, known as 'Bertie'.

Edmund chewed on his lip; the year had changed him. He'd seen a new side of himself. As the saying goes, he was older and wiser, but it had come at a high price. In a way, he was more patient, considerate, and rounded, with a better understanding of the fragility of life and how precious it was. However, the journey had been intolerable, more than he and his darling wife Violet could bear. They'd lost a significant part of themselves, which he doubted would ever return.

He reflected on everything that had happened, but as hard as he tried, his mind drew a blank. His heart felt heavy, it was filled with longing and despair, and there was something else - fear, an all-consuming fear leaving him feeling hopeless and powerless. He shook his head in exasperation; he wanted and needed to remember – why had he shut everything out?

He searched his mind for pleasant, heartening memories, and eventually, dear old Reverend Anslem came into his thoughts. He considered what the Reverend had said to him during their private prayers in church last Sunday following the service. The Reverend saying Edmund and his dear wife Violet were having an 'annus horribilis', and he should believe in the power of prayer and not lose hope because God worked in mysterious ways.

Indeed, God did. Edmund wanted to believe that more than anything. For months through prayer, he'd been trying to do a deal with God. Edmund wasn't sure he believed in the power of prayer, but he tried his best, thinking to himself the things we do for love, although in his case, it was desperation. However, God didn't seem to hear him, leaving him feeling desperate and despondent. Annoying tears pricked at his eyes; he thought of his beautiful wife Violet and what the past year had done to her; worry had made her a shadow of her former self. He tried to stop his tears but couldn't; they came from deep within his soul.

He couldn't remember exactly when the thought had come to him, but he decided he must take control and find his own miracle; he'd given God a chance and it wasn't working; perhaps God was too busy. Edmund did what he thought any educated and resourceful person would do and sought other solutions, even those outside the orthodoxy. He banished all forms of negativity from his mind, fearing that if he didn't, the worse would happen. He called his search 'the path to restoration'.

He sought out new wisdom and hoped to make discoveries to help himself and others; nothing was off-limits. However, those closest to him, including Reverend Anslem, told him he had to stop denying what was happening close around him, particularly at home; he needed to accept the inevitable and God's will. At times, the Reverend questioned Edmund's sanity and judgment. It was like Edmund believed the answers he craved were blowing somewhere in the wind.

He considered Edmund's actions wild, reckless, and dangerous, telling him he was meddling with things he didn't understand and would face God's reckoning. The Reverend knew desperation could do strange things to people and drive them away from God's righteous path. Of course, Edmund wasn't the first to seek new forms of wisdom, and he wouldn't be the last. But in Edmund's case, it just seemed to add to his trauma and distress; he appeared to be losing his grasp on reality.

Edmund had an inquiring mind and was convinced the answers he sought were out there; he just had to find them. The Reverend knew this; he'd served in the parish for many years, knowing Montague Rothery, Edmund's father, the town's highly respected magistrate. He'd admired Montague's thirst for knowledge, and in many ways, Edmund was just like him. However, the Reverend felt it was his duty as God's messenger to guide Edmund through what he considered to be a period of severe emotional trauma, religious conflict, and cerebral confusion.

He didn't hold back and raised his concerns, warning Edmund of his actions and associations. The Reverend knew little of Edmund's surreptitious behaviour but continually feared the worse. The Reverend insisted Edmund was committing heresy and should follow God's righteous path, devoting his attention to the Bible, putting himself entirely in God's hands, not ancient cults with pagan beliefs, spells, and magic.

Of course, people in the village sympathised and questioned what they would do in his situation. His family were hardly the first to succumb to illness and sadly wouldn't be the last; the church graveyard could testify to that; it grew bigger almost by the day. 'There for the grace of God go I', as the saying goes. However, Edmund had grown tired of people's sympathy and pity; what good did pity ever do anyone, he thought. Decisive actions were needed; they spoke far louder than words and people's prayers.

He stood on the landing, distracted from his solitary revere by the sound of gusting wind. It rattled the glass in the windows, howling like a demon as a brooding full moon appeared from behind a dark ragged cloud, the white-gold light cutting through the inky darkness. The house creaked as if it was responding to the violent wind and sudden light - creaks were a familiar sound in this groaning old house, particularly at night.

Edmund glanced across the dreary landing lined with portraits of his ancestors. Their sombre faces had watching eyes; they all looked to be staring at him disapprovingly. Sometimes he talked to them when he needed guidance or to gather his thoughts; he smiled, not that they ever answered back. However, Edmund didn't feel like talking today; he wasn't in the mood. It was getting darker in the house; he wished he'd brought an oil lamp and rubbed his arms again.

He could hear the steady tick-tock of the stately grandfather clock downstairs in the hall, another familiar sound; it was like the beating heart of the house. The clock had stood there for many years, long before Edmund was born, watching the comings and goings in the house while marking the passing of time; if only it could talk. He found the slow, rhythmic, tick and tock comforting; it had always been a constant in the household; it took him back to happier days and childhood memories. Edmund was meticulous about his clock winding in the house, just like his father had been - it was a weekly ritual.

The constant tick-tock made him wonder about the time; for some reason, it had taken him longer than usual to reach the landing. He patted his waistcoat pockets, searching for his gold pocket watch – how strange, he didn't have it. His heart sank; it had been his father's and grandfather's before him; it was precious to him. He couldn't remember putting it down anywhere and hoped he hadn't lost it. Perhaps Violet would know where it was; he always seemed to forget things these days.

In the gloom, he tried to recount his movements; where had he put his watch? The windows had frosted in the cold night air; he wrote his name on the clouded glass before rubbing at another window. He peered out at the moody dark sky; it twinkled with stars – the stars playing a game of hide and seek among the ominous grey clouds. One of the clouds caught his eye as it drifted across the night sky; he thought it looked like a mythical ice creature from a children's fairy tale, breathing vast plumes of snow across the night sky.

The sky looked heavy as lacy snowflakes fell at speed, swirling and twisting in a merry dance, clinging to everything they touched, forming deep drifts across the gardens, against the stables, the stone outbuildings, drystone walls, the undulating fields, and bare hedgerows beyond. As far as the eye could see, snow covered everything in a perfect, crisp white blanket, creating a cocoon, muffling all sounds. Everything was still, so silent. No matter how hazardous and impractical, the snow made everything look better – pure, smooth, and perfect; it hid all imperfections, making everything look like it had been enchanted by a fairy queen.

The falling snow cast eerie shadows across the walls and portraits on the landing; Edmund shuddered again; he still had the feeling something wasn't right. 'Pull yourself together man,' he said aloud to himself, a note of irritation creeping into his tone. Why did he feel so unsettled and out of sorts with himself?

He worried it could be the start of miasma and prayed he wasn't coming down with something. Of all people, he couldn't afford to be ill. Surely after everything he'd been through, Reverend Anslem's God wouldn't do that to him. Although in his search for wisdom, he'd recently been told that miasma didn't exist and had been replaced by something called the germ theory of diseases. This news comforted him; it gave him hope, proving his point that new wisdom was out there.

Edmund stood almost hypnotised, watching the snow as it silently settled on the gnarled bare trees which lined either side of the cobbled drive up to the house. They stood rigid and firm against the chilling seasonal gusts, like circus acrobats poised to show the world their grace. Edmund was relieved the horses were in the stable and felt sorry for any living thing caught outside in the freezing weather, fearing they would surely perish.

His feelings of unease returned; he trembled and blew on the window. He couldn't understand why his breath didn't frost in the freezing night air. He ran his hands over his body, patting himself; why didn't he feel cold? Why did the house feel empty and lifeless? He cupped his ears with his hands, listening carefully for a long moment. He sighed with relief, hearing voices coming from somewhere in the house. He concentrated hard, but as he listened, he couldn't make out the words or recognise the voices. Surely, they couldn't have visitors, he thought, not in this awful weather. Then he wondered if they might be the voices of travellers stranded in the treacherous weather seeking shelter. The sounds seemed strangely distant and faraway; Edmund assumed it was due to the muffling effect of the snow.

The falling snow focused his mind on the temperature inside; he insisted the house should always be kept warm day and night in the winter months. Peripneumonia was the devil; it had taken many in the towns and villages, both young and old. And those it didn't take, it weakened; it showed no mercy in picking out its victims. And it wasn't the only killer; lately, death and disease seemed to be all around them; bronchitis, consumption, and dropsy were common. He must find the servants and set them to work on the fires and see the stable boy checks on the horses.

Something held Edmund back; he hesitated, standing on the landing for a long moment looking out of the window; the snow was coming down faster now. He remembered he'd come upstairs to check on something, but he couldn't think what it was; neither could he remember what he'd been doing before he came upstairs. He banged his fist on the wall in frustration - what was the matter with him? He couldn't shake off the overwhelming feeling something wasn't right with him or the house; he felt stuck - like he was treading water....

Chapter 2

England 1931 The Present.

The noted spiritual medium Jocasta Bradman shook her head, 'Nooo,' she declared, hanging onto the word as her nostrils flared. She let out a long sigh of defeat, breaking the circle of the séance and standing up, trying to hide her annoyance. 'No, nothing, nothing at all, I'm afraid. I'm not sensing anything, no spirits, no psychic energy,' she stood rigid with her arms behind her back and sniffed the air as if sneering. 'And certainly not any ectoplasm, which is always a sure sign of a spiritual presence or ghostly visit,' she shook her head again. 'Yet I'm sure this grand house is no stranger to ghosts - they rarely are; I'd put my reputation on it. In older properties and historic houses, people tend to live in perfect harmony with ghosts, never knowing they exist; it's quite natural.'

Jocasta bit her lip, still shaking her head. 'It's most unusual. I may need to consult my crystal, tarot cards, or even go into a trance.' She glanced at her Gladstone bag on the floor next to her, then looked at me; well, to be more specific, her eyes locked onto mine, 'Jasper,' she said firmly as her eyes widened. 'What about you? Do you sense anything? I know you're very sensitive where any spiritual matters are concerned.'

As a time-travelling ghost, it came with the territory, not that anyone knew I was a ghost, and I obviously didn't leave a trail of ectoplasm! I glanced around the room as the roaring fire spat and crackled like it was trying to tell me something, its amber glow helping to throw light into the elegant, darkened room. On the table, the flames from the candles, held in their stylish silver candle holders, danced and flickered. Outside, a branch from a shrub tapped against the window in the whipping wind, like a message in morse code.

I'd been slightly distracted by all the Christmas cards, the colourful, sparkling Christmas tree, and the comforting smell of pine and bitter holly. I loved Christmas; we didn't have it back in my day - that is, when I was alive. I've only experienced it as a ghost, so I always try to make the most of it.

The spruce tree almost touched the ornate high ceiling. It was weighed down with colourful, sparkling decorations and dried sliced oranges tied to fragrant cinnamon sticks, scenting the room with their warm, spicy, slightly fruity, peppery fragrance. We were told some of the ornate decorations were treasured family heirlooms dating back to the 1840s, the early Victorian period. People think the Christmas tradition as you know it began thanks to Prince Albert, Queen Victoria's husband, but no, the honour of establishing this tradition rightfully belongs to good Queen Charlotte, the German wife of George III.

Initially, Queen Charlotte decorated a single yew branch, a shared Christmas tradition in her native Mecklenburg-Strelitz, to celebrate Christmas with members of the royal family and the royal household. In December 1800, the Queen set up the first known English Christmas tree at Queen's Lodge, Windsor. She held a large Christmas party for the children of the families in Windsor and placed a whole tree in the drawing room, decorated with tinsel, glass baubles, fruits, and sweet treats, illuminated by small wax candles.

I know it to be true because I was fortunate enough to be there. It was my introduction to Christmas traditions, so you could say I was there at the start of it all. I had another Christmas experience in 1850 in London with Jocasta; it was grim and fabulous all at the same time. It involved the Covent Garden workhouse and a grand house in exclusive Belgravia. They're both rather complicated stories which I can't explain now; the latter involved me taking Jocasta back in time; I'd done it with her once before, not that she could remember!

'No, I can't say I do.' I replied, looking at Florence and Winston, hoping they may have sensed something. That's Florence Dearden, the white witch and the noted historian and Cambridge scholar Winston Hatherton. We were all members of the famous Pluckley Psychic Historical Society; you may have heard of us.

Florence and Winston sat at the table unmoved; Winston was savouring a glass of aged malt whiskey. In contrast, and because of the séance, Florence had hardly touched her schooner of sherry. I could tell she feared missing the slightest tap or knock – or any glimmer of a spiritual presence, let alone a full-blown ghostly manifestation, although they were rare.

'I think we've finished our séance for today,' said Jocasta, still sniffing the air. 'I feel we've done as much as we can for now - we'll call it round one,' she smiled casually, raising an eyebrow. 'Or our starter for ten.'

'Oh, is that it?' Asked Clementine Nantwich with a note of surprise in her plummy tone, looking somewhat deflated.

Jocasta nodded, 'Yes, I'm afraid it is for this evening unless I get a sudden presentiment leading to an eventuation. I believe the moment has passed in the Astral Plane; I can feel it most strongly in my vibrations and base chakra,' she pondered for a moment closing her eyes, centring her core. 'If we continue, I fear we'll waste time and energy flogging a dead horse,' she gave a wry smile. 'Or spirit - not that we're beaten, of course, oh no, we're far from it. We'll try again tomorrow and really put our backs into it. I'm starting to get a feel for this house - sometimes it can take a little time for things to warm up and eventuate.'

'Base chakra!' Exclaimed Clementine, fanning herself with her hand; she looked like she might faint; I was pleased she was sitting down. I sensed she had a delicate nature, rather like me!

Jocasta nodded, 'Oh yes,' she replied, looking at Clementine like she'd asked a silly question. 'Chakras are energy centres; there are 114 in the body. You probably won't know anything about them, Miss Nantwich, chakras are quite an esoteric subject, but the human body is a complex form of meridians and energy, sensitive to vibrations.'

As Jocasta said this, all colour was draining from Clementine's carefully made-up face.

'You see, chakras enhance our spiritual, mental, emotional, and physical wellbeing,' Jocasta shook her head, pursing her lips, lost in thought. 'But they must be balanced and clear without a glimmer of interference or congestion, particularly where elementals are concerned - now they can be most troublesome.'

'Elementals?' Asked Clementine hesitantly, going white, even ghostly! She shuffled uncomfortably in her chair, crossing her legs tightly together.

'Yes, elementals,' replied Jocasta matter of factly. 'An elemental is a mythical being described in alchemical and even occult works from around the time of the European Renaissance. They were described in the 16th-century works of Paracelsus. He was a Swiss physician, alchemist, lay theologian, and philosopher of the German Renaissance. He also had a substantial impact as a prophet or diviner. According to Paracelsus, there are four categories of elementals: gnomes, undines, sylphs, and salamanders. These correspond to the four Empedoclean elements of antiquity: earth, water, air, and fire, respectively.'

Silence...

'Now, if you don't mind, I'll take you up on your kind offer of a mince pie and a glass of sherry,' continued Jocasta dreamily, anticipating the sweet shortcrust pastry filled with a mixture of sweet fruit and spices of cinnamon, cloves, and nutmeg. Then there was the nutty, dried fruit and saline flavours of sweet sherry to wash it all down. 'I make it a rule never to drink alcohol before a séance. It interferes with my vibrations and increases the chances of making errors, you know, contacting a demon or summoning a poltergeist, that sort of thing, which would never do; they can be most troublesome. Although with a séance, one never knows for sure what might eventuate,' Jocasta glanced over her shoulder at the raging fire and mumbled something to herself... 'Now, where was I?'

'You were talking about not drinking alcohol before a séance,' I replied, trying not to sigh; Jocasta was easily distracted; I wanted to keep us on track.

'Ah yes, of course, although occasionally I do allow myself the driest of martinis. For some reason, totally unknown to me, a martini doesn't interfere with my chakras. And I think Titus has a secret liking for them.'

'Titus,' muttered Clementine wearily, quite lost; I wasn't surprised. 'Is Titus your pet dog?'

I tried not to laugh.

'No, of course not, and please keep your voice down; Titus might hear you,' bristled Jocasta wide-eyed. 'I don't have a dog; they're such needy animals. I have a black cat, Cassiel; he's named after the archangel and guardian of Capricorn, my star sign – Titus is my spirit control on the other side. A most gifted Native American Indian,' Jocasta lowered her voice to a whisper rubbing her chin. 'However, he can be - hmm, how do I put it, he can be – well, for want of a better word, highly-strung,' she nodded. 'Yes, I think that's a fair way of putting it; the truly gifted often are – but I wouldn't have him any other way.' She gave a righteous smile.

Silence...

'All self-respecting mediums have a control,' said Jocasta stiffening and looking severe as she started finger-wagging. 'Miss Nantwich, never trust a medium who doesn't have a control; they're usually charlatans, and sadly, there are still quite a few around. Although it's not as bad as it used to be - the Victorian period was the worst; it was full of them. And it's not that long ago when you think about it.'

You could say Titus was the fifth member of our team residing in the complex world of the Astral plane and Twilight Zone. He'd helped us with many cases, but he was a diva, terrible hypochondriac, and name-dropper. The last time Jocasta spoke to him, he told her he was assisting the film star Rudolph Valentino with his poetry. I'm sure you'll be meeting him.

'And I find dealing with the spirit world always gives one such an appetite,' declared Jocasta tapping her stomach rhythmically with her fingers. 'One needs a well-nourished, robust constitution in my line of work, and I do like a nice homemade mince pie at this time of year, particularly my own,' her eyes twinkled. 'This will sound like I'm blowing my own trumpet, something I don't make a habit of, but I'm very good with pastry,' she glanced at her hands. 'You see, it's all in the fingers; I take after my late mother – mince pies make me feel so Christmassy.' Jocasta smiled distractedly, her mouth-watering. 'Luckily, I'm not a slave to my figure like some women; I gave all that up years ago.'

I tried my best not to laugh; I'd never met anyone with an appetite that even came close to Jocasta's. That said, I supposed Winston and Florence could give her a run for her money. Winston was particularly partial to tea and cake, anything sweet. You'll get used to it!

'Oh, where are our manners, would you like something to eat, Miss Bradman?' Asked Clementine. 'I can ask our maid, Ethel, to prepare you something; she never retires until we do; she's always busy doing her embroidery. Ethel is so kind; they don't call her Goodbody for nothing,' Clementine smiled. 'That's her surname. She's devoted to the two of us and looks after the few house staff we have here; nothing is ever too much trouble for her,' Clementine clutched her pearls, glancing at her sister, Agnes. Clementine looked slightly flustered, her cheeks turning a rosy shade of pink. The two spinster sisters were of a certain age and quite delightful, elegant, and charming. We were at their magnificent home Rothery Hall, situated in a quiet corner of the picturesque town of Brenchley in Kent.

'Oh, please call me Jocasta, and yes, that's so kind; some food would be lovely, thank you; after that séance, I'm quite ravenous.' Jocasta moved to one of the windows, slightly pulling back the heavy burgundy velvet fringed curtains. She glanced out of the sash windows at the falling snow, moonlit sky, and stars. The gardens and bare trees looked like they'd been covered in cotton wool. She turned to Winston,

'I'm so pleased we're staying the night; the sky is heavy with snow - it's full of it, and it's settling fast; the roads will be treacherous.'

He nodded, taking his pipe from his jacket pocket, 'The Rover is not too bad in the snow,' he replied, pursing his lips. 'Although I don't like driving in such horrid weather, but I suppose it looks nice if you don't have to go out in it.'

Which it did, not that the snow and cold bothered me, of course.

Clementine nodded obligingly, looking at her sister Agnes and then back at Jocasta, 'What would you like, Miss Bradman – sorry, Jocasta?' She asked with a grin, over-enunciating her words. She was so posh I dared hardly speak. I wondered if the two sisters had received elocution lessons. They had such perfect diction, like one of those announcers on The British Broadcasting Company radio news or a narrator on those new Pathé newsreel films shown in the cinemas.

Jocasta shrugged thoughtfully, rubbing her chin, 'Hmm, perhaps a few delicious sandwiches, a slice of game pie, a few well-seasoned sausage rolls, some cheese, and biscuits. Stilton, if you have any? I do like a good Stilton at Christmas, followed by some spiced, fruity Christmas cake and a few shortbread biscuits, and, as I said, a few mince pies - something quite light and simple. I never like too much food at this late hour; it affects my sleep. You see, like most mediums, I have an active mind; it never rests with such vivid dreams,' she smiled, looking far away.

'You must understand the spiritual highway is very active at night; I frequently get presentiments and find myself communing with wandering spirits. There are so many of them who want to be heard or have a message to pass on to someone,' she smiled. 'They're literally forming a queue.'

Clementine and Agnes were hanging on to Jocasta's every word.

'Take last night - I dreamed I was a Lady in Waiting to Queen Elizabeth I; her face was a startling white thanks to her heavy makeup. She used a type of makeup known as 'Venetian ceruse', a mixture of vinegar and lead - a potential killer,' Jocasta grimaced and shuddered.

'She was very demanding and not happy with the court. Her majesty felt she wasn't getting enough attention,' she chuckled to herself. 'But I digress.'

What did I tell you! That's something you'll get used to, digressing! However, Jocasta was right about Queen Elizabeth I; she was like that and needed lots of flattery from her court. She put great importance on her appearance and spent hours getting ready: she had over two thousand elaborate gowns and never wore an outfit in public more than twice, but that's also another story!

Clementine stood up and shivered, pulling her pale pink cashmere cardigan closer to her against a sudden chill; she was unsure how to respond to Jocasta's comments, thinking she lived in another world, a world of the dead, or was quite mad. Agnes jumped up, smoothing down her tweed skirt, adjusting her diamond brooch, and taking a lace handkerchief from her cardigan pocket, 'You sit down, sister dear; you've had quite a turn with all the recent events at this house.' She blew her nose loudly and glanced around the room nervously before moving around, switching on several ornate fringed lamps.

'You must be quite exhausted. Let me find Ethel, and we'll soon sort out some supper for Miss Bradman, well, everyone,' she looked over in Jocasta's direction and gave a wry smile. 'Sorry, I should say, Jocasta,' she took a deep breath shaking her head as if annoyed with herself. 'You must excuse us; my sister and I are so used to formality. It was drummed into us from childhood - everyone said we were old before our time,' she rolled her eyes and smiled. 'Our father had strong Victorian principles, just like his father before him; you know, children should be seen but not heard. I don't know how our dear mother put up with him. God rest her soul, but she was always like a ray of sunshine; people say we take after her. I hope we do.'

They did!

Jocasta briefly turned from the window, looking distracted and returned the smile, 'Yes, a different generation,' she said, turning her attention back to the falling snow and night sky. 'How still everything is; the snow muffles all sound.' She glanced at a vase of holly on a walnut side table, admiring the red berries. 'The Holly has such a bitter smell at this time of year, but it's not unpleasant.'

Agnes agreed, 'Yes, I love holly at any time of year; I like the shiny leaves and curly edges, although they can be sharp,' her thoughts returned to food. 'Oh, would you like some mushroom vol-au-vents? I can't resist the delicate, flaky puff pastry.' I made them myself; I fell in love with vol-au-vents on a trip Clementine and I made to the Ritz in London in 1922; we decided to treat ourselves.'

'Vol-au-vents!' Exclaimed Jocasta as her stomach rumbled and her taste buds danced with excitement. 'Goodness, you're spoiling us; yes, that would be delicious. I do like a nice earthy mushroom. As for puff pastry, I love it,' she flexed her arm. 'I wish I had the patience and arm muscles to make it.'

Agnes agreed, 'Yes, it is an effort, but it is nearly Christmas, and Christmas is a time for treating oneself and feasting, although these days, Clementine and I always seem to be on a diet.' She smiled graciously and left quietly, closing the door behind her.

'Clementine, you say you inherited this beautiful house?' Asked Florence, admiring the stylish room while sipping her sherry. It was expensively and tastefully decorated with sophisticated antique furniture, fine art, delicate porcelain, silver nick-nacks, expensive silks, velvets, and textiles; a grand piano stood in a corner near one of the heavily draped windows.

Clementine nodded, 'Yes, we moved here last year in the early summer, the house is beautiful, but I hope it doesn't become a burden as old houses and large estates can. We've had quite a few upsetting years with family deaths. You see, we are the last of the Rothery's on my mother's side of the family. Sadly, she died in 1928. Of course, we're Nantwich with our father's surname; we lost him in 1926.

As the Male Primogeniture Rule dictates, our mother's younger and only brother, our uncle, Edmund, inherited the house and estate after their father died. Of course, by that time, our mother had long married our father. Edmund lived here, running the estate for many years, although our mother always took an interest and involved herself whenever she could.'

'What was your mother's name?' Asked Jocasta.

'Beatrice,' replied Clementine smiling. 'I think it's a lovely name.'

No one said anything.

'Didn't Edmund ever marry?' Asked Florence casually. 'This is a big house for just one person.'

'Oh yes, of course, he was married to Violet. She was a member of the wealthy Rattigan family. You may have heard of them; they lived in a grand castle near Truro. I think members of the family still do. Her father made his fortune from the Cornish tin and copper mines. Violet was gorgeous and always immaculately dressed, with a fabulous wardrobe from the fashion house of Callot Soeurs in Paris. She was one of their first customers when they opened their salon in 1895.

Violet moved her patronage from Charles Frederick Worth, who had sadly died that year. Like her mother, she'd been a loyal client of his and knew him well; she even attended his funeral in the Avenue de la Grande Armée and burial in the grounds of his villa at Suresnes.' Clementine's eyes moved to an elaborately framed portrait above the ornate fireplace. 'That's Violet in all her finery and beauty painted in 1899 by William-Adolphe Bouguereau.'

'Never heard of him,' said Florence, admiring the portrait. 'But it's a beautiful painting; she's quite a vision.'

Clementine agreed, 'Yes, she was a great beauty.'

'William-Adolphe Bouguereau was a French academic painter,' said Winston. 'He made modern interpretations of classical subjects, emphasising the female body,' he paused thoughtfully, then continued rather pompously. 'Hmm, and a Rattigan, you say. They're one of the wealthiest families in England. And you're right; I can see Violet was a great beauty.'

Which she was, with a heart-shaped face, blond hair in an

elaborate updo, and piercing blue eyes. Her magnificent lace-trimmed and beaded silk gown matched her eyes, and she held a delicate lace fan. She looked quite the elegant lady.

'She was known far and wide for her great beauty, and yes, the Rattigan's,' continued Clementine conspiratorially. 'Violet had many suitors, but there was only one man for her, and that was Edmund. They were married in 1888; we believe it was a very grand occasion with the cream of high society,' she hesitated, frowning. 'Although they always seemed such an odd match, Violet liked luxury, grandeur, and glamour, whereas Edmund enjoyed the quiet country life, but Violet seemed to quickly adjust. However, Edmund spoiled and indulged her; they seemed blissfully happy together. I never heard her complain.'

'What happened to Violet?' I asked.

Clementine's face clouded; she took a deep breath, 'Sadly, she died nearly thirty years ago in 1902. She was only thirty-six; it seems like only yesterday. They say she died from a broken heart; you see, the year before, they'd lost their only son Thomas to peripneumonia on Christmas Day of all days. He was only six years old and such a lovely little boy, so full of life,' Clementine's lips trembled; she took her handkerchief and dabbed at her eyes. 'Violet also died on Christmas day at exactly the same time as Thomas; it was like she wanted to ensure she'd be with him. It was both tragic and somehow strangely romantic.'

Silence...

'Yes, tragic and terribly sad,' said Florence clearing her throat, although I could tell she was intrigued. 'Heart-breaking, but what you have to say is also fascinating. Had Violet been ill?'

Clementine hesitated, wondering how she should answer, 'No, not really, well, not in the traditional sense,' she paused for a long moment, lost in the memory of it all. 'We were still quite young, but neither Violet nor Edmund was ever the same after Thomas died; he was the apple of their eyes,' she dabbed at a tear that ran down her cheek. 'It was awful - as if they died with him. Thomas had always been a strong, robust child, a proper rough and tumble little boy, but he suddenly fell ill. He struggled on for about a month; Thomas was a fighter. At times we thought he'd turned a corner and would pull through, but, well - he didn't. Edmund did everything he could to find a doctor and chemist or druggist who could help them find a cure to get him better; he left no stone unturned.'

'Peripneumonia has taken so many over the years,' said Winston. 'Young and old, tragically, it's touched many people's lives.'

Clementine stood up and put some logs on the fire, taking the poker to stir up the flames. 'It's hard to describe, but Edmund and Violet were both broken; they wanted a big family, but Violet struggled with pregnancy suffering several miscarriages, but they kept on trying. They were thrilled when Thomas was born, over the moon. However, Violet was told it wasn't safe for her to have more children. But that didn't matter to them; they had Thomas, an heir to the estate.'

Clementine paused again, lost in her memory. 'Once Thomas passed, well, Violet seemed to just slowly waste away, like her life force was gone.' Clementine put the poker back in its stand and sat down, smoothing down her skirt. 'Edmund almost gave up completely after Violet died. It hit him very hard; she was the love of his life - they were so happy together. I think it was this house and the estate that kept him going. Our mother tried her best to help, but there was only so much she could do - she was always there for Edmund.'

'So, he never remarried?' Asked Winston lighting his pipe, blowing plumes of fragrant smoke into the air from his oriental tobacco.

Clementine shook her head with disbelief at the question clutching her pearls, 'Goodness, no, he was far too in love with Violet; he never stopped loving her. For him marrying someone else would have been a great betrayal of their love for each other,' she sighed, shaking her head. 'As I say, he was a broken man; he had no interest in anything or anyone after her death and was very angry with God. I don't know how Edmund managed to keep this house and estate going; it was like he was soulless. That said, I'm sure the estate was the only thing keeping him alive unless it was his anger with God. Without that,' she shrugged and hesitated. 'Well, I dread to think what would have happened to him. He would have died from a broken heart years ago like Violet – although I'm sure he did in the end. I don't believe you can ever mend a broken heart, no matter how hard you try,' she glanced at the portrait of Violet. 'Of course, he never talked about it; I think British people keep their pain to themselves, keeping it locked away.'

'Yes, the British stiff upper lip,' agreed Winston. 'It has a lot to answer for.'

The door opened, and Agnus walked in, 'Yes, sister dear, he died of a broken heart; I've never been surer of anything in my life. Although the doctor said his official cause of death was angina - so a heart attack. But in truth, he died when Violet passed. After that, he became nothing more than a shadow of himself, an empty shell.

'How old was he?' I asked.

'Sixty-nine,' replied Agnus sitting opposite Clementine near the blazing fire. 'So not a bad age, I suppose. But he was taken too soon.'

'Do you really think so?' Asked Clementine thoughtfully. 'After Violet died, I always had the impression he couldn't wait to join her.'

Agnes nodded, 'Hmm, true, but anyway, we only hope he can finally rest in peace, and he's now with Violet and Thomas, having the family life together they always dreamed about.'

'When did Edmund die?' Asked Winston.

'Ah, well, this is where the story takes another turn,' said Agnus moving to the drinks cart and pouring herself and Jocasta a large sherry. 'Edmund died in 1929 on Christmas Day, at exactly the same time as Thomas and Violet.'

Silence...

'And exactly what time was that?' Asked Winston, furrowing his brow, disturbing thoughts of past cases flashed into his mind.

'Three o'clock in the afternoon,' replied Agnes taking a sip of her sherry. 'Hmm, that's so good, nectar; this is Bodegas Hidalgo La Gitana manzanilla sherry. I think it's the best. The Spanish are so good with sweet sherry,' she smiled. 'I'm getting flavours of fresh Cox's apples and salted almonds,' she quickly passed a glass to Jocasta... 'Now, Edmund is buried with Violet and Thomas on the estate in a family plot. Clementine and I put fresh flowers on their grave every Sunday, whatever flowers are in season. Edmund and Violet wanted to be close to Thomas after he died. Edmund wanted to be close to both Thomas and Violet once she passed. Naturally, it was his dying wish to be buried with them, so they could all be together.'

Jocasta turned from the window glancing at me, then at Winston and Florence. 'How deeply touching; I'd like to see the grave, I'm sure we all would. What you have to say is interesting and may even be significant, yes, I'm sure of it,' she took a sip of sherry and smiled with delight. 'Hmm, you're right about this sherry; it's absolutely delicious, like nectar, and so warming,' Jocasta wrinkled her nose, going all comfy and cosy. 'Now, you say you heard noises on your first Christmas here last year, and they've started again?'

Agnes returned to her seat by the fire, 'Yes, we moved here in the early summer of 1930, it took a while for Edmund's affairs and will to be finalised, and we had things we needed to sort out. For us, it's been a huge undertaking, but we want to make the Rothery family proud for our mother and Edmund. By the time Christmas came around, we were still finding our feet in this house and with the estate. The noises started exactly twelve days before Christmas, just like they have done this time.'

'How can you be so sure?' I asked. 'You know, be so specific about dates.'

'Oh, I keep a diary, and my birthday is on the 12th December,' said Clementine. 'That's when I heard the noises for the first time, just as I explained to you Jocasta in my letter.' Her eyes glazed over; the four of us could see she was recalling her memories. 'Such disturbing sounds, sobbing, moaning, noises of pain, heartbreak, and suffering. And a child, a child in pain, in desperate need. I can't tell you how disconcerting they are. Then just as quickly as it all started, the noises stopped on January 5, Twelfth Night or Epiphany Eve; we know it as the

12 Days of Christmas. Over the months that followed, we didn't think that much of it; I think we pushed it to the back of our minds; Agnes and I were so busy with the house and estate, it seemed to consume all our time.'

'You say you've both heard them?' asked Jocasta.

The two women nodded, 'As clear as day,' said Agnes. 'Exactly as Clementine has described.'

'And just like last year,' I said. 'The noises have started again in precisely the same way?'

The two women nodded again. 'Yes, six days ago on my birthday,' said Clementine with a weary sigh. 'I don't think either of us have slept since it started.'

I nodded, 'Are there any specific times of day when the noises are worse?'

Clementine pursed her lips and looked at Agnes, 'Hmm, it's hard to say. To me, they appear random, almost like, oh, this will sound silly, but almost like they recall events as they happen or happened.'

'Have the servants heard them?' Asked Florence finishing her sherry.

'Yes, of course,' said Agnes. 'Once they start, you can't miss them, no matter how hard you try. They start softly, as gentle whispers or moans, but gradually they get louder and louder, almost echoing around the house. The servants were initially reluctant to admit it, fearing what people would say. Folks thinking they'd gone quite mad and were hearing voices. You know how people like to gossip in small villages, particularly about large old houses.'

'You can't mistake the sounds of distress,' said Clementine. 'It's so hard to take because of the feelings the noise generates within you. Feelings of sadness and inadequacy at being unable to help or stop it. It makes you feel desperate, exasperated, afraid, upset, and anxious. We've heard a mixture of noises; they all involve raw, emotional pain. The first is a consumptive child crying and pleading desperately for its mother, but the mother never comes. Then there are the sounds of adults in complete turmoil and anguish; they are broken and in despair. It's unbearable.' Tears ran down her face.

Agnes moved to comfort her sister, 'Clementine, dearest, calm yourself,' she looked at Jocasta almost pleadingly. 'I'm sure Jocasta and her associates here will get to the bottom of all this.'

I looked at Clementine and Agnes, knowing we would, but it wasn't as easy as that. Once we understood the reasons for the problem we had to find a solution, a way to make it disappear, which was never simple.

Clementine tried hard to compose herself, grabbing her beaded evening bag, 'Oh, please excuse me, I'm being rather silly.' She grabbed her powder compact from her purse and began powdering her nose and cheeks. 'Goodness, sister, I look a sight, like the wreck of the Hesperus.'

'Not at all,' said Jocasta trying to sound sympathetic. 'From what you've described, your reaction is perfectly natural and understandable. For some reason unknown to us right now, it sounds like the suffering of Thomas and the emotional trauma and pain felt by Edmund and Violet following the death of Thomas are trapped here in this house. It happens more frequently than people realise. Malevolent spirits can attach themselves to trauma and pain; it forms an energy source they can feed on,' she paused. 'Of course, there could be other explanations – that is what we must find out.'

The door opened, and Ethel walked in with a tray of food, quickly returning to the kitchen and returning with another; it was a feast. She carefully put everything on an elegant walnut side table; with the fussing assistance of Agnes, I could see she was a perfectionist. Once she was happy, Agnes thanked Ethel, who left.

'Do pour yourself more drinks,' said Clementine with a warm smile. 'Let's not be dull and try and find some Christmas spirit.'

'I don't mind if I do,' said Winston feeling all convivial, taking Florence's glass and moving to the drinks cart, pouring himself another whiskey with more sherry for Jocasta and Florence. He looked at Clementine and Agnes, sherry bottle in hand, 'Ladies.'

'I don't mind if I do,' said Clementine. 'But please don't think we make a habit of drinking, but as I say, it is almost Christmas.'

'I'm in,' said Agnes with a smile. 'We could both do with some good Christmas cheer and spirit.'

Of course, as a ghost, I didn't eat or drink; Winston knew better than to ask me after all the years we'd worked together. I'm sure he, Jocasta and Florence thought it very strange, but they'd come to see it as one of my eccentricities or little quirks, and anyway, in our line of work, they were used to the unusual and irregular.

We spent the next half-hour in front of the raging fire, chatting about nothing of any importance. As the snow continued to fall outside, the five of them ate the delicious finger food toasting each other's good health. Once the food was finished, and I mean finished! Agnes moved to the piano and started playing a seasonal tune, Silent Night, Holy Night, one of my favourite Christmas carols; as she played, the wind howled outside like a demon.

***

Edmund stood on the landing in the dark, watching the falling snow dancing in the moonlight. He was sure he could hear music, was Violet playing the piano? He listened hard; it sounded like a carol, his favourite, Silent Night, Holy Night....

Chapter 3

Violet Rothery pulled back her silk-trimmed cashmere blankets and carefully arose from her mahogany four-poster bed, pushing several hand-embroidered silk cushions out of the way. She sat for a moment, gently rubbing her forehead; the dizzy spells had finally passed. Violet found lying in a darkened room was the only thing that helped.

The dizzy spells had started about a week ago; Violet felt like she was in a dark, spinning tunnel heading towards a blinding bright light; the spinning made her head throb, leaving her feeling lightheaded and faint. She wondered if it was due to lack of food; she had no appetite these days and couldn't remember the last time she'd eaten or even drank anything; she seemed to exist on nothing.

Violet smoothed down her heavy black wool and silk dress, wishing corsets were more comfortable. She slipped on her embroidered bedroom slippers, taking her shawl from the back of one of the silk upholstered chairs and moved to a heavily draped window, pulling back the deep-pink, silk velvet curtains. It was snowing heavily; Violet stood by the window in the moonlight, watching the snow swirling as it cascaded from the starlit sky, settling across the gardens, the rolling countryside, and woodland beyond. It was beautiful, delicate, perfect, and peaceful, covering everything in a sparkling white blanket of pure perfection. The snow made even the ugly and mundane charming; it looked magical; she found the falling snow surprisingly calming.

She wondered why life couldn't be the same as her thoughts returned to her anguish. Why was life given and then so cruelly taken away? She shook her head in despair, it was a question she'd asked herself a thousand times, but she had no answers. It was a question she'd asked Reverend Anslem many times, and he always said the same thing, 'Faith is about trusting God when you have unanswered questions.' It offered her no comfort or resolution.

We are all born, she thought; we have a bit of life; for some, that life is long; for others, it's short. For some, it's mostly happy, while for others, it's sad, full of pain and suffering, then we die - what was the point of it all? She had the same thought about feelings and emotions. Why are we given all these feelings and emotions we can't control? Yes, they can bring happiness, but they also cause so much distress, pain, and suffering - why, why, why? She wondered if life would be better if we all felt nothing.

Violet took a monogrammed handkerchief from her pocket and dabbed her eyes; tears seemed to overwhelm her most days; how many tears had she shed - how many more did she have? That she couldn't answer other than to say, far more than she'd ever imagined possible.

She wrung her hands; it was something she did unconsciously, sometimes rubbing them until they were red and blistered. Edmund was with young Sam, their stable boy, bedding down the horses. He was known as young Sam because his father was also called Sam. Old Sam had worked on the estate all his life; he was now their groundsman. Violet hoped the two of them wouldn't be out long in the freezing snow and was thankful the stable block was dry and well maintained.

She and Edmund were both lost in their sorrow, lost to the depths of darkness. Violet tried to recall how she knew Edmund was with Sam in the stables, but as hard as she tried, she couldn't remember; everything was a blur these days. However, she found it comforting to know Edmund was close by, to know he was there; it calmed her.

She sighed wearily; these days, Violet dreaded the cold weather and winter months; it filled her with foreboding and fear. She thought of the spring, and golden daffodils, such an optimistic time of hope, new life, regrowth, and rebirth; she used to look forward to it but not anymore. Now everything was just a vague jumble, the days, nights, and even the seasons merging into each other. Often, she didn't know what day it was, nor if it was day or night, let alone the month or season; what was left of her meagre existence was consumed with grief and misery.

Her thoughts returned to her dear Edmund, knowing how deeply he felt her pain, not that she wanted to add to his suffering. Outwardly he'd been so strong for everyone, but she knew he was just as broken as she was. Her lips almost curled into a smile. People thought of him as a tall, handsome man, slightly arrogant, with an aloof and unapproachable demeanour. But once people knew him, they soon learned he was quite the opposite with a kind and generous nature; at least, that's how he used to be.

She dabbed at her eyes full of self-loathing; Violet had become the thing she detested most in a woman, a clingy wife. She despised herself for being so needy, wishing she could be strong and not so weak and feeble.

Outside, the wind blew the snow in swirls, making it dance across the gardens, forming deep drifts. Violet glanced at the ornate fireplace wondering why the fire hadn't been lit. Edmund insisted all the fires should be kept burning in the winter months, not that she felt cold; she didn't feel anything.

Her thoughts turned to the house staff; they'd been so kind and understanding. She looked around her beautifully decorated and furnished bedroom, grateful they looked after the house with such care. Keeping everything just as it always had been when Edmund's father was alive - she was neither use nor ornament. These days the servants moved around the house like ghosts; she couldn't remember the last time she'd seen or heard any of them. Since Thomas passed away, she'd lost interest in everything, even herself. Now the house was quiet and lifeless; it existed but had lost its beating heart and felt cold and empty, like a private museum or morgue.

A shiver ran through her; she pulled her beautiful, French embroidered wool shawl around her shoulders, admiring it for a moment. It was made for her in happier days in Paris, France, by the

House of Worth. A time when she enjoyed such things as silks, satins, chiffons, and the fripperies of fashion, precious jewellery, dinner parties, grand balls, and the gilded world of polite high society. Thinking about those days now - well, it seemed like a lifetime ago, like it happened to another person.

She sighed again; none of those things mattered anymore - nothing did. Violet felt annoyed with herself for ever thinking such things were necessary or even important. Before she married Edmund, the gilded cage of high society had been her playground, visiting her wealthy family or staying with aristocratic ladies at grand houses and attending smart soirées. How could she have been so vain and self-indulgent? How misguided, vacuous, and pleasure-seeking she was. Violet hated how unquestioning and naïve she had been, allowing herself to be so cosseted, blind, and immune to what was happening around her, even on her own doorstep.

Men, women, and children were begging in the streets or suffering in workhouses; worse, they died from hypothermia or starvation. Many lived in appalling, cramped conditions without even a modest roof over their heads or warm clothes to wear, walking about in bare feet. How could she have been so blind to it all? All she had cared about were those grand parties, the tug and pull of innocent flirtations, beautiful jewellery, and wearing the most luxurious and expensive fashions, hats, and furs. They had seduced her; she'd never given a moment's thought to the people and world that existed outside her gilded one. She wondered if God was punishing her for being so selfish and indulgent.

Violet trembled and sighed, consumed with the gnawing emptiness she'd endured since Thomas died. She found it hard to believe nearly a year had passed - his death still felt so new, so raw. Reverend Anslem had agreed to hold a remembrance service for Thomas at the church; Violet hoped it might comfort them or offer some contentment, that God might give her a sign, telling her why he took her precious boy. The Reverend told her Thomas had joined God's Heavenly

Angels and would bring peace and joy to others doing God's work; how she wanted to believe that. The Reverend quoted words from The Excursion, a poem by William Wordsworth saying, 'The good die first'; it gave her no consolation or resolution.

She thought of the women in the village, mothers with young children. It was ironic; she'd always been seen as an untouchable, the grand lady of Rothery Hall. Someone far removed from the rigours of life by her status, breeding, social class, carriages, and fancy clothes. She was surrounded by servants and beautiful things, her every whim taken care of; at least she could now look those mothers in the eye with solidarity.

Like her, many had lost a child through childbirth or sickness; she knew their pain and suffering. Rich or poor, it was universal and something all the money in the world couldn't resolve. Not that money made Violet feel any better; she'd always had money but had never known what it was like to be poor. However, even in her grief, money made her an outsider; people saying it was alright for her. She could at least be miserable in comfort. Of course, they were right, not that it made her feel any better. Rothery Hall was paradise, a place she had loved, but it had become a prison full of pain. A prison Violet could never leave because it was the only place Thomas had ever inhabited.

She forced herself to think of happier times, cherished memories - she would always have those; nothing could take them away. But even they felt like a burden, reminding her of what she had lost. Memories of when Thomas was born, oh the joy she and Edmund had experienced, their hearts bursting with happiness. At that moment, she had everything she ever wanted; life was as perfect as possible. She tried to take some comfort from that; how many people could say their life had been as perfect as it could be, even for a moment?

Violet thought of Thomas - when he first started crawling, then walking, his first words, first pair of shoes. Him playing outside in the warm summer sunshine, their picnics by the river and in the summer house. Thomas took after Edmund; he loved nature and animals.

Edmund had started teaching Thomas to ride his pony, which he adored, even though it made Violet nervous, bringing out her over-protective nature. Another thing Thomas loved was his little dog, Patch; they were devoted to each other.

Thomas thought he was indestructible; he liked playing at soldiers and being a hero; he particularly liked pretending he was a pirate. Then there were the funny things he would say, the unexpected things children say. He enjoyed listening to the story Treasure Island by Robert Louis Stevenson, a tale of buccaneers and buried gold. Violet lost count of the times she'd read it to him. In fact, the book made Thomas eager to learn to read.

As much as Violet tried to think of these happier memories and keep them at the front of her mind, she couldn't. Her mind was consumed with misery, repeatedly returning to the same thoughts. Thomas becoming ill, his suffering and her feelings of helplessness and despair. Because there was nothing - nothing they could do to help him other than be there, trying to offer comfort and their unwavering love, devotion, and prayers, endless prayers.

She glanced at the large portrait above the fireplace, a treasured painting of her and Thomas by the famous portrait artist John Singer Sargent. It was painted in the house gardens during the summer of 1900; Thomas was five. Sargent had perfectly captured the colourful gardens, the glorious summer light and the two of them playing with Thomas's little dog, Patch. Sargent had remarkable technical skills, particularly his ability to draw with a brush, which was consistent with the grand manner of portraiture. The happy, sunny picture made Violet feel close to Thomas; she sat for hours each day staring at the painting, trying to lose herself in it...

What was that? Violet listened hard; she was sure she could hear someone playing the piano; it sounded distant, far away. Who on earth could be playing her piano? She moved to the door but didn't open it. She listened for a long moment; she could hear someone playing the Christmas carol Silent Night Holy Night. She wondered if it was Nora, her maid - well, it had to be Nora; no one else in the house could play the piano, although Nora didn't usually play very well - perhaps she'd been practising.

Violet moved back to the window, watching the falling snow, listening to the music, singing the words aloud to herself:

Silent night, holy night!
All is calm, all is bright.
Round yon Virgin, Mother and Child.
Holy infant so tender and mild,
Sleep in heavenly peace,
Sleep in heavenly peace.

She and Edmund loved that carol; it reminded her that Christmas was fast approaching, traditionally a joyous time of family, friends, feasting, gifts, and celebration. But now, it could never be a happy time; tears ran down her cheeks, Violet made no effort to stop them. It was almost the first anniversary of Thomas's death, a time of sadness and remembrance, not celebrations and parties. Violet could never enjoy any festivities; she would always wear black and be in mourning, she would never celebrate Christmas. She doubted she would ever be able to smile again, let alone have any joy in her life.

***

While the others were sleeping, I'd planned to explore the grounds and house in incorporeal ghost mode drifting through walls, looking for any hidden passageways, underground tunnels, lost or trapped spirits, hoping, of course, I wouldn't find a demonic presence or poltergeist. Jocasta said they could be troublesome, which was putting it mildly. However, all that went out the window when I suddenly found myself in Constantinople in 1454, an ancient city in modern-day Turkey, now known as Istanbul.

Suddenly finding myself in a new place from history wasn't unusual; I've come to think of the past as a foreign land, a place where things are done differently. Time moves in mysterious ways; I'd been there for days helping some of the enslaved people to escape from Mehmed II, known as Mehmed the Conqueror; he was an Ottoman sultan. Slavery was an ongoing battle there, along with many other atrocities; it was a brutal time.

I'd probably have to return there at some point; I tried not to think about it. You see, I never know where they might send me from one moment to the next, and don't ask me who 'they' are because I've no idea; that's how it works. After all these years, I'm used to it.

Here at Rothery Hall, the house servants had battled their way through the snow, arrived early, and had been very busy. The fires were blazing in the ornate fireplaces casting a welcoming amber glow into the rooms and elegant entrance hallway. The house looked perfect and dust-free, with not a piece of furniture, curtain, cushion, or ornament out of place, yet despite its grandeur and size, it still had a homely feel. I could hear the steady tick-tock of the grandfather clock in the hall; it was like the beating heart of the house.

We were in the breakfast room, one of several rooms in the house decorated with tasteful trimmings, mistletoe, holly, and greenery for the Christmas season. I stood at one of the windows admiring the gardens; the scene looked like a winter wonderland. The snow clung to everything, buildings, trees, shrubs, walls, and fencing. It had stopped snowing for the moment, leaving everything covered in a thick layer of perfect, gleaming white. I had to narrow my eyes; the glare was almost blinding.

The icy sky was awash with silver hues; the sun shone a cool yellow, mostly hidden behind the playful clouds. The winter sun trying its best to break through and make its presence known, wanting to add some warm respite against the freezing chills of the biting wind. I could tell more snow would fall soon; I pitied anyone working outdoors.

Clementine and Agnes smelt delightful and looked immaculate in tweed, silk, cashmere, pearls, and tasteful diamonds. They were busy fussing over the others as they finished a hearty breakfast of eggs, bacon, kippers, sausage, mushrooms, hot buttered toast, marmalade, honey, and strawberry jam, all washed down with several cups of tea.

I was waiting patiently on the velvet-covered window seat; we were to take a tour of the house and grounds with Clementine and Agnes. I could see the two ladies weren't breakfast people, only having black coffee, but they seemed to enjoy watching Jocasta, Winston, and Florence tucking in - tucking in being the operative words!

'Do you know, I think this is some of the best butter I've ever tasted,' said Jocasta, generously buttering her fourth slice of toast. 'It's so rich, creamy, and, well, buttery.'

'Isn't it,' agreed Florence, savouring every mouthful. 'It's so good; I don't think I've tasted anything better.'

Agnes smiled, 'It's good to see people enjoying their food. Most of the produce we use is local; it comes from the farms on the estate, including the delicious butter; Ethel says it makes fabulous cakes. I always say you can taste the summer grass, wildflowers, and Kent sun in it,' she smiled with satisfaction, finished her coffee, and poured herself some more from an elegant silver coffee pot.

'Yes, you can,' agreed Jocasta with her mouthful of toast. 'I couldn't have described it better myself; you make it sound so romantic,' she picked up the honey, 'This is the same; it tastes of wildflowers and the hedgerows - pure nectar. I must make sure I buy some local produce before we leave; I like to support local suppliers, and it's even better if one can make new culinary discoveries.'

Clementine looked at Winston; he was emptying the teapot. It was his third cup, 'Shall I ask Ethel to get you some more Tea, Winston? It's no trouble.'

His lips curled into an appreciative smile, 'Well, only if you're sure? You'll find I never say no to a nice cup of tea,' he said almost with relief. 'I find it sets me up for the day and helps me think as we try to sort out any historical, ghostly, or spiritual conundrums,' he smiled, tapping his head with his hand. 'If I have a mental block, tea seems to sort it out and get the old grey matter working.'

Winston never turned down a cup of tea. How well Clementine already knew him; I've never known anyone drink so much tea; I think it ran through his veins. Right on cue, Ethel walked into the room looking like a hospital matron in a poorly fitting navy-blue dress. Her grey hair was severely scraped off her well-scrubbed face; her unusual grey eyes were framed with round, horn-rimmed glasses, making her look like the headmistress of an all-girls school.

'Ah, Ethel, I was just about to ring, perfect timing,' said Clementine. 'Could we have another pot of tea, please? She glanced at Jocasta and Florence, 'Do you ladies require anything else?'

'No, we're fine,' said Jocasta eyeing the last of the sausages. 'It's all been most delicious, thank you, it set me up until my mid-morning snack.'

Ethel glanced at Clementine, nodding obligingly, her lips curling into a half-smile as she whispered something. Well, I think she said something; her lips moved, she grabbed the teapot and left. Ethel appeared to be a lady of few words.

'Now, Jasper,' said Agnes in her plummy tones, like she was about to make an announcement on the BBC radio; I could feel everyone's eyes focus on me. 'Clementine and I are interested in dialects,' she gave a wry smile. 'The King's English was drummed into us from an early age - you know, the skill of clear and expressive speech, especially of distinct pronunciation and articulation; we can't abide loose vowels,' she gave an ironic smile. 'While not wanting to sound boastful, we consider ourselves experts on the subject. Poor diction is even worse than sloppy posture; we can't abide sloppy posture; good deportment is another essential. We've even given classes at The Royal Academy of Dramatic Art, a London drama school providing theatre, film, and radio training - It was granted a Royal Charter in 1920.'

I could feel my back and shoulders straightening, but what did I tell you! I knew they'd had elocution lessons.

She continued authoritatively with her precise articulation, 'Now, your voice has us both fascinated; it has a most unusual sing-song cadence infused with European accents. It's peculiarly personal, with an unaccustomed rhythm that develops into a flat drawl that ends in a childlike query. It has a quality of heartbreak.'

I had no idea how to answer. Since our arrival at the Hall, I didn't think I'd spoken very much, certainly not enough to warrant such detailed analysis and attention.

'Yes,' agreed Clementine thoughtfully. 'I would say your voice is intelligent and alert, wistful but enthusiastic, frank yet tactful, assured without conceit and tender without sentimentality.'

I smiled, I didn't think I could blush, but if I could, I'm sure I would have been bright red, 'Ladies, you make me sound like a paragon of virtue.' I was going to say I'm only human, but I stopped myself!

'We're being serious,' said Agnes sincerely. 'Now, where does your accent come from? Is it Dutch, a place famous for the delightful tulip?'

How to answer? 'Hmm, well, I was born in London, an orphan; I never knew my parents.'

'Oh, how awful,' said Clementine looking at Agnes, alarmed. 'We're so sorry; that must have been dreadful for you. I once heard a child cry in hospital - it was awful.'

I nodded, trying to be polite, 'Was it? But please don't be sorry - it's all in the past,' I was going to say it was a long time ago, but I stopped myself. 'I've travelled quite a lot,' all of that was true, but, of course, I was missing out the ghostly time travel part of it all. 'I suppose I've managed to do a lot in my lifetime - I think all the places I've visited and the people I've met have influenced me in so many subconscious ways,' I shrugged, shaking my head. 'I don't have any other explanation to offer you.' I smiled, hoping we could move on.

'Jasper makes a valid point,' said Winston sipping his tea. 'In our line of work, we have so many unique experiences; it's hard to explain to others. Of course, these experiences affect us in ways we don't always realise at the time. They also increase our knowledge and aid our unique work at the Psychic Historical Society.'

'I think there are many subliminal influences at work,' said Florence picking up the sugar tongs and taking some cubed sugar for her tea. 'We are all affected by our experiences,' she glanced at Winston, Jocasta, and me. 'In our line of work, we tend to accept and believe in things that sit outside the norm because we know them to be true. We don't generally talk about them because we know people would either be frightened or find it difficult to comprehend.'

'Or think we're quite mad,' said Jocasta casually, finishing her toast, wondering if she should have any more to tide her over until mid-morning. She always needed to keep her energy levels up during psychic investigations. 'It's complicated,' she proffered. 'People fear what they don't understand, often putting it down to madness in another because they have no alternative explanation to offer. To believe in something, people need to see proof, which is difficult to provide in our line of work. Often, we see things others can't - it's a gift.'

The door opened, and Ethel came in with the tea looking flustered - saved by the bell!

Once tea and breakfast were finally out of the way, we moved into the wood-panelled hall with its fine works of art, and chequerboard flooring, past the stately grandfather clock and the huge fireplace with its blazing fire.

'How many bedrooms does the house have?' I asked, glancing around the elegant entrance hall.

'Eight, not a lot for a house this size, but they're big rooms and rather draughty,' said Agnes with a shiver. 'Of course, there are also several bedrooms in what used to be the servants' quarters, up in the attic.'

'Actually, it's rather nice up there and quite warm,' declared Clementine. 'Of course, the heat rises, and there are fabulous views across the estate.'

We moved up the sweeping staircase with its ornate carved

wood balustrade and across the carpeted landing to what had been Violet's bedroom. Clementine turned the polished brass handle and opened the oak-panelled door, and in we went. The room was flooded with sunlight and just as elegant and grand as I expected, with high ceilings, a four-poster bed, and opulent décor; there was no mistaking this was a lady's room.

'This room is untouched,' said Clementine with a shiver, her breath frosted in the air; the fire hadn't been lit; it was freezing, not that I felt the cold. 'Just how it was when Violet was alive. Edmund insisted that nothing should be touched or changed. I think it was his way of keeping her memory alive, and strangely he has; I always sense Violet when I come in here,' she laughed. 'Oh, listen to me; I sound all spiritual,' she looked at Jocasta and smiled. 'What was that word you used? Ah, I have it, 'presentiment'; I sound like I'm having a presentiment.'

Jocasta didn't look amused or impressed as her lips tightened.

'What I mean is, I always think of Violet when I come in here,' Clementine glanced around her. 'It's such a beautiful room, full of elegance, and that's just how I remember her.'

Which it was.

'Yes, it is,' agreed Jocasta moving to one of the windows; the glass had misted in the cold. She rubbed at it with her hand. 'What a lovely view Violet had across the gardens and fields beyond... Hmm, that robin is very angry.'

'Robin?' I asked, bewildered.

Jocasta nodded, narrowing her eyes, 'Yes, there's a disgruntled robin in the garden; for such a little bird, they are so aggressive and territorial - the weather won't be helping,' she smiled. 'But I do like to see them with their little redbreast at this time of year; I always look for Christmas Cards with robins on them. We'll have to ask Ethel to put some food scraps out for them.'

'Yes,' agreed Agnes, moving to the window. 'I wonder why the robin is such a Christmas symbol?'

'Oh, it goes back to Victorian times,' said Winston going into history mode. 'That's where the tradition of sending Christmas cards first started. The Royal Mail postmen wore bright red uniforms, which earned them the nickname of 'robin' or 'redbreast'. Artists began illustrating Christmas cards with pictures relating to the delivery of letters, such as post-boxes or the postmen. Eventually, they started drawing the familiar little brown and red bird delivering letters instead of the postmen. This trend became very popular and continues to this day, with many robin-themed items being seen during the festive period.'

Jocasta turned from the window, taking in a portrait above the fireplace. 'What a charming picture - Violet and young Thomas, I assume?'

'Yes, it's by John Singer Sargent,' said Agnes proudly. 'It was painted the year before Thomas died,' she sighed hopelessly. 'Just look at them; they were so happy, with no idea what was to come.' She took her lace-trimmed handkerchief from her pocket and dabbed her eye.

'Indeed,' replied Jocasta thoughtfully. 'Let us focus on the joy they felt when the picture was painted, remembering that Violet did know happiness as did young Thomas. Sadly, some people never do.'

'Jocasta's right,' said Florence admiring Violet's bed and expensive, French, silk-covered furniture. 'Some people never know happiness. Of course, if you've had happiness and lost it, it's all the harder to bear, but you could argue people have their memories; it depends on your point of view,' she paused, shaking her head. 'As the poet Alfred Lord Tennyson said in his long elegy for the death of a friend, 'Having experienced real love in one's life is worth the pain of losing it, compared to never having experienced such love in the first place'.'

Silence...

'So well said,' agreed Winston. 'Tennyson is one of my favourite poets. But still, to lose a child and one's wife so close together must have been unbearable for Edmund.'

'It was,' said Clementine solemnly, joining Jocasta and Agnes by the heavily draped windows.

'Did Thomas have a nanny?' Asked Florence, admiring the portrait.

'Oh no,' said Agnes earnestly. 'Violet wouldn't entertain the idea; she was a very hands-on mother, totally devoted to Thomas and Edmund, although Thomas was always her priority, not that Edmund minded.'

Jocasta cleared her throat, sniffing the air, 'Agnes, Clementine, these noises you've heard in the house,' she glanced around the room. 'I'm sure Violet has been here very recently; I'd put my reputation on it.'

Clementine clutched her pearls, looking at Agnes nervously, 'How - how do you mean?'

Jocasta sniffed the air loudly as she moved around the room, 'Tell me did Violet wear perfume with,' she sniffed the air repeatedly, 'Amber,' Jocasta sniffed the air again. 'Bergamot... hmm most unusual I'm getting Deer musk... Leather... Civet... and... Tonka bean.'

'Goodness,' declared Clementine, 'You can smell all that?'

Jocasta nodded proudly, tapping her nose, 'Yes, I have a very sensitive sense of smell, just like an African Elephant.'

'Err - indeed, you have,' replied Clementine, hesitantly pulling her mouth to one side. 'Violet always wore Excellence de Fleurs Ambrées by the French perfume house of Guerlain. I'd recognise it anywhere.

'Well, I can smell it, and more importantly, there's something else in this room - ectoplasm; I can smell that strongly too,' Jocasta moved to the bed, still sniffing the air. 'Yes, I'd put money on it. Violet has been here – but she's not here now, although that doesn't mean she won't be back,' she slowly glanced around the room and moved back to the windows, stopping in front of one studying it, still sniffing the air. 'She's been here at this very window, I'm sure of it.'

'Are - are you sure?' Asked Agnes doubtfully, going pale.

Jocasta nodded, 'I've never been more certain of anything in my life spiritually speaking. I can sense her presence,' she paused. 'And don't ask me how, but I can feel her pain and anguish; it's strong.'

Jocasta looked at me, Winston, and Florence. 'I'm sure her attachment to this place, Thomas, and her pain are some of the things holding her here,' she chewed on her lip for a moment... 'Hmm, but I feel there's something else...'

'What?' I asked nervously, glancing at Winston and Florence.

Jocasta looked at me like I'd asked a stupid question, 'That dear boy is the million-dollar question and what we must find out,' she stiffened. 'But something else is at play here, I'm sure of it.'

Jocasta continued to walk around the room, sniffing the air while running her hands over Violet's things. She moved to one of her closets, carefully rummaging through her beautiful dresses and evening gowns, admiring them. They were works of art and fine examples of French haute couture, made from the best fabrics and decorated with delicate lace, hand beading, and intricate embroidery.

'It's a pity fashions change,' continued Jocasta. 'These are so beautiful, although the necessary Victorian corset was an instrument of torture for many women. Have you thought about donating them to a museum? I'm sure the Victoria & Albert Museum in London would be delighted to have them for their Textile and Fashion collection. Such gorgeous things need to be seen and admired.'

'We might get around to that one day now Edmund has passed,' said Clementine. 'As we said, he wanted time to stand still, to keep everything just as it was; he couldn't move on,' she looked puzzled. 'But tell me, what are you looking for in Violet's closets?'

'Oh, nothing in particular,' replied Jocasta. 'I'm trying to make a connection to Violet through her possessions; if we look long enough, I'm sure we'll find something, but it may take time. Tell me, where is Violet's jewellery?'

'Jewellery!' Exclaimed Clementine.

Jocasta nodded.

'Well, on the advice of Edmund's solicitor, we keep all of Violet's precious jewellery in a safe at the bank,' replied Agnes. 'Edmund left it lying around in drawers for years; I'm amazed it was never stolen. But as I've said, he wanted everything to be kept just as Violet had left it, not that it brought him any joy.'

Agnes moved to a deep drawer pulling out a beautiful French burr cedar tulipwood crossbanded Jewellery Box, with an Ebony and boxwood inlay and canted corners. She put it on the dressing table and opened it. Inside it was lined with turquoise and gold padded silk with several trays. Each tray contained an assortment of semiprecious jewellery with extravagant and complex compositions of flowers and foliage picked out in coloured gemstones.

'I believe some of this jewellery belonged to Violet's mother,' said Agnes. 'We've been so busy with the house and estate we've barely had a chance to look at Violet's things.'

'They look beautiful,' said Jocasta, quickly studying them. 'I'll take a good look at these later. I don't want to interrupt our tour of the house. But they are exquisite - you never know, I might be able to make a connection to Violet. It can come from anything related to the person.'

'Talking about the house, what do you know about it?' I asked, wanting to keep us on track.

'Oh, a little,' said Clementine. 'We've grown up with it. Our grandfather, Montague Rothery, had the house built in the Georgian style, which he admired. The land had been given to him by his father, it was ten acres back then, but over the years, Montague bought up many hectares of the surrounding land. He and our grandmother Elspeth moved into the house in 1854, and, over the years, they added the stables with a barn and more outbuildings for carriages. He wanted the house to be private; you will have noticed that it was not visible from the gated entrance when you arrived here. Agnes and I always think the long sweeping tree-lined drive creates a sense of ceremony with its impressive final reveal of the Hall.'

'Yes,' I agreed, 'it's impressive. Tell me, do you know if there was anything on the land before the house was built?'

'Goodness,' now you're asking me something,' replied Clementine reflectively, clutching her chest and chewing on her lip; she looked at Agnes. 'Like what exactly?'

I shrugged, 'Anything really, former dwellings, a farm, church, that sort of thing.'

Clementine shook her head slowly, 'It's such a long time ago, but not as far as we know; I think it was just an open field or meadow. Why do you ask?'

'Oh, no reason, really; I'm just curious.' Jocasta and Florence glanced at me; Jocasta tapped the side of her nose. That was code for we needed to find out, which we did.

'Is that how the family made their wealth?' Asked Winston. 'Through land ownership?'

Agnes nodded, 'Yes, as far as we know. It goes back to the early part of the 19th century, and Montague's father, Bernard Rothery, our great grandfather, he died in 1861. Bernard had poor health; we never knew him. He started the family fortune and must have been a savvy businessman, making a lot of money from buying land and renting it out,' she smiled. 'Although I don't think you could ever describe the family as the landed gentry, at least not in the earlier days. As his only child, Montague inherited everything after his father's death and, as I've already said, continued in his father's footsteps and bought a lot more land. Like Bernard, he had a good business head. I think most, if not all, of the family records, are in the study cum library; if they're not there, they will be at the bank or family solicitors.'

Winston's ears pricked up, 'Oh, you have a library, I'd hoped you might have; houses like this usually do. You must allow me to look at it; I love nothing more than a library full of books; the older, the better.'

Which he did; I hoped we wouldn't have to spend hours in there. Don't get me wrong, I like books, but with Winston, they were more like an obsession.

'Of course,' smiled Agnes. 'Montague loved books, like his father before him. And like his father, Montague also worked as a Magistrate; he was highly respected in Kent, sitting on several committees.'

Montague and Elspeth were quite philanthropic,' said Clementine proudly. 'Helping several causes like the opening of the church school in Brenchley, Elspeth loved children. Montague sat on the Board of Guardians and contributed significant funds to help maintain the Tonbridge Workhouse, the new one had opened in 1836. The workhouse had outbreaks of smallpox, and he helped to fund the building of an isolation block. And in the 1850s, he and Elspeth helped set up the hospital there, along with a working farm and pig farm - they wanted the workhouse to be self-sufficient.

Montague also contributed funds to the London Ragged School Union, established in April 1844. It provided free education, food, clothing, lodging, and other home missionary services for poor children, and he helped spread ragged school ideals across the country.'

'Hmm,' mused Winston curling his bottom lip. 'They sound like a pillar of the local community. Montague being a magistrate and his father before him is interesting but not unusual. From the 18th century, magistrates were taken mainly from the landed gentry. Magistrates were very powerful men. As the need for a professional police force became apparent, so did the need for professional magistracy. This led to the first paid professional magistrate being appointed in 1813.'

'Didn't they combine the roles of Policemen, Judges, Civil Servants, and Local Government authorities?' Asked Agnes.

Winston bobbed his head, 'Yes, and it's a changing institution that continues today. But one mustn't underestimate the status, prestige, power, and function the magistrate had during Montague and particularly Bernard's time. It could take in far more than minor crimes such as drunkenness, fighting, and theft, and they dealt with crimes without the benefit of a jury. Offenders were issued fines and periods of imprisonment, leaving the higher courts, such as the Old Bailey, to deal with only more severe cases of felony. Sadly, many magistrates were easily corrupted, with some saying, the greatest criminals of the town were the officers of justice.' He smiled. 'Not that I'm suggesting Montague and Bernard engaged in such things, but they could have upset many people and given them a thirst for revenge.'

Winston was right. I remember it well; corruption was rife in London back in my day.

Agnes glanced around the room, looking at her gold watch, 'Well, if we've finished here, let's continue our tour. We've lots to see, so we need to speed up a little, or it will take us all day,' she smiled. 'Not that we're in any rush.'

Chapter 4

Elspeth Rothery sat in her white night clothes, tightly wrapped in a thick wool blanket, trying to compose herself, rocking backwards and forwards in the nursery rocking chair; she had no idea how long she'd been sitting there, losing all sense of time. She wiped away her tears, but as fast as she did, more came. Apart from the rhythmic creak of the chair, the house seemed unnaturally still and quiet. She was tired of people fussing around her like she was ill, not that she was herself; how could she be? Elspeth sighed, feeling relieved to get away from everyone, to finally be alone.

Grief consumed her as she sat by the ornamented iron crib, rocking herself backwards and forwards. She ran a trembling hand lightly over the crib, thinking of the bundle of joy that should have been lying there. She and Montague had the crib specially made for the baby they had named Raymond. It would have been Rosemary had it been a girl. She glanced around the beautiful nursery, thinking it felt out of place in the house and a cruel reminder of her misfortune. Their home seemed so lifeless; Elspeth didn't remember the place ever feeling so quiet and empty.

She gently touched her still swollen stomach, finding it hard to believe her baby was stillborn. Elspeth closed her eyes tightly, wanting to shout, scream, and cry simultaneously. Her hopes of being a mother had disappeared at that moment; the dreams she had of holding her boy and watching him grow were gone, shattered to pieces. Everything she wanted and planned for was lost, leaving a raw, festering wound inside her.

Now, she just wanted peace and quiet, to be left alone to grieve and come to terms with what had happened. Elspeth couldn't imagine a day when she would ever heal and find tranquillity. Montague told her they would recover and be stronger but said it would take time, not that she could think about the future. Elspeth knew she would always feel their loss like a dagger at her heart.

Strangely, part of her wished for the sound of laughter and a crowd. Elspeth thought it might be a brief distraction, giving her some respite from her despair and a glimpse of normality, particularly at this festive time. It made her think of Queen Victoria, Prince Albert, and Charles Dickens. Dickens had become known as Mr Christmas due to his now-famous book A Christmas Carol. Christmas was a time when people were supposed to celebrate the birth of Jesus and be full of joy and happiness. The thought only served to add to her despair and make her feel more hopeless and wretched.

Elspeth shook her head, wiping away her tears. Happy, she thought as her body heaved; how could she ever be happy? She couldn't imagine ever feeling content with life, and herself, let alone smile again. Elspeth reflected on that awful moment, the moment they realised Raymond had been taken from them. The scene repeatedly played in her mind in a constant loop; it was endless torture. Montague had held her tightly, telling her life would go on, trying his best to hide his grief and comfort her. Never had she been more thankful for his kindness, love, and devotion, wanting to be in his strong arms forever.

Yet, in her grief, she didn't have the energy to disagree with him but wondered how her life could ever go on; she would never be the same again. It was like time froze when Raymond was born so perfect, yet... dead. *Dead...dead...dead...* that awful word seemed to echo all around her getting louder... *dead...dead...dead....*

Elspeth closed her eyes tightly, shaking her head violently, trying to snap herself out of her misery and focus on something else. She could hear the steady tick-tock of the grandfather clock in the hall and concentrated on its melodic rhythm, taking comfort from its familiarity. As she allowed her mind to wander, she found herself thinking of the pompous, round-bellied, self-satisfied Charles Blair and his haughty and pushy wife, Cynthia. This evening she and Montague should have been going to a drinks party at their grand historic house, Blair Manor, to see in the New Year; it would have been her first social outing as a new mother.

When they received the invitation earlier in the month, Elspeth had protested, saying she didn't want to go. Her advanced stage of pregnancy gave her an excuse; she felt very uncomfortable and was sure she wouldn't be able to attend. But Montague, ever the optimist, had insisted, saying it would take her mind off things. He then spoilt his thoughtfulness by talking about the advantages of polite society and his business interests, but that's men for you. He'd sent one of the servants with a note giving their apologies saying Elspeth was indisposed. Not that anyone expected them to attend. Servants talk, and news travels fast in a small town - particularly bad news.

In truth, Elspeth couldn't abide the social-climbing Blair's. She particularly despised the social butterfly Cynthia, who fluttered around with her ornate Eugene Rimmel fans wearing the latest French silks, lace, and chiffons, dripping in diamonds like the fairy from the top of a Christmas tree. There was nothing subtle about Cynthia; if you'd been to paradise, she had a season ticket.

Cynthia had recently met His Royal Highness Prince Albert at a supper party in London's smart Belgravia and made sure everyone knew about it, insisting the prince was quite taken with her. The prince probably smelt her long before seeing her; Cynthia always wore a heavy, cloying, jasmine French perfume. Elspeth felt sure fluttering Cynthia would have thrown herself at him in the most vulgar fashion, overdressed in her frills and flounces sparkling like a beacon. Not that avoiding the party was any consolation to Elspeth, but at least she wouldn't have to face Cynthia or people's pity. She shuddered at the very thought of it.

Fluttering Cynthia already had five children and seemed to have no problems in that department, effortlessly popping out babies like a cork from a champagne bottle. She also managed to maintain her twenty-three-inch waist with the help of a determined lady's maid and robust corsetry. Cynthia waving goodbye to comfort, all for the sake of high fashion and keeping up appearances... 'Stop it, stop it,' Elspeth said out loud, annoyed with herself. She didn't want to sound bitter or be unkind, but Cynthia had five healthy children, and she had none; her lips trembled as more tears rolled down her face. Why was life so cruel and unfair?

Elspeth dug deep, trying to summon her resolve. She thought when the day came for her to face fluttering Cynthia, along with the ladies from the afternoon tea brigade, her various charities, good causes, and church committees, she would stand tall, gracious, and proud. She would be strong, thanking people for their kind words and condolences, showing no emotion.

Elspeth would smile sweetly and serenely, going about her business, keeping up appearances, no matter how much her heart was breaking inside. She decided that she and Montague would never talk about Raymond with anyone; it would be as if he had never existed. Not because they didn't love him, he would be permanently etched in their hearts, but it was the only way she could see herself moving forward and getting over the loss.

More tears rolled down her face. Elspeth suspected something wasn't right towards the end of her pregnancy. The baby stopped kicking at around seven months, but the family doctor, Dr Clutterbuck, told her she was imagining things due to nervous exhaustion. He said it wasn't uncommon in women of breeding due to their delicate nature. She didn't know if she should feel complimented or insulted but leaned heavily towards the latter.

As a man of medicine, he informed her that the heavy burden of pregnancy interrupted a woman's menstrual cycle. He reminded Elspeth that menstruation was a time of illness, debilitation, and temporary insanity. Dr Clutterbuck believed this temporary insanity could present itself during pregnancy and linger, causing melancholy. He firmly believed that women had drawn the short straw in their biological evolution, making them the weaker sex. He argued that women were condemned to weakness and sickness because of their female physiology and nature, and put quite simply, it was something they must accept and endure.

Elspeth let out a long sigh. She disagreed with his beliefs about women and didn't see men in any way superior to women, particularly men like the stuffy Dr Clutterbuck. She reminded him that in many cultures throughout history, women were seen as unique and worshipped because of their ability to produce a child. Dr Clutterbuck bristled, saying that on the continent, much of history was recorded by uncivilised savages. Savages who did childlike drawings on cave walls while worshipping pagan gods like the sun, walking about half-naked, waving their what not or spears, while chanting rambling coarse words of indecency and barbarity!

Elspeth tried to move her thoughts to the future, hoping and praying the new year would be better. She never imagined she'd be happy to see the end of 1856; after all, it had been a year full of hope, joy, and happiness. Yet it had all come to this, nothing but unbearable grief and misery. More tears spilt down her cheeks.

Raymond was stillborn on Christmas day; Elspeth's fear and anxiety had proven correct. Dr Clutterbuck was sympathetic but unmoved by the event, shaking his head and distancing himself from any responsibility, giving a long list of possible causes for the stillbirth to a distraught Montague. They included haemorrhoids, gastric irritation, coughing, sneezing, and anaemia, along with excessive joy, grief, rage, sorrow, and apprehension, not to mention the bedroom attentions of an overzealous husband. So, anything really, take your pick.

Truth be told, he had no medical explanation other than it being one of the risks and dangers of pregnancy for a young woman, not that it was the woman's fault. He was familiar with infant mortality; deaths were not uncommon. Mrs Nora Edmonds was a respected midwife in the town; she sympathised and, like Dr Clutterbuck, was all too familiar with stillbirths. However, in her experience, stillbirths didn't always inspire grief and sadness; many women from poorer and larger families were often relieved to have a stillbirth; it was one less mouth to feed and child to care for.

Dr Clutterbuck felt sure Elspeth and Montgomery would go on to have a large family; telling them the first child could be difficult for a young woman. Privately, he told Elspeth it was the wife's duty to look after her husband's every need, acquire all the skills of domesticity, preserve morality, and provide him with a God-fearing home and robust, healthy family. She found his words of no comfort and was grateful she had not married such a man. Unlike most men of her acquaintance, Montague treated her as an equal, not as a possession and something he owned.

Old Reverend Dewhurst managed to visit with the holy bible in hand, battling his way through the heavy snow in his religious robes to offer his condolences and bless the child. He told Elspeth to find comfort in God's righteous path, saying God was testing her and Montague, but God would guide them through if they let him, and to put themselves in his hands. Like Dr Clutterbuck, the Reverend's words offered her no comfort or contentment, but she was grateful for his visit, kindness, and blessing.

She stopped rocking and stood up slowly, pulling her blanket around her and moved to one of the cupboards taking out a beautiful music box. It was a recent gift to celebrate her forthcoming birth from an acquaintance of Bernard's, Montague's father. She couldn't recall who had sent it, thinking she must remember to check so she could write a thank-you letter. It was exquisite and of the finest quality, depicting heavenly angels and the baby Jesus. She placed it on the writing table, admiring it but didn't wind it up or switch it on; she was in no mood for music, only silence.

Elspeth moved to the window. A single star shone brightly in the night sky like a beacon; it was snowing heavily, the snow settling on everything it touched, forming deep drifts across the gardens; she was pleased she didn't have to go out. Elspeth trembled, pulling her blanket closer to her, glancing at the fireplace, wondering why the fire hadn't been lit; she hadn't noticed it earlier, not that she felt cold. She hoped she was coming down with a fever, not that she felt feverish.

Elspeth rubbed her head; her vision swam. She put her hand on the wall to steady herself. Over the past week, she'd started having dizzy spells, something she'd never had before. She put it down to weakness caused by childbirth. It was a strange kind of dizziness; she felt like she was in a dark, spinning tunnel heading towards a bright light. It made her feel lightheaded and faint; she must remember to carry her smelling salts. She should probably eat something but had no appetite.

She glanced around the room. Something felt different, yet everything looked just as it always had. Why did she have a nagging feeling of unease? She thought of Montague, wondering where he was and what he was doing; she knew he grieved as much as she did. She heard a creek; her eyes moved to the rocking chair; it started rocking backwards and forwards. She could hear something in the distance; it sounded far away; she listened hard; she was sure it was a child crying....

***

'Obviously, this is the nursery, said Clementine, swishing in ahead of us. I caught a whiff of her lavender cologne; it was sweet, floral, evergreen, and woodsy; it suited her. 'Like Violet's room, Edmund insisted the nursery shouldn't be touched with everything left just as it was,' she sighed, looking in all four corners of the room, recalling her memories. 'God bless him,' she sighed again, shaking her head. 'He used to sit here for hours lost in his grief, oblivious to the outside world; I hope it comforted him.'

'I think it did, sister,' said Agnes mournfully, holding her perfectly manicured hands together as if praying. 'May he rest in peace.'

'Is everything just as it was in 1901 - when Thomas passed?' Asked Winston, looking doubtful, he glanced around the room, taking his glasses out of his jacket pocket.

'I think so - well, what I mean is, we haven't touched anything in here,' said Clementine smoothing down her hair, not that it needed it. 'Other than taking the dust covers off everything. This house holds so many beautiful things; they deserve to be seen. We want the house to look like a home, not a warehouse or storage facility. This is another room we've not had time to look at properly. We've been concentrating on the areas of the house we use the most, but I'm sure we'll get around to it soon.'

Her eyes fell on the bed, and she exhaled heavily. 'Little Thomas lost his fight and passed away in that bed with Violet and Edmund by his side - when he slipped away,' she paused, looking at Agnes like she would know what she was about to say. 'Well, in many ways, he took Violet and Edmund with him; they were never the same after that,' she shook her head, lost in compassion. 'How could they be? In their grief, they couldn't even comfort each other.'

Silence...

Despite the nursery's associated sadness, I have to say it was a charming room with several draped windows; it was expensively decorated in the Victorian style. In addition to Thomas's bed, it contained beautifully made bespoke oak cupboards, closets, an ornate marble fireplace with an iron fireguard, and an iron crib with a colourful mobile hanging above it.

Vine-patterned wallpaper lined the walls, and a vibrantly patterned carpet graced the floor. The furnishings included a green velvet upholstered sofa and chairs, a rocking chair, and a writing table. Toys were dotted around the room, including a rocking horse. Some toys were on shelves; I could see a Noah's Ark, Doll's House, card games, dolls, books, and jigsaws. It was strange, but I was sure the rocking chair was moving but stopped as we entered the room. None of the others seemed to notice it, but I was sure of it; call it ghostly intuition.

'This room has known great joy and sadness; I can feel it strongly,' declared Jocasta, touching everything, trying to make a spiritual connection. 'But, as a nursery, one can't deny it's quite delightful, and for the purposes of our investigation, I think it's good the rooms are as Edmund left them. The more things are untouched, the better,' she moved around the room, carefully running her hand across the walls. 'The rooms may hold residual energy and clues from their past - think of each room rather like a crime scene, and we are the constabulary or detectives investigating.'

'A crime scene!' exclaimed Agnes, looking alarmed, but she quickly brightened. 'You make it sound like a Sherlock Holmes story by Sir Arthur Conan Doyle; you know the 'consulting detective',' her eyes smiled playfully. 'Clementine and I loved his short stories in The Strand Magazine; we were sad when they ended in 1927. The two of us had great fun guessing who had committed the various crimes and atrocities.'

Jocasta nodded, clutching her hands behind her back as she paced the room, 'And were your guesses correct?' She asked, raising her eyebrows.

Agnes hesitated... 'Ah, well, I must confess we were quite hopeless,' she sounded deflated, shaking her head and forcing a laugh. 'But we enjoy a good mystery, romantic suspense story, or anything by Elizabeth Gaskell.'

'Hmm, I see,' replied Jocasta, like she already knew that, and continued to pace the room. 'I do enjoy a well-written and researched mystery or anything with a strong female character. I can't be doing with weak, besotted women fainting at the drop of a hat or the moment a man looks at her - Although I must admit, I have a soft spot for Jane Austen and her Pride and Prejudice and the aloof Mr Darcy,' Jocasta paused, wrinkling her nose, and sneezed loudly, 'Oh, do excuse me, it must be the dust.' She pulled her handkerchief from her divided skirt pocket, blowing her nose loudly.

'Dust!' exclaimed Agnes indignantly.

'Yes,' declared Jocasta tapping her nose and putting her handkerchief back in her pocket. 'Like most mediums, I have a very sensitive nose and a heightened sense of awareness, that's why I get sudden presentiments - But anyway, back to our investigation. You see, human interference can disturb the spiritual highway, sending everything into disarray in the Twilight Zone.'

Agnes and Clementine looked at her blank.

'It's complicated. Think of it this way - some of the rooms in this house are caught in the semidarkness, between the physical and spiritual worlds.'

Jocasta put her hands on the rocking horse and breathed deeply, shaking her head. 'No, nothing here... Now, if I'm right, we must move whatever is captured in this semidarkness back to where they belong in the spirit world. But to do that, we must discover the root cause of what's holding them here. If we can do that, we can also free them from their pain and anguish.'

Jocasta took another deep breath as if fortifying herself, 'And it's interesting, you should mention Sir Arthur Conan Doyle; he has a longstanding interest in mystical subjects and remained fascinated by the idea of paranormal phenomena. In 1889, he became a founding member of the Hampshire Society for Psychical Research. In 1893, he joined the London-based Society for Psychical Research; he even showed an interest in joining our society in Pluckley, such is the group's fame.'

That was a bit of an exaggeration, but I didn't say anything; Jocasta was on a roll.

She looked at Agnes and Clementine like they should both be impressed and continued, 'Sadly, he died last year, but he wrote many books about paranormal activity,' she chewed on her lip thoughtfully. 'Although many of his theories have been challenged and disproven, but I've always admired him,' she smiled. 'Anyway, I digress; we must stay focused and not allow ourselves to be distracted.'

I laughed to myself; I couldn't see that happening; Jocasta,

Winston, and Florence were easily distracted, particularly by tea, food, and in Winston's case, books or history!

Agnes wavered, looking at Clementine nervously, wringing her hands, 'Hmm, semidarkness - it does sound complicated. I'm afraid this is all new to us; we've never thought about such things before.'

Jocasta stopped pacing, looking earnest as her eyebrows knitted together, 'No, you won't have, and why should you? Like illnesses, we only tend to become aware of things when they affect us directly, and the spirit world is no different. You, we, are now in the uncharted waters of multidimensional astral chambers and spiritual domains. You see, there are limitless doorways in the spirit world leading to many unknown worlds in the Astral Plane and darker areas of The Twilight Zone - as I've said, it's complicated.'

Clementine and Agnes looked at each other, trying to remain calm, then at Jocasta as if she were addressing them in a foreign language.

Jocasta continued her pacing, 'But let me assure you, you are not the first, and you won't be the last to experience spiritual phenomena; it can come in numerous forms... You know, in many ways, you're quite fortunate; most people never get the chance to experience the spirit world. I always feel they're missing out. Not, of course, that anyone would wish to encounter a demon or poltergeist; they can be most troublesome and unpleasant.'

Jocasta made it sound like they'd won a major prize in a competition, but I was pleased she said that about demons and poltergeists. I was impressed by Jocasta's descriptions, not that I knew anything about astral chambers. Still, the spirit world was undoubtedly full of new surprises and just like life, it was constantly evolving.

Agnes swallowed hard, trying her best to stay composed, 'Anyway, this was also Edmund and our mother's nursery. We used to play here from time to time when we were girls visiting our grandparents with mother and father; it brings back many memories. This room gets flooded with light in the summer,' her eyes moved around the room. 'I think Violet made minor changes when she knew she was expecting Thomas, but the room still looks as I remember it when I was a girl.'

Florence was using her witching ways trying to detect any magic or magical objects in the room and moved to a round music box on the writing table; it depicted two heavenly angels on a gold stand admiring the baby Jesus in his manger. The words 'Oh come let us adore him' were written in white letters on the gold background. She switched it on, and the angels started moving around in a circle to the tinkling music of the Christmas carol, Oh Come, All Ye Faithful. We all stood in silence as if hypnotized, listening to the tune until it stopped.

'How lovely,' said Jocasta dreamily as if taken to the heavens. 'I love music boxes, but I've never seen one like this before.'

'Strange, I don't remember ever seeing it,' said Clementine looking bewildered. 'Do you, Agnes?'

Agnes shook her head, 'I can't say I do, but isn't it lovely? Quite charming, it draws the eye.'

Clementine stood admiring the box from different angles. 'I'm sure we would have remembered this; it looks new and has probably hardly ever been used. I bet it's not seen the light of day for three decades,' she curled her lip and stroked her chin. 'But how odd. I wonder how it got here on the writing table.'

'Perhaps one of the servants was dusting, found it and put it out on display,' said Florence. 'After all, we are approaching Christmas. For Christians, the true meaning of Christmas is the celebration of the birth of Jesus Christ, which this depicts so romantically.'

'We must remember the word 'Christmas' is a shortened version of Christ or Christian Mass,' said Winston going into history mode. 'I think people forget that. Christmas began to be widely celebrated with a specific liturgy in the 9th century and over many years has evolved into what we have today.'

'Yes - the servants, of course,' agreed Agnes with a relieved expression, trying to hide her growing feelings of unease as she glanced at Florence. 'That makes perfect sense; it's just the sort of thing Ethel would do; she's so thoughtful and very religious. I must remember to thank her – it's so lovely. I'll come back later to collect it and put it on prominent display downstairs near the Christmas tree; such a lovely thing deserves to be seen and appreciated at this time of year.'

'It looks French to me, but perhaps made for the British or American markets,' said Winston putting on his glasses to scrutinize it closely. 'It's outstanding quality, probably from the mid-19th century. The round base, the box part is made from gilded brass, mother of pearl, and white marble. The angels are hand-painted in gold and made from fine porcelain. I would say this music box was made for a fine lady, not a child.' He carefully picked it up, looking for a maker's mark but didn't find anything.

'Is there anything in it?' I asked, standing on my tip toes, peering over his shoulder.

'Ah, good idea,' he said, putting the music box on the desk and carefully opening it. The box had a satisfying click, revealing a gold, padded silk lining; Winston peered inside. 'It seems empty,' he ran a finger around the inside. 'Hmm, I may have spoken too soon; there is something here.' He took out a tiny roll of paper; it looked like a small cigarette. We all held our breath as he carefully unrolled it; the paper was so thin it was almost translucent. A mark was drawn on the paper in dark red ink, a symbol.

'Do you recognise the symbol?' I asked.

He shook his head, 'No, but this could be the maker's mark; I'll try to find out.' He took out his wallet and carefully put the paper inside.

My ghostly senses told me it wasn't a maker's mark. Jocasta moved in to have a better look; she ran her finger gently over the music box but quickly pulled her hand away as a chill ran up and down her spine.

'What is it?' I asked nervously; the others quickly stepped back.

'Hmm, I don't know,' she replied softly, looking far away, shaking her head. 'I just had a strange feeling - a feeling this is - hmm, connected to something,' she glanced around the room and then out towards the windows. 'I can't tell you what, but I don't think it's - good.'

Just what I wanted to hear, but then again, in my experience, house hauntings were rarely good.

Florence agreed, 'I think Jocasta's right; I sense this music box is somehow enchanted and linked to magic.'

'But how could that be?' I asked, feeling bewildered. 'Do you think it's linked to dark magic?'

Florence pursed her lips, shaking her head, 'I'm not sure, but I sense a mystical force,' she hesitated. 'It's a strange one, I feel the box is mostly dormant, but it sits in waiting for... for something.'

'Waiting for what?' I asked eagerly; it was getting worse. That was the last thing we needed, something sinister sitting in waiting for something unknown.

Florence shook her head again, looking apologetic, 'I don't know, but I'm sure I'm right.'

'Hmm, it's interesting you should say that Florence, I agree and feel this beautiful object is somehow connected to whatever is happening here,' agreed Jocasta, her face contorting in frustration; she looked dumbfounded, shaking her head. 'What is it about this place? For some reason, this house holds onto pain from Christmases past, and I'm sure it's deliberate. Whatever holds the pain here thrives on it, and this music box could somehow be part of that.'

Jocasta scratched her head with both hands as if rallying her thoughts, 'Someone or something wants it that way, almost like it's some kind of - well, I want to say revenge,' she stiffened, pulling her shoulders back as she looked at Clementine and Agnes. 'That's why you've heard the sounds, voices from the past. I can't explain why, at least...' Jocasta stopped mid-sentence and started sniffing the air, 'Ah, I thought so; I can smell ectoplasm; someone has been here,' she sniffed again. 'But this time, it was someone different, not Violet.'

'Another ghost?' I asked. 'Do you think it's a demon?'

Jocasta shook her head, still sniffing the air, 'No, I don't think so. I'd feel that in my base chakra, although a cunning demon could be involved, we must always be on our guard,' she moved around the nursery and stopped by the rocking chair, holding onto the chair for a long moment. 'The ectoplasm is very strong here; whoever it was, they were sat in this chair for some time.'

Clementine and Agnes were turning paler by the second, fidgeting with their hands and feet. Their breathing became uneasy as they tried to control their fluttering heartbeat.

'I'm pleased you've said that.' I replied, feeling relieved. 'When we came in here, I was sure it had been rocking but stopped abruptly when we entered the room.'

All eyes turned to me.

'How interesting,' said Jocasta looking me up and down knowingly. 'You have the sharpest eye for these things, Jasper. I didn't see that - I really need to fine-tune my chakras the next time I go into a trance.'

Silence...

'Could it be Edmund?' Asked Agnes meekly, swallowing hard.

Jocasta shook her head, 'No, it was a woman, of that I'm sure, a woman in pain, full of grief, just like Violet.'

'Full of pain,' said Clementine uneasily, taking a deep breath, trying to calm her fluttering pulse. 'The only other woman who ever lived here apart from us was our grandmother Elspeth, Montague's Wife - she died in 1899... Although, there would have been the female house staff. I imagine there would have been quite a few of those over the years, and our parents had a nanny; could it be her?'

Jocasta shrugged, wrinkling her nose solicitously, 'Hmm, I suppose it could be,' she proffered. 'But whoever it is, I wonder what they could have been so upset about; we know it can't have been the death of Thomas because he didn't have a nanny - perhaps it was the death of a friend or relative,' she shrugged. 'Of course, I'm only guessing, but whatever it was, it was certainly distressing news.'

'When did Montague die?' I asked.

'Montague?' Said Agnes, all aflutter. 'Goodness, I haven't thought about it in years - it was the winter of 1897... on...'

'On Christmas Day,' I replied.

'Yes...' replied Clementine slowly in a faint whisper, the cogs turning in her brain. 'I don't know why, but we hadn't made that connection, although Agnes and I were quite young when he died.'

'Hmm, the mystery deepens,' said Florence pulling her thoughts together. 'First, we have Montague, then Thomas, then Violet, then Edmund, all dying on Christmas day. And I'd put money on it that Montague died at exactly the same time as they did.'

Silence...

'Remind me, when did Bernard die?' Asked Winston.

'1861,' said Agnes, digging deep into her memory; she shook her head. 'For some reason, the date has slipped my mind; I think his death was sudden and unexpected, probably his heart. He used to visit this house but never lived here.'

'What about his wife?' I asked.

'He was married to Dora; to my knowledge, she never lived here either,' replied Agnes chewing nervously on her lip. 'I think she died in 1865; the details might be here in the study. If they're not there, they're bound to be in the church records; they're both buried there. We haven't been to their grave for a while; we never knew them.'

'Yes, we must check,' muttered Florence. 'It may be relevant; they could somehow be connected. If magic is involved, it can transcend generations,' she did a 360-degree turn, looking at the floor, the walls, and the ceiling. 'Whatever is happening in this house links to pains of Christmases past. I feel that for some reason, agony and tragedy must be re-lived every Christmas by those who experienced it.'

'But why?' Asked Clementine, baffled. 'Why would someone want to do something so wicked?'

Florence shook her head, 'That is what we must find out; dark forces can feed on powerful emotions; that's how they sustain their existence in The Twilight Zone.'

Jocasta agreed as we continued to look around the nursery, examining the contents of cupboards and closets; everything was of the finest quality.

'Why did I get a bad connection from that rocking chair?' Mused Jocasta out loud, although I think she was talking to herself. 'Because as I've said, I'm also sensing the grief here was overtaken with joy, that is until Thomas died in 1901. Then everything changed.'

There was a knock on the door. It was Ethel all of a dither, 'I've stoked up the fire and put tea, some of my shortbread biscuits, spiced cinnamon, and marzipan buns in the drawing-room,' she said softly. She had the same severe hairdo, and her face looked like she'd cleaned it with a scouring pad. Today she was dressed entirely in black, which washed her out; she looked, well, for want of a better word, ghostly.

'Thank you, Ethel,' said Clementine, almost relieved. 'We'll come straight down; I'm ready for a cup of tea, I'm sure we all are,' she turned to the writing desk. 'And thank you for finding this music box; it's charming. I'm going to bring it downstairs and put it near the Christmas tree,' she glanced at Florence. 'That is, if you think it will be safe?'

Florence smiled, trying to look reassuring, 'Good idea, best keep it out in the open, where we can keep an eye on it.'

Ethel looked mystified, 'Music box?' she said curtly. 'I'm sorry, I don't know anything about a music box,' she glanced at the object sitting on the writing table. 'Is that it?'

Clementine nodded.

Ethel stared at it for a long moment, 'How charming? It looks so refined and elegant. I do like to see religious objects at this time of year; we must remember that Christmas is about Jesus, the church, and the good lord,' her mouth tightened, and she frowned, looking pensive. 'Not trinkets, baubles, and grotesque overindulgences.'

'But if you didn't put it out, dear,' asked Agnes. 'Then who did?'

Ethel shook her head, pulling her mouth to one side, 'I've no idea; no one's said anything to me, but I'll ask the others. Oh, and you haven't forgotten that Reverend Sommersby and Miss Duckworth, the church organist, are calling this afternoon to discuss your duet at tomorrow's fund racing carol concert for the restoration of the churches-stained-glass-windows? Miss Nugent from the drapery told me they're expecting the mayor, his wife, and members of the administrative county to attend the concert.'

'Goodness is it today?' said Clementine glancing at her watch and fiddling with her diamond and emerald ring. 'Do you know we've been so wrapped up with this house and ghosts, it's slipped our minds. But not to worry, as you know, we've been rehearsing at the piano and are fully prepared.'

Ethel turned pale at the mention of ghosts, crossing herself before grabbing the door to steady herself.

'What are you singing?' Asked Florence, trying to move the conversation away from ghosts for Ethel's sake. 'I love a good carol concert. Carols are such joyful songs bringing people together, connecting them to shared experiences and feelings. In church, I particularly like rousing hymns of communal praise.'

'It's Charles Wesley's Hark the Herald Angels Sing,' replied Agnes. 'Clementine and I are both sopranos; we were tutored by the renowned Florence Perry; she was famous for her Yum Yum.'

'Yum Yum?' I asked hesitantly, trying not to laugh.

Agnes nodded, 'Yes, you know from the Mikado; Florence was huge with the D'Oyly Carte Opera Company, but she was a hard taskmaster. The carol is one of our favourites, and the church choir is wonderful; they sound like heavenly angels thanks to our choir mistress, Miss Lovage. The church has been decorated with wonderful greenery and floral displays for Christmas. They have a nativity scene and a beautiful tree, all decorated by the ladies' church committee.'

Agnes smiled wryly. 'The ladies are very competitive when

decorating the church for festivals as they take it in turns. This year it's Mrs Mottershead, Miss Ryder, and Miss Bush; you couldn't wish to meet a more determined group of women; they started planning their displays with military precision in April. But it's all very hush-hush and top secret. There's also a Christmas bring-and-buy sale; Ethel's made some Christmas cakes, mince pies, and chocolate fancies. Both the Reverend and verger love a nice fancy; they can't keep their hands off them – and it's all for a good cause. Anyway, you must all come to the concert - I insist.

'Yes, you must join us,' said Clementine, adjusting her expensive silk scarf. 'But come, sister dear, I don't want our tea to go cold; I can't abide cold tea,' she glanced at the window, nodding towards it. 'It's starting to snow again; the sky looks full of it. I wonder if we're going to have a white Christmas? - I do hope so.'

'Oh, I can't think about Christmas properly,' replied Agnes brusquely, her voice going up an octave. 'Snow is the least of our worries; I won't be able to rest in my bed until we get to the bottom of whatever is going on in this house; I'm sure the devil possesses it.'

'Calm yourself, sister,' said Clementine, putting her arms around Agnes's shoulders while trying to calm herself. 'Take some deep breaths and think about dolphins or whales; I always find them relaxing.'

As she said this, I was sure I could hear whispers coming from the walls - Jocasta put out her hand. 'Shhh, what's that?'

Be gone...be gone...be gone... The words echoed in a faint whisper around the room.

Jocasta put her finger to her mouth, glancing in every direction, 'Who's there? Reveal yourselves to me... I command you to reveal yourselves at once.'

Silence...

'I'm assuming you all heard that?' She asked in a whisper.

We all nodded, looking at each other uneasily. I glanced at Clementine and Agnes and whispered, 'Have you heard that before?'

They were huddled together with Ethel, shaking their heads, 'It's hard to say with the noises,' said Clementine breathlessly. 'But I don't recall hearing the words 'be gone'.'

'Fascinating,' muttered Florence reflectively, recovering her composure. 'I think the 'be gone' is for our benefit, for me, Jocasta, Winston, and Jasper. Someone or something doesn't want us here. Perhaps we're getting nearer to the truth.

Jocasta straightened her back and glanced at the three women stoically, 'Now, stay calm, ladies. I may need to consult my crystal. But first, I need some of those restorative shortbread biscuits, spiced marzipan buns, and a reviving cup of tea to get my chakras and energy centres flowing. If I let my energy levels drop, it could affect any presentiments, and I do like a nice bit of marzipan at this time of year.'

Chapter 5

Montague Rothery sat in his study; he could finally let his tears flow. It was the only room in the house he could guarantee he wouldn't be disturbed, the only place he felt safe to let his emotions and grief surface. It was something he had to do in private, away from prying eyes and loose tongues.

He found himself thinking about the famous expression of the British stiff upper lip, questioning why public expressions of grief were seen as a sign of weakness, not that he saw himself as weak, just human with all of life's foibles. He quickly pushed the thought out of his mind; he needed to be strong and stoic for his darling wife and keep his dignity in front of the house staff.

The servants never came into the study uninvited and had a strict timetable for cleaning and attending to the fire. Montague told them he didn't want to be disturbed and would be busy. They wouldn't bother him unless it were something unexpected or urgent. He knew the house staff were just as shocked and upset as he was. However, they liked to gossip; bad news and scandal were currency in the village. Today's events at the Hall would keep loose tongues wagging and people speculating for weeks with morbid curiosity.

Now that Dr Clutterbuck and Reverend Dewhurst had finally left, Elspeth was with Stockton, her lady's maid, resting. Montague didn't want her to be left alone and would join her later, knowing she was in good hands. Of course, Elspeth was in torment; how could she not be? He wished he could endure it for her and would do it willingly, but he couldn't; nobody could. Now, he needed some time on his own to compose his emotions, find some inner strength and muster his resolve.

A heavy lump formed in his throat; he held his head in his hands for a long moment and sat taking deep breaths, trying to silence irrational thoughts and calm his bleeding heart, telling himself everything would be alright - it had to be. How would his darling wife ever recover? He would never forget the look on her beautiful face when he told her their child was... he couldn't bear to think of the word, let alone say it. The look on her face would haunt him forever; he felt so insignificant, helpless, and powerless.

After he'd finished his prayers and just before he left, Reverend Dewhurst held his crucifix and bible tightly, looked to the heavens, and said, 'When the Lord closes a door, somewhere he opens a window.' Montague mulled the Reverend's words over in his mind, trying to take some comfort and nuggets of wisdom from them.

He took his handkerchief from his jacket pocket and quickly wiped his eyes and nose, determined to be strong. Naturally, he was shocked and stunned by what had happened earlier, never realising how quickly excitement, expectation, and joy could turn to tragedy and grief. Powerful emotions coursed through him, the likes of which he'd never experienced nor wanted to experience again. Tortured feelings he didn't know anyone could feel, let alone be expected to endure. He'd discovered a whole new side of himself.

Of course, like everyone, he knew pregnancy could be dangerous, but he'd never expected their child to be anything less than perfect - a stillborn child had never crossed his mind. He thought of the scruffy yet endearing urchins from the farms on the estate; their life was far from easy, but at least they had food and a roof over their heads. He took an interest in their wellbeing and always stopped to talk to them when he could, offering them some boiled sweets or mint humbugs, their little faces lighting up with delight. The little mites were always pleased to see him, calling him Squire Sir. They always waved and tried to attract his attention whenever they saw him and had an amusing tale to tell.

Montague felt responsible for his farming tenants and their families and had done a lot to improve the farm cottages and their lives on his estate. He didn't want to be like his father; he always believed his father had treated the tenants on his estates harshly and without due care and compassion. His father saying, he wasn't a charity. He was only interested in making money; if his tenants paid their rent on time, things ticked along nicely. However, the minute they didn't, trouble loomed, and they'd be out if they didn't come up with the money quickly. There were always plenty of others waiting to take their place.

His father lacked empathy and believed the poor faced their situations because they deserved it, either due to laziness or because they were not worthy of fortune; he was far from alone in that belief. He believed uncompromisingly in the need for self-sufficiency. He disagreed with wealthy people in society giving to the poor as a Christian duty. He felt it created weakness and dependency, believing the poor and growing criminal element would take advantage, seeking charity and handouts when they didn't need them. His father never questioned the social and political factors that kept people poor and drove them to crimes.

If his father wanted something, he schemed and ruthlessly went after it, regardless of the cost to the lives of others. He didn't follow the rules of fairness and decency; he made up his own to suit himself and somehow managed to stay on the right side of the law. Money, power, and position were his master. To him, masculinity meant the military, patriotic virtue, and unwavering courage. He felt men should behave like hunters, adventurers, and pioneers, striving to become successful, self-sufficient, and independent.

Montague's thoughts drifted to the poor wretches who ended up at the Tonbridge workhouse, wondering how any of them managed to survive due to their misfortune. Most came from the streets or slums, and many children were orphaned, having the worst possible start in life. He was trying hard to make radical reforms with his own money. And here he and Elspeth were, able to give a child the best of everything, yet their child had been taken away from them before taking its first breath. It made no sense, and he felt outraged.

Reverend Dewhurst said some children are born to help the

angels and go straight into God's loving care, anchored in his heavenly heart. Montague wasn't an atheist, but neither was he a religious man. He had his views of God and the soul but preferred to keep them to himself; he knew the Reverend's words were meant to be kind and helpful, but they gave him no comfort.

Yet despite his feelings about religion, Montague found himself praying to God, asking why his child had been taken; he needed answers but didn't receive any. He also asked God to give Elspeth strength and help her find some relief, comfort, and contentment.

His mind went around in circles, asking the same questions, looking for reasons and answers, but he had none. Could it be their fault? Had they done something to cause the stillbirth? He mulled over what Dr Clutterbuck had said regarding the possible causes. Montague shook his head, he wasn't a medical man, but Dr Clutterbuck's explanation didn't make any sense. To him, it sounded more like quackery.

He reflected on the past year; 1856 had, up to this point, been the best of times, a year of great joy and celebration; he'd felt reborn and energised at the idea of becoming a father; the future seemed so bright and exciting, it had new meaning. The lump returned to his throat. Now, it had turned into the worst of times.

When he had the house built, Montague saw it as the perfect place to raise a large family; he could see it clearly in his mind, his own happy brood. In keeping with the Victorian tradition of the upper classes, he and Elspeth wanted a big family; they loved children and had both experienced the loneliness of being an only child. They didn't want that for their family.

Upon learning Elspeth was with child, he ensured she had the best possible care and attention during her confinement. As far as he knew, she wasn't exposed to any danger and hadn't had to exert herself unnecessarily. In fact, she became irritated by his constant fussing and attention, telling him she was pregnant and neither ill nor an invalid.

He glanced around the study, thinking how quiet and empty the house felt. He'd managed to send a short note with the servants to his parents and in-laws telling them what had happened. He couldn't face any of them right now, particularly his mother. He'd speak to them when the time was right, when he felt more decisive, more able to hold himself together and maintain the composure and demeanour of a gentleman. He supposed Elspeth's mother would come to stay for as long as Elspeth needed her; he hoped that would give her some comfort.

Montague thought of his childhood; his father was a cold and distant figure, always stern, preferring the company of his peers and business associates in London. Not that such behaviour in men was uncommon. The wife was responsible for the home, domestic life, and children; his mother was a huge influence in his life. She had a kind heart and willingness to help others less fortunate than herself. It was something she did through several church societies, all unbeknown to his father, who would never have approved. It was on a need-to-know basis, and he didn't need to know.

His father was often away and only appeared at certain times and on certain days. When he was home, these times became rituals where they all gathered, usually for no more than an hour before dinner. Montague supposed his father loved him in his own way, but he vowed he wouldn't follow in his footsteps; he'd be a hands-on father, creating a warm, loving home. He didn't want his children to endure a childhood they would spend their lives recovering from.

He had to admit his father had mellowed with age, probably due to his failing health. Whatever he might think of him, his father had worked hard to provide for his family, even if they always came second to business success and money-making. They were his priority, but Montague benefitted greatly from that. His house and extensive land ownership wouldn't exist if not for his father's business acumen and generosity; he'd given him a good start.

Under his father's influence, Montague attended Eton College and worked hard to become a gentleman and sit comfortably with the upper class. He'd done this with determination and the impeccable morals he received from his mother. It annoyed him greatly that he lived in a time of such extreme social inequality. As a gentleman, inner values were far more important to him than people of position and wealth. And although he'd had a relatively privileged upbringing, he didn't always see eye to eye with gentlemen whose wealth had been purely inherited rather than earned.

Montague was proud not to be a man of leisure, valuing his moral qualities of altruism, benevolence, culture, and education. He felt lucky to have met Elspeth; like him, she came from a good family, but neither could have married purely for social position and gain, only for love. He could never understand the conflict and snobbery between the aristocracy and the middle classes.

However, the poor were another matter; they were frequently misunderstood. All too often, the wealthy controlled their circumstances, giving them an uncertain and perilous future – life was cheap. The rich and poor were like two nations ignorant of each other's habits, thoughts, and feelings. It was as if they were dwellers in different zones governed by different morals and laws.

How lucky Montague had been to find Elspeth. Victorian society created many restrictions on how men and women could meet and interact. Like many of their wealthy peers, they met at a ball, this one given by Lord and Lady Stroud at their grand townhouse in London's smart Eaton Square. Lady Stroud was worried she didn't have enough young men and encouraged the single gentleman to bring along a respected friend, emphasising it had to be a gentleman, which is how Montague ended up there. He wasn't generally in the inner circle of the aristocracy nor London's polite high society.

On his arrival, he spotted Elspeth almost immediately hiding behind her fan. She held her gaze on him, catching his attention. He was relieved when their host finally introduced them. A lady had to be formally introduced to a gentleman. However, as hard as he'd tried, he struggled to maintain a dignified reserve, which was essential in a gentleman when hoping to court a woman.

A man was expected to display a calm and restrained demeanour. Montague's mouth curled into a brief smile; he was not the most accomplished dancer but tried his best and was careful not to damage Elspeth's elaborate and delicate gown. He ensured he escorted her into supper and afterwards escorted her back to the ballroom; there wasn't a moment's awkwardness between them or lull in polite conversation.

Montague had been impressed by Elspeth's forthright spirit and feminist views. Her parents had encouraged her education and allowed her to cultivate a mind of her own; she was filled with intellectual curiosity, campaigning for women's education and equality. Eventually, Elspeth introduced him to her family, and he slowly gained their approval, leading to the ritual of their courtship. The rest, as they say, was history.

The wind howled outside, causing the snow to swirl in a ghostly dance forming deep drifts across the gardens. Montague jumped as something tapped at the window - it was a gnarled tree branch covered in snow; it would blossom in the spring. His thoughts turned to Elspeth, hoping she would do the same and blossom. He wondered how you could mend a broken heart – he had no answer but would try with every part of himself.

Montague didn't like to overthink the future or his own mortality, yet he found himself wondering what the future might hold for the two of them. What if they couldn't have a family? What if their fate was only with each other? He took some comfort from that; whatever happened, they would always have each other.

He looked around the study at the rows of leather-bound books perfectly lined up on the bookshelves. He shook his head, something felt different, yet it looked the same. He had a strange feeling of déjà vu as he glanced at the fireplace and couldn't understand why the fires hadn't been lit or why he hadn't noticed it earlier, particularly given the freezing weather, not that he felt cold. The mantel clock had stopped at three o'clock, the exact time of the ill-fated birth; Montague shuddered.

He rubbed his head as his vision swam; over the past week, he'd been getting strange headaches making him feel lightheaded. Montague felt like he was in a dark spinning tunnel heading towards a bright light; he couldn't explain it, wondering if he had eye strain or was developing a head cold.

He glanced at the side table. It seemed to glow with a peculiar luminosity; he noticed a book. He wondered who could have put it there; no one other than Elspeth was allowed to touch his books; she often joked about it. Montague trembled as he stood up and moved to the table; he was surprised to see his pocket watch and, without thinking, felt his waistcoat pocket. 'How on earth did that get there?' He muttered to himself, picking up the watch and carefully putting it in his waistcoat pocket; it had belonged to his father; he gave it to him on his eighteenth birthday.

His attention turned to the leather-bound book; he'd never seen it before. On the cover, it said, 'My Diary 1861' and had a dark red mark or symbol above the words. He opened the book flicking through the pages; they were blank with no diary entries, or so he thought. Montague blinked several times, trying to focus his eyes, unable to believe what he could see. As he ran his fingers across a page, an animated picture of his father appeared; he looked disturbed and troubled as if he was trying to say something - something urgent... What was that? Montague glanced around the room; he could hear a noise – distant, far away; he stood motionless, listening hard... it sounded like a child crying in distress...

**

'I must ask Ethel to give me the recipe for those delicious, spiced marzipan buns,' said Jocasta dreamily as we headed towards the study. 'I loved the soft marzipan centre, and the amount of nutmeg, ginger, and cinnamon was just right. The buns looked so lovely and seasonal with that light dusting of icing sugar - like snowy mountains,' she smiled, looking quite satisfied with herself. 'I like a nice little sweet snack with my mid-morning tea, even if it's only a ginger biscuit or humble garibaldi. And I'm pleased you have china tea; it's so much better for my vibrations.'

Clementine nodded, more out of politeness than understanding.

Jocasta continued, 'As a noted medium, I need to be careful about what I eat and drink, particularly before a séance. I always need to be prepared; I never know when I might get a presentiment that requires my immediate attention.'

As much as I was tempted, I didn't say anything. I could tell Jocasta had enjoyed the buns when she took the last one from the cake stand, her fourth, not to mention the several shortbread biscuits she'd devoured. She said her chakras were quite drained and needed replenishing, blaming it on the strong presence of ectoplasm in the house!

'I'm pleased you liked them,' said Clementine with a warm smile. 'But good luck with the recipe, Ethel has a secret ingredient, and she won't reveal it to anyone; it's caused quite a stir at our local branch of the WI, the Women's Institute, with everyone trying to guess what it is and get her to reveal the secret. Mrs Goodridge from the post office is quite frustrated; she sees herself as a baking expert and something of a domestic goddess. I suggested to Miss Frinton, our local WI chair, that we should have a competition to raise funds for the church or some other good cause. The prize winner getting the secret ingredient on the condition they don't reveal it to anyone else.'

'What an unusual but good idea,' agreed Jocasta. 'The Women's Institute is a sterling organisation; I've judged several of their baking competitions, for some reason, they see me as a bit of a cake expert. I've also given a few lectures on paranormal phenomena at my local branch in Folkstone; they were very well attended. I find women are much more open and receptive to the spirit world. Men tend to lean towards scepticism; their central chakras tend to be closed,' she paused, pursing her lips, waving a finger. 'But there are a lot of charlatans around, so scepticism is not necessarily a bad thing. Of course, like Jasper and Winston here, there are many gifted men who are exceptions to the rule.'

I felt my halo glow! Winston grunted modestly.

Clementine nodded, not looking convinced, thinking Jocasta probably did know a lot about buns and cake; she certainly seemed to eat enough. 'I see,' she said unconvincingly. 'I must admit I love marzipan and could easily eat several of those buns, but Agnes and I are always watching our weight,' she sighed. 'These days, it's a constant battle. I wish I was like you, Jocasta, and not bothered about my appearance and figure. Agnes and I have always been slaves to fashion and the latest silhouettes from Paris,' she groaned wearily. 'It's an expensive pastime. I blame women's magazines. Of course, these days, every woman wants to look like Greta Garbo or some other Hollywood starlet.'

'Oh, but it's expected and necessary,' said Agnes almost apologetically. 'We're lucky to have the social occasions to wear nice things, and thankfully many places still have strict dress codes. Accessories are also important; a daytime occasion always requires a hat, gloves, and some tasteful jewellery. In the evening, it's a cocktail dress or gown,' she smiled. 'I just wish I could find a comfortable pair of heels for my poor feet, but women have always suffered for beauty and fashion.'

Winston looked like he was going to say something but wisely thought better of it.

The six of us were walking towards the back of the house as Clementine stopped by a panelled oak door with an engraved brass fingerplate and opened it, 'Anyway, here we are - this is the study.'

Jocasta had stiffened, not knowing if she should be insulted by Clementine's comments about her weight and fashion sense. She surreptitiously smoothed her hand over her divided skirt, breathing in slightly; the waistband was getting a bit tight. She decided to ignore it and focus her attention on the study and task at hand, 'What a charming room, such a good size with a very pleasing aspect,' she declared, trying to centre herself. She breathed deeply, 'Ah, the smell of old books,' she glanced at Winston. 'I love it; it's so distinctive, dry, dusty, musky, even woodsy, someone should bottle it,' she smiled, sniffing again. 'And the light fragrance of wood polish, the beeswax and turpentine are so distinctive,' she continued sniffing the air. 'And there's something else; I'm getting a hint of lavender.'

'Ah, that will be Ethel,' said Agnes. 'She'll only use Town Talk Lavender Furniture Wax. She swears by it and buys it in bulk; her mother used it; apparently, she wouldn't entertain any other brand.'

Of course, Winston was drawn to the rows of books perfectly lined up on the oak shelves, taking his glasses out of his jacket pocket to inspect them in more detail. 'I do like a well-maintained and stocked library,' he proclaimed with satisfaction. 'Books take us into another world - their ink on papery leaves speaks their words and stays constant and unchanged as the years pass, waiting to entrance a new reader,' he patted the book spines. 'They spark curiosity, educate, and invite unspoken conversations with the mind that can leave a lasting impression. One of the greatest pleasures in life is finding a good book,' he put on his glasses and scanned the shelves. 'Who is responsible for this collection?'

'You make it sound so poetic, Winston,' declared Agnes with a twinkle. 'We can't take any credit for this collection of literature. As you know, we're book lovers, but our collection of fiction is still in storage in one of the outbuildings; I'm sure we'll get around to them one day, we might donate them to the local library. Montague, our grandfather, loved his books,' she gestured to the shelves. 'This collection is all down to him. I think many are first editions; he collected all the classics and closely followed the literary trends back in his day.'

Winston nodded, 'Yes, I can see that,' he said as he studied the shelves, pulled out a book, and scrutinised it.

'What have you there?' Asked Florence, looking over his shoulder before moving to one of the windows admiring the silver sky and carpet of white. The garden undulated with deep snowdrifts and sparkling icicles, the white of the snow punctuated by the occasional splash of green from the conifers and the green and red of the holly bushes. Florence could hear birds chirping, their clicks, whistles, warbles, and trills, but couldn't see them.

'It's The Christmas books of Mr M. A. Titmarsh, by William Makepeace Thackeray; this one appears to be a first edition published in 1857. It caught my eye due to the word Christmas - and it's a book I've always wanted to read.'

'Oh, I love his Vanity Fair,' said Clementine with a beaming smile. 'It's such a classic as it follows the lives of the lively but cynical social climber Becky Sharp, and the effete sentimental Amelia Sedley, along with their friends and families, during and after the Napoleonic Wars,' she sighed nostalgically. 'I do like a good Regency romance; I'm always drawn back to Jane Austen. She had such a sharp observational eye for the social norms of the day - and what woman didn't fall in love with the proud and aloof Mr Darcy?'

'Hmm, so true,' agreed Jocasta. 'As I think I mentioned, Pride and Prejudice is one of my favourite novels; I like the complex character of Miss Elizabeth Bennett; I like a woman who stands up for herself, her beliefs, and her family. History doesn't accurately record the role and importance of women; they get overlooked,' she smiled mischievously, raising her eyebrows. 'Probably because history was mostly written and recorded by men.'

'Actually, Vanity Fair was seen as quite 'risky' when it was first published in 1848,' said Winston, carefully putting his book back on the shelf. 'Thackeray was such a brilliant British novelist, author, and illustrator known for his satirical works. His books are full of wit and humour. I always think Vanity Fair to be a panoramic portrait of British society in that period.'

As we wandered around the study, it was, as expected, a large room with a high ornate ceiling. It was well organised, with row after row of oak bookshelves groaning with colourful leather-bound books, their titles picked out in gold lettering. A leather-topped oak desk with a leather-covered chair stood in the centre of the room. Several side tables and comfortable chairs upholstered in green tartan fabric and green velvet were dotted around the study; an ornate marble fireplace dominated part of one wall. The mantlepiece held elegant 18th -century French ormolu candlesticks and an elaborate mantel clock in the same ormolu style. The clock had an urn-shaped body with foliate scrolls, bouquets of rosettes, and acanthus leaves; the white clock face featured Roman and Arabic numerals. You couldn't miss its soothing, melodic tick-tock. This was a house of clocks.

The windows were draped with green velvet to match the chairs; the deep pile carpet matched the green tartan upholstery. The windows looked out over the back of the house across the beautiful snow-covered gardens, fields, and mature woodland beyond. The snow made everything sparkle - the vista looked magical, like a winter wonderland.

'I don't think Edmund came in here that often other than to do his paperwork,' pondered Agnes. 'It was his father's domain,' she looked at the shelves. 'I bet these books haven't been touched in years. I can remember my grandfather sat at that desk,' she glanced at one of the easy chairs by the fireplace. 'And I can see him sat in that chair lost to the world in a book. He was such a bookworm and had a great mind and thirst for knowledge.'

'He did, didn't he,' agreed Clementine. 'Goodness, it's funny the things you remember; I haven't thought about this in years. When we were quite young, I remember the fire raging, the clock ticking, the two of us sat on the floor mesmerised, and Montague, our grandfather, sat in that chair reading Lewis Carroll's Alice in Wonderland to us by candlelight. He was so good at telling stories; he brought them to life and did a different voice for all the characters.'

It sounded perfect, like the childhood I dreamed of having when I was in the orphanage. 'When Edmund married Violet, did they live here with his parents?' I asked.

Agnes nodded, 'Yes, Edmund never lived anywhere else; he

loved it here, and it would have been such a big house for just two people and a few house staff. Edmund and Violet married in 1888. Edmund took over the running of the estate before both his parents passed. His father died in 1897, and his mother in 1899.

Our grandparents were thrilled when Thomas was born in 1895, they were near the end of their lives, and his birth brought them great joy.' Agnes moved to the window staring at an oak tree, its branches bowing under the weight of the snow as the wind began to pick up again. 'I think they thought children would never happen for Edmund and Violet. As I told you, Violet had quite a few miscarriages; I think Elspeth gave Violet a lot of emotional support,' Agnes paused, recalling her memories. 'I'm pleased they didn't have to experience the grief of Thomas's passing; that would have been an awful thing for them to take to their graves.'

Clementine sighed woefully, 'Ahh, life... we never know what's around the corner, which is probably a good thing. You've probably wondered why Agnes and I never married?'

Silence...

'Hmm, well, I must admit the thought had crossed my mind,' said Jocasta trying her best to be tactful. 'But it's not polite to ask, and it's none of our business.'

'Not at all,' replied Clementine nobly. 'In truth, neither Agnes nor I were in any hurry to marry. We wanted to see the world and enjoy our freedom while we could; marriage is a life-changing responsibility, particularly for a woman. We were both betrothed, but sadly, our fiances were killed in 1914 at the start of the war.'

'Oh, I'm so sorry,' said Jocasta, her face crumpling. 'That happened to so many women and must have been heart-breaking for you both.'

Clementine nodded, 'It was - I suppose the two of us were naïve; we didn't think we'd ever get over it. It changed us, but as they say, time is a great healer. They were so young, their lives over before they'd really started. Our fiances were both part of the 4th Middlesex division. They were among the first army units of the British Expeditionary Force to cross the English Channel to France. Their unit took up positions near the village of Bettignies, beside the canal, running through the town of Mons, when they came under heavy enemy fire.'

Clementine exhaled hopelessly. 'We often talk about them and what might have been,' she shrugged, bobbing her head. 'Neither of us had any appetite for marriage after that. During the war, we lost a whole generation; people had a sense of disillusionment. It made everyone want to return to a simpler, idealistic past.'

'People think we've had a cosseted life,' said Agnes earnestly. 'Which I suppose we have. We tried to do our bit during the war and were among London's first female ambulance drivers; we witnessed some awful sights - things we will never forget. When the war ended in late 1918, life took on a whole new meaning, and in the greater scheme of things, marriage didn't seem as important or a priority. The passions of youth had faded as fate and life took over,' she smiled. 'Although we both received several more marriage proposals. I suppose we were lucky in that we have financial independence.'

'That's rare for women and is worth a great deal,' said Florence. 'Financial independence transforms lives.'

'The war was a terrible time,' agreed Winston mournfully. 'With many casualties and a huge loss of life. Peace comes at a great price; we must never forget that, nor take it for granted. That's why history is important; it can teach us many lessons, so we don't repeat the same tragic mistakes.'

That was true, but I knew it was far from a guarantee. Propaganda is a powerful thing. As the generations pass, history is forgotten. The powerful and those who shout the loudest tend to be heard, only telling the parts of history they want you to hear, changing or misrepresenting the facts for their own convenience and agenda.

Clementine nodded slowly, 'Yes, the war was tragic. Of course, we were far from alone in our loss. As you said, Jocasta, many women lost their fiancés and husbands, not to mention the terrible impact on families and whole communities,' she sighed again and smiled forlornly. 'All this reminiscing and family talk made me think about them.'

As a time-travelling ghost, I've found myself helping in many war zones around the world, including the 1914 world war; the memories will never leave me. I remember the desolation and emptiness of it all. The mud and scorched earth, the split, shattered, burnt trees, and the explosion of shells; one could look for miles and see no human being. Yet in those miles of country lurked thousands, even hundreds of thousands of men. Men planning and plotting against each other, never showing themselves as they battled with bullets, bombs, aerial torpedoes, and shells.

Little cylinders of gas were waiting for the right moment to spit forth their nauseous and destroying fumes. And yet the landscape showed nothing of this - nothing but the shattered trees, trenches, scorched earth, and three or four thin lines of earth and sandbags. Those and the ruins of towns and villages are the only signs of war and its devastation.

I will never forget the feeling as you enter no man's land from the front line and trenches. Fear leaves you for terror; you don't look, you see. You don't hear; you listen. Your nose is filled with fumes and death. I witnessed many acts of courage. I shook my head, trying to shake all thoughts of it away, forcing myself to think of the spirit of Christmas, the ideas of togetherness, kindness to others and being selfless. A time for forgiving and taking stock of what's important in life while trying to be a better person and make the world a better place.

'Few people came out unscathed, said Florence lost in her memories. 'The war left many scars from injury, loss of life, and numerous atrocities. I don't think we'll ever know the full scale of it, but some people will never heal.'

The room took on a sombre tone; we all had our own recollections of the war years. Wars destroy cities, communities, and families, disrupting the social and economic fabric of nations. They cause long-term physical and psychological harm to children and adults; the trauma and human costs are vast and far-reaching. In addition, one mustn't forget their negative consequences on infrastructure, public health provision, and social order. These indirect consequences are often overlooked and unappreciated.

Jocasta stood by the desk pondering, 'Sometimes we are taken into troubled waters, not to be drowned but to be cleansed,' she said philosophically, sniffing the air. 'Anyway, this house, this place must have witnessed many things over the years. It's quite fascinating, and I can smell ectoplasm again. I've never known a house like it; a spirit has been sitting here at this desk – I'm sure it was someone troubled.'

'Is it the spirit from the nursery?' I asked nervously.

Jocasta shook her head, 'No, I don't think so, although it's hard to be sure.'

'Do you think it's our grandfather Montague?' Asked Agnes. 'This was always his place. I don't have your gift, Jocasta, but I always think of him when I come here; I sense him in this room.'

'It's a possibility, isn't it, Jocasta,' said Florence, turning from the window having spotted a robin redbreast. 'Spirits tend to be drawn to places that mean something to them - although that can be for both good and bad reasons.'

'Whoever these spirits are,' said Jocasta pensively. 'They all have something in common; they are all in a moment of raw pain and anguish,' she looked at Clementine and Agnes. 'Hence, the awful noises you've both heard in this house. But I'm still puzzled as to why it's only at this time of year. I'm sure the spirits are not always here, which is most unusual for house hauntings. It's as if something compels the spirits to return here at Christmas to suffer past pains. And why so much tragedy on Christmas day? That's something else I feel is significant.'

I moved to one of the side tables. A book sat proudly in the centre; the cover said 'My Dairy 1861'. It immediately piqued my interest; you never know what secrets a diary could reveal, confessions, intrigues, seductions, and debauches. I tried to steady my imagination turning to Clementine and Agnes, 'Do you know who kept a diary?'

'A diary!' exclaimed Clementine glancing at Agnes; she looked as intrigued as me. 'How interesting; I didn't know any of the family kept a diary. Mind you, I don't suppose there was any reason for us to know; what have you found?'

I shrugged, 'I'm not sure it's anything of any importance,' I held up the diary. 'Have you seen this before?'

The two women looked at the diary and shook their heads. 'No,' said Clementine wistfully. 'We've never seen it before, and I can't imagine who found it and put it there.'

'Hmm, just like the music box in the nursery,' mused Florence, intrigued. 'That also seemed to appear out of the blue - strange.'

I couldn't explain it, but I had a peculiar feeling as I opened the diary, quickly flicking through the pages; they were all blank... 'Hmm, that's disappointing, nothing, it doesn't look like it's ever been used.' I closed the diary, and as I did, something caught my eye. 'Oh - but hang on a minute,' I recognised something. 'Winston, pass me that piece of paper you found inside the music box in the nursery.'

He looked at me puzzled, taking his wallet out of his jacket pocket, carefully removing the piece of paper, 'What is it?'

I took the paper from him, 'Ah, I thought so, look, the marks match.' I showed them the cover of the diary with the piece of paper.

'Don't you think that's strange?' I asked.

Silence...

Winston cleared his throat, 'Hmm, it does seem odd,' he curled his lip reflectively. 'I know it's unlikely, but I suppose someone could have copied the mark and put it in the music box. We need to find out if the mark means anything,' he scrutinised the symbol again. 'As I said, I think it's most likely a maker's mark; this diary could be from the same company. It's not unusual for things like diaries and jewellery or music boxes to be in the collections of luxury goods manufacturers,' he smiled. 'They make nice gifts for the people who have everything.'

'Let me see the diary,' said Jocasta eagerly.

I passed it to her; she took it and immediately dropped it on the table like it was burning hot, jumping back. 'Goodness, that's powerful,' she swayed and had to steady herself, putting her hands on the table.

'Jocasta, are you alright?' I asked, touching her on the shoulder.

She nodded breathlessly, trying to calm herself, 'Yes – yes, I'm fine. I had a sudden presentiment; it sent my chakras spinning. I feel this diary holds a warning,' she turned to Florence. 'Put your finger on the diary and tell me what you sense.'

Florence looked puzzled, stepping forward, but did as she was told, putting her middle finger on the diary. She jumped and jolted back but held her finger on the book for a long moment closing her eyes as we all watched expectantly.

She looked at Jocasta, amazed, 'That's fascinating; this diary is enchanted just like the music box upstairs in the nursery,' she chewed on her lips for a moment, pinching the space between her eyebrows. 'I can't explain it; I sense a mystical force, although it's unusual. I feel the box and this diary are mostly dormant, but they hold something.'

'Or someone,' said Jocasta drumming her fingers on the table. 'I have a theory; I think this diary and the music box have been enchanted by the same person, group, or perhaps a coven. But the items are specific to one person, or in this case, one ghost.'

'So, you don't think it's the house that's haunted?' I asked. 'But the diary and the music box.'

'Oh no, the house is most certainly haunted; they're all connected,' declared Jocasta, examining the diary. 'I think the diary and music box are what you might call 'extra insurance'. And the date 1861 might be significant,' she glanced at Clementine and Agnes. 'Does the date 1861 mean anything to either of you?'

The two women looked at each other bewildered, shaking their heads. 'No, other than the year Bernard Rothery died.'

'Yes, of course,' replied Jocasta thoughtfully. 'Hmm...'

'But why was extra insurance needed?' I asked. 'There must be a reason.'

There was a sudden whoosh, then a whisper; Jocasta glanced around the room, putting her finger to her mouth...

Be gone – be gone – be gone... echoed around the room.

Agnes and Clementine went pale, clinging to each other as those words echoed in a whisper around the study.

'I don't know how much more of this we can take,' said Agnes nervously, glancing in every direction. 'This house is possessed.'

Florence moved to the desk doing a 360-degree turn. 'It's like there are watching eyes everywhere in this house.'

'But only it seems at Christmas,' I said.

Be gone...be gone...

'Who's there,' demanded Jocasta sticking her chin out and stiffening. 'Reveal yourself to me.'

Silence...

'Hmm, so that's how it's going to be,' she muttered, contorting her face. 'I need a cup of tea.'

'What a good idea,' said Winston, brightening. 'Tea helps me to think, and it's so reviving.'

Ah yes, tea, that great panacea, why wasn't I surprised!

'Tea!' Exclaimed Clementine.

'Yes, tea, and I need to consult my crystal,' replied Jocasta looking at Clementine and Agnes. 'Have faith, ladies, we'll get to the bottom of whatever is going on here, but remember Rome wasn't built in a day.'

Chapter 6

The pallid sun sat low in the silver sky; it was still snowing. The feathered ice crystals kept the gardens and surrounding countryside a glistening blanket of white, the sunlight emphasising the uniform purity of the snow. We all sat in the drawing-room in the shadow of the sparkling Christmas tree and the warm amber glow from the raging fire, the others with tea and mince pies. Having finished her third, Jocasta commented on the lightness of the pastry, reminding everyone she was noted for hers. She sat at a table consulting her crystal. 'Tell me, where are Montague and Elspeth buried?' she asked, wiping pastry flakes from around her mouth.

'Here in the grounds,' said Clementine finishing her mince pie, savouring every tiny mouthful; she was making it last. 'These are delicious and so morish. They're naughty but nice,' she smiled mischievously, glancing at Agnes. 'I'm going to be on a big diet after Christmas – but I must admit, at this time of year, I like a nice mince pie with a generous splash of brandy in the filling - they make me feel so cosy and Christmassy.' Clementine hunched her shoulders, wrinkled her nose, and grinned, almost intoxicated; she then carefully dabbed her mouth with a linen napkin, trying not to spoil her meticulously applied rose-pink lipstick.

'We're always on a diet, sister dear,' declared Agnes resignedly. 'We're famous for our boiled egg and water biscuit regime,' she smiled, looking at the four of us. 'And yes, it is as dull as it sounds. Although Evangeline Sudbury, the famous socialite, recommended the new elimination diet to us, she says it's marvellous and was introduced to it when she took the waters for her health in Bath... If I understand it correctly, you don't eat anything.'

'That sounds like a fast and not a diet,' declared Winston sipping his tea, pulling a disapproving face. 'And surely not at all conducive to good health and wellbeing.'

'Oh, I can't eat too many boiled eggs; they're not good for my constitution,' professed Jocasta virtuously. 'And I always say a bit of what you fancy does you good - it's food for the soul. I always listen to my body where my diet is concerned; I need to think about my chakras and vibrations. I always need to be at one with the spiritual highway; it's easy to get my meridians convoluted and out of line.'

I was saying nothing!

Out of politeness, Clementine nodded, knowing if she asked any questions, she'd be even more confused. 'Hmm, but I'm not sure I'll think that when I can't fit into my clothes,' she said pointedly. 'In the spring, we've been invited to a society wedding in the lovely town of Chipping Norton. The wedding ceremony is at St Mary's church which is quite delightful. Agnes is wearing lilac crepe de chine, and I have a wonderful pink silk ensemble; both are from Lachasse in London – anyway, I digress – I thought I'd mentioned Montague and Elspeth's grave?'

'No, I don't think you did,' said Florence, thoughtfully finishing her tea. 'So, all the family, Montague, Elspeth, Edmund, Violet, and Thomas, are all buried here?'

'Yes, that's right,' confirmed Clementine. 'It was Montague who created a family plot in one of the fragrant rose gardens - the white garden; it's heavenly in the summer. The sweet, musky fragrance of the roses is intoxicating. Although our mother, Beatrice, isn't buried here, she's with our father in the Nantwich family plot at All Saints, the village church. It sits in the middle of the village; it's another magnificent church, a historic place hidden behind an avenue of yew trees with lovely views of the surrounding countryside. It was built in the 12th and 13th centuries. Of course, there have been later additions. It has some beautiful stained-glass windows.'

'And you say your great grandfather, Bernard, and great

grandmother, Dora, are also in the church graveyard?' Confirmed Jocasta; she was such a stickler for detail.

Clementine nodded, glancing around the room, 'Yes, this house was never their home; we never connected them with this place. Although I believe Bernard gave Montague a considerable amount of money and the land so he could build the hall and fulfil his vision to develop the estate. However, given Bernard's business reputation and acumen, I'm sure he will have kept an eye on things and how Montague was spending his money. I assume he and Dora used to visit from time to time - why do you ask?'

'Oh, I'm just trying to get a picture of the direct family in my mind,' replied Jocasta committing everything to memory. 'Sometimes, graves within the grounds of an estate can be significant to house hauntings. Admittedly it's rare, but we can't rule anything out at this stage in our investigation.'

Agnes clutched her pearls and swallowed hard, 'Significant in what way?' She asked, her voice going up an octave.

'Well, there can be all manner of things,' mused Jocasta breezily, taking a sip of tea; she was still staring into her crystal, looking bewildered. 'We've come across death-dealing spirits, elaborate rituals and spells on graves linked to immortality, along with resurrection prophecies and supernatural terror where spirits are trapped and can't transcend to the Astral Plane. Then some are lost or refuse to accept they have passed over, wandering aimlessly among the maelstrom in the many celestial spaces or the much more sinister Twilight Zone; they can pop up anywhere. We'll have a better idea after we've visited the graves.'

'I - I see,' said Clementine unconvincingly, taking a deep breath, trying to look composed. 'You read about such things in the newspapers and fictional horror stories, but you never expect them to be true.'

Oh, I disapprove of such fantasy fiction; they're inaccurate, misleading, and full of nonsense,' said Jocasta with a sneer. 'And don't get me started on newspapers; they're always using spiritual matters to create some cheap and vulgar newspaper sensation. Why only last week I saw a ridiculous headline about some woman finding her dead mother's ghost in a chiffonier.'

Clementine bobbed her head, trying her best to be gracious, 'I see; I must say, Agnes and I are having quite the education. I'll think of graveyards quite differently from now on,' her mouth sunk at the corners. 'In fact, I think I'll avoid them.'

'Oh, but you mustn't,' protested Jocasta rubbing her crystal vigorously on her divided skirt. 'Most of the dead are quite harmless and like to mingle among the living; it perks them up - it's all part of nature and the natural order of things. We are all a part of the great universe, although there is still a lot we don't understand - Professor Wimble from The Society for Psychical Research in London says you're never lonely in a graveyard, and he's right. Of course, it's different for me,' Jocasta gave a self-satisfied smile. 'One can become overwhelmed with messages from the other side or by a spirit with a query - they can be most persistent.'

She put her crystal on the table, shaking her head, suddenly looking severe. 'The only graveyard I would avoid is Greyfriars Kirkyard in Edinburgh,' she said sternly with a warning in her tone. 'It's a seemingly idyllic cemetery dating back to the 1560s. But it has strange goings-on and attracts a steady stream of amateur ghost hunters and thrill-seekers. I disapprove of such things; these amateurs can cause havoc with their meddling, calling up all manner of troubled spirits, poltergeists, and werewolves.'

'Werewolves!' Exclaimed Agnes clutching the arm of the chair.

Jocasta nodded, 'Yes, Scotland is noted for them. They're also known as lycanthropes or shape-shifting humans. I'm reminded of a complicated case Jasper and I investigated within the Highlands of Scotland in 1916; it involved a particularly nasty werewolf,' she glanced at me; the thought of that case made even me shudder. I can't be doing with werewolves and vampires. 'And you haven't aged a day, Jasper,' she held my gaze knowingly. 'Anyway, I can't focus on werewolves right now; it's a long and complicated story. I've had some disturbing presentiments when I've been at Greyfriars Kirkyard. Particularly where graverobbers were concerned.'

'Good heavens, it gets worse, Graverobbers?' Uttered Clementine feeling lightheaded, taking her smelling salts from her bag, quickly taking a sniff, and passing them to Agnes, who almost snatched them out of her hand.

Jocasta nodded, wrinkling her nose and narrowing her eyes, distracted by her crystal.

'Yes, they were known as resurrectionists,' said Winston taking his pipe out of his jacket pocket. 'Although they were nothing more than body snatchers and were commonly employed by anatomists during the 18th and 19th centuries to exhume the bodies of the recently dead.'

'A dark period in history,' said Jocasta grimly. 'A shocking business, it traumatised many of the newly deceased. Some couldn't pass over to the other side because they felt they had to stay and guard their earthly bodies. I'm not surprised people think graveyards are haunted.'

Winston's eyes widened as he continued, 'Hmm, yes - anyway, to address this issue, Parliament passed the Murder Act in 1752, which allowed judges to allocate executed criminals' bodies for dissection, a fate generally viewed with horror. But such was the demand; this proved insufficient to meet the needs of the hospitals and teaching centres that opened during the 18th century - corpses became a commodity.'

'It sounds horrific,' said Clementine fanning herself dramatically with her hand. 'One never thinks of such things.'

'It was organised crime,' continued Winston fumbling in his pockets for his tobacco. 'Resurrectionists worked in gangs and usually found corpses through a network of informers. People like sextons, gravediggers, undertakers, and local officials who all conspired to take a cut of the proceeds.'

Jocasta tutted loudly, shaking her head, 'It was an abomination.'

Winston continued, 'Measures taken to stop the resurrectionists included high walls around graveyards, increased security, and night watches patrolling gravesites. The rich placed their dead in secure coffins and installed physical barriers such as mortsafes and heavy stone slabs to make extracting corpses more difficult.

However, the bodies of the poor in mass or paupers' graves remained easy prey for the resurrectionists. The Anatomy Act of 1832 was supposed to end the practice of body snatching, but the resurrectionists remained commonplace. Reports of body snatching persisted for some years. Nevertheless, by 1844, the trade had more or less stopped, although I believe there was an isolated case in 1862 at Wardsend Cemetery in Sheffield in the West Riding of Yorkshire.'

Clementine shook her head, entranced with a morbid fascination, 'Goodness, that all sounds terrible; relatives of the newly deceased must have lived in constant fear. Now, I can understand why Montague set up a burial plot here,' she grimaced, taking a sip of tea to comfort herself. 'We think of these things as happening in the dark ages, yet, it wasn't that long ago,' she exhaled loudly. 'But in terms of the graves here, I don't think you'll be able to see much in this weather; it will be covered in deep snow.'

'Oh, we'll brush or dig the snow out of the way if needed,' said Jocasta screwing up her face as she stared at her crystal. 'And I'm sure if there is anything, I'll sense it in my vibrations, or I may get a Presentiment,' she held her crystal up to the light. 'The weather's affecting my crystal's clarity, but it's clearing... Hmm, I don't know why, but I keep seeing a stone with the letter R on it. Does that mean anything to you?'

The two women glanced at each other, 'The letter R,' said Agnes, bemused, pulling a face... 'Hmm, I can't think of anything. Do you mean a gravestone?'

Jocasta looked into her crystal, shaking her head, curling her lip, 'It's hard to be sure; it doesn't look like a gravestone, at least, not a traditional one, and I keep seeing a frothy lilac tree - it's quite charming.'

'Well, there are several mature lilac trees in the gardens,' pondered Agnes reflectively, picturing them in her mind. 'They are magnificent when they flower and smell delightful, so sweet; I always think lilac flowers smell of roses, milky almonds, and green leaves - they are a sure sign summer is on its way.'

'Could it be old Mrs Rochester?' Asked Clementine pouring herself more tea. Her hand shook slightly; her nerves were jangled from all the strange goings-on at the house. I could see she was trying to put on a brave face.

'Who is she?' Asked Jocasta, still studying her crystal. 'I think I spoke too soon; my crystal is clouding again. It's most annoying; it's the weather, although there could be a lot of elementals about.'

Clementine nodded, not that she understood, stirring a spoonful of sugar into her tea, 'Mrs Rochester lived on the estate for many years in one of the farm cottages and was famous for her clog dancing. She died last year and was buried in her clogs - she insisted on it. They were her most prized possession, a gift to her from the famous pantomime performer Dan Leno. He won the title of World Champion Clog Dancer - do you think it could be her?'

'Clogs! - was she Welsh?' asked Winston finishing his third cup of tea.

'Welsh?... Err, I'm not sure,' said Clementine shaking her head looking doubtful. 'We didn't know her very well, but she was marvellous at straddle jumps and jumping over chairs as part of her clog dancing routine, particularly given her age.'

'Hmm, I see,' replied Winston, thoughtfully filling his pipe with tobacco. 'How old was Mrs Rochester?'

'Eighty-nine,' said Clementine. 'Mrs Rochester had a long life, which she put down to lots of gin and plenty of fresh air. But she looked her age, that is, until she put on her clogs, and then there was no stopping her. She was like a twenty-year-old, performing in the streets, in pubs, at social occasions, and, of course, at clog dancing competitions all over Britain.'

'Where is she buried?' Asked Jocasta chewing on her lip, eyeing the last of the mince pies; it was topped with a generous dusting of icing sugar and was proving irresistible; I could tell her mouth was watering.

'In the church graveyard,' said Agnes putting more logs on the fire. 'She's buried with her late husband, Alfred,' she smiled wryly. 'I was surprised she wanted to be with him; she never had a good word to say about him when he was alive, calling him a lazy good for nothing. I don't think he appreciated her clog dancing and felt neglected, probably due to her constant practising and gin habit. I don't think we ever saw her sober.'

'Ah, I see, the demon drink, it's been the undoing of many – I suppose it could be her,' muttered Jocasta turning her crystal in her hands. 'Although I can't help thinking it's something closer to home. I could try contacting her or ask Titus to find her - you know, to see if she knows anything. If she's a lover of clog dancing, she should be easy to find – heel and toe clog dancing is very popular in the music halls on the other side.'

Silence...

'You make it sound like a phone call,' said Agnes with a nervous smile, sitting down next to Clementine. She shook her head, 'Oh, listen to me; I can't believe I just said that.'

Jocasta laughed, still looking into her crystal, 'Well, in some ways, I suppose it is... Hmm, and I keep seeing a gold pocket watch, a stone tablet, and - a mirror.'

Clementine and Agnes looked at each other amazed. 'I'm astonished you should mention a gold pocket watch,' said Agnes. 'It's probably nothing more than a coincidence, and it's hardly uncommon, but Edmund had a gold pocket watch. It was passed down the family line and belonged to his father and grandfather. Edmund wasn't particularly materialistic, but the watch was one of his most treasured possessions; I think he felt a connection to the family line through it.'

'Do you still have the watch?' Asked Jocasta eagerly, wide-eyed.

'Yes, but not here. As I think I mentioned, after Edmund died, items of value were moved to the bank for safekeeping until his will was sorted out. Many items of jewellery, including several diamond tiaras and his pocket watch, are still there.'

'Ah, I see - well, we must try to get it,' said Jocasta, still studying her crystal. 'We need to examine it; I'm sure it's linked to whatever is happening here. When I saw it, I felt something in my base chakra - that's always a sure sign.'

I moved to the window and stood watching the falling snow; a gust of wind blew clumps from the tree branches, causing the snow to crash to the ground with a soft thud, disturbing the perfect carpet of white, sending clouds of powdery white ice into the air.

'A mirror?' I repeated to myself nervously, turning from the window. 'You've seen a mirror?'

Mirrors were funny things; they could hold dark energy, spirits, and hexes. The Greeks believed that one's reflection on the surface of a pool of water revealed one's soul. It was Roman artisans who learned to manufacture mirrors from polished metal surfaces. They believed their gods observed souls through these devices. To damage a mirror was considered so disrespectful people believed it compelled the gods to rain bad luck on anyone so careless. Over centuries those adept in the dark arts have found more sinister uses for mirrors.

'Jocasta, tell me more about the mirror. What does it look like?'

'Patience, dear boy, I'm still tuning my core vibrations, trying to get a good look at it,' she sighed, screwing up her face. 'Hmm, it's as if someone or something doesn't want me to see it; everything's gone cloudy again.'

'Is it a mirror in this house?' I asked. 'There seems to be quite a few,' I looked at Clementine and Agnes. 'Are all the mirrors on display?'

'Yes, there are a lot,' agreed Clementine guiltily, glancing at a decorative wall mirror near the piano. 'We've always loved the mirrors in this house. They're so ornate, many are French, but I've no idea how many there are or if there are any more in storage. Most big houses tend to have many rather grand mirrors, and this house is no exception.

I'm guessing, but I think many of the mirrors have been here since Montague and Elspeth's time. Violet added more; she took great pride in her appearance before Thomas passed and said mirrors brought a room to life and made it sparkle. She bought several impressive mirrors during her trips to the fashion houses in Paris.'

'Hmm, I don't think it's a particularly grand mirror,' said Jocasta twisting her mouth to one side and wrinkling her nose. 'I can't make out its size. My crystal is too cloudy; it could be big or small,' she rubbed her chin. 'And I don't know why, but I'm sure it's not on display,' Jocasta looked bemused. 'It's almost like it's a hidden or a secret mirror – most strange, why would someone want to hide a mirror? And we mustn't forget the stone tablet; what could that be about?'

'I wonder if it's a curse tablet?' Pondered Winston. 'In history, it wasn't uncommon for curses to be placed on stone tablets; the people of the Greco-Roman society used curse tablets. The ancient Greeks feared the power of these tablets. They believed they could use magic to control the natural world.'

There was a knock at the door; it was Ethel looking flustered, 'Sorry to disturb, but Reverend Sommersby and Miss Duckworth, the church organist, are here. Mrs Pumphrey's broken off from her dusting and is taking their coats; she wanted to talk to the Reverend about the Christmas bell ringing rota,' she paused, folding her arms tightly across her chest. 'All I can say is, it must be important; you know how obsessed Mrs Pumphrey is with her dusting - she worries someone might spread rumours in the village about dust in the house. Anyway, shall I show them in?'

Clementine glanced at the mantel clock, 'Goodness, look at the time - I thought I'd heard the doorbell; they had slipped my mind again,' she sighed wearily. 'I don't mean to sound rude, but the Reverend and Miss Duckworth are the least of our worries with everything that's going on in this house.'

Ethel stiffened and nodded in agreement pulling her cardigan closer to her like it would offer some protection from ghostly presences.

'Quick, Ethel, take away the tea things and bring us more tea and cakes; the Reverend has such a sweet tooth, it's no wonder he has hardly any teeth. And you'd better bring in the drinks cart; you know how the Reverend likes his brandy and Miss Duckworth her sherry. Although if they're chilled to the bone, I suppose it will be warming in this weather,' Clementine heaved another sigh shaking her head disapprovingly. 'I'm not surprised he's often seen staggering back to the vicarage singing hymns to himself. One evening Miss Lee from the library found him talking to a lamppost in the moonlight; she said he was quoting passages from the bible about hell and damnation with gusto.'

Jocasta quickly snatched the last mince pie as Ethel grabbed the cups, saucers, and tea things, piling them on a tray with a clatter. 'I'll take these to the kitchen; then I'll bring them through. I think they'll need to sit by the fire they both look perished; it's bitter out. Although it's hard to tell with the Reverend, his face is always bright red.'

Ethel swished out of the room, still flustered, and as she did, I caught the faint smell of lavender wood polish. Agnes and Clementine stood up in a commotion, smoothing down their skirts, arranging their blouses, jewellery, and hair. Then they started plumping up the chair cushions. Agnes glanced at the piano; her music was laid out and ready; she looked at Clementine, 'I hope you're in fine voice, sister dear?'

Clementine smiled, 'Of course, or I should be after all the rehearsing we've done. You'd think we were performing at La Scala in Italy.'

'Shall we leave you to it?' Asked Jocasta, carefully putting her crystal in her Gladstone bag. 'We don't want to intrude; we'll get ourselves well wrapped up against the weather and tour the grounds; the bracing fresh air will give us an appetite for dinner, although I'll need my late afternoon snack to keep my energy levels up and chakras burning.'

'Oh yes, I'm pleased you've reminded me; I've been meaning to ask,' said Agnes. 'What would you like for dinner? Do you have any special dietary requirements?'

'Please don't go to any trouble for us; we're easy to please food-wise,' replied Jocasta. 'I always like three courses, something simple like reviving soup, perhaps leek and potato, followed by a nice roast - beef, lamb, venison, or pork with all the vegetable accompaniments, and Yorkshire pudding; I do like a crisp Yorkshire pudding with onion gravy. And for dessert, a lovely warm, comforting pudding with lots of creamy custard would be most welcome,' she licked her lips with anticipation. 'I'm fond of steamed treacle sponge pudding with lots of delicious golden syrup. That should carry us over until breakfast, but as I say, don't go to any trouble for us - Now, we need to find the family grave and get a feel for the estate, and this moment seems like an interlude and a good time. Do you have a spade?'

Agnes went pale, clutching her pearls, 'A spade! What do you need a spade for?' She asked meekly, gulping hard, steadying herself on a chair.

Jocasta looked at her like she'd asked a silly question, 'To remove any snow from the graves, of course.'

Agnes relaxed, looking relieved, 'Ah yes, of course - but you're more than welcome to stay, it looks freezing out, and I'd hate for you all to catch a chill on our account,' she lowered her voice. 'However, I should mention that we haven't told the Reverend about the unusual things happening here. He's not,' she hesitated, whispering. 'The Reverend, well, he's not what you might call spiritually-minded - if you know what I mean?'

Jocasta put up her hand, 'You don't need to explain; we come across it all the time from some fractions of the church and constabulary,' she put her thumb and finger together and ran them across her mouth. 'Mum's the word.'

'The constabulary!' exclaimed Clementine looking confused.

Jocasta nodded, 'Yes, the constabulary is often involved in our line of work. We've helped them solve many cases, not that they would admit it.'

'Ah, there you are, ladies,' said Reverend Sommersby smiling from ear to ear, briskly rubbing his hands together, his face glowing like a beacon. 'Miss Duckworth and I are quite chilled to the bone.' Miss Duckworth nodded, hovering uncomfortably in the background, rolling her hands. The Reverend glanced at the four of us with surprise. 'Oh, I'm sorry, I didn't know you had visitors. Are we interrupting something?'

'Not at all,' said Agnes trying to be convivial. 'These are our guests; they're staying with us for a few days to help us with – with the house, as you know, we're still finding our feet here. They're just about to take a tour around the gardens.'

'What! in this weather?' Asked the Reverend, his eyebrows shooting to the top of his head as he glanced at the windows. 'It's bitter out and most inclement - It's a pity you weren't here last summer; the grounds were delightful. I don't think you'd find better anywhere in England. Mr Tadworth, the head gardener here, helps us maintain the gardens at the vicarage. I keep telling him he should write a book; what he doesn't know about the horticultural world, well, it isn't worth knowing.

Mr Tadworth says you can bury any number of headaches in the garden, and anyone who has time for drama isn't gardening enough,' the Reverend smiled righteously. 'I keep telling my parishioners to get their hands dirty and involve themselves with gardening and nature. As it says in Corinthians 9:6, 'Whoever sows sparingly will also reap sparingly, and whoever sows generously will also reap generously,' you reap what you sow,' he gave a self-satisfied smile. 'And I'm unanimous in that.'

Florence stood at one of the windows observing the falling snow, 'Indeed, you do,' she agreed. 'But a little bit of snow never hurt anyone. Personally, I find the cold invigorating; it gets the circulation going, it makes you feel alive and at one with nature and the seasons.'

'Do you think so?' Asked the Reverend thoughtfully. 'These days, I don't tend to feel the cold too much. I think it's from all my years in draughty churches, vestries, and church halls in a cassock. Although I must say, even I'm finding this cold spell a bit of a challenge, it's quite vexing, but then, I'm not getting any younger as my joints keep reminding me,' he exhaled loudly. 'Anyway, ladies, may I say what a beautiful Christmas Tree you have, quite magnificent; they do put one in the festive spirit,' the music box caught his eye. 'And what a charming ornament of heavenly angels with the infant, Jesus, quite delightful. It's good to see people remembering the true meaning of Christmas.'

'It is charming, isn't it,' agreed Agnes. 'A recent discovery in the house. I'm sure there will be many more as we find our feet; we're still settling in.'

Agnes did the introductions, and we all shook hands; the Reverend's hands were freezing. He was in his late forties and clearly a man who liked his strong spirits. Not you understand, in the ghostly sense, but the brandy and whisky kind. Miss Duckworth was in her mid-forties and spoke softly. Without wanting to sound disrespectful, she was a rather grey and dull bespectacled figure. I found it heartening to know she liked a glass or two of sherry. I hoped it might add some colour to her character. She was the sort of person you barely noticed; I thought she'd make a great spy or gossip columnist.

'When I glanced out of the study window at the vicarage earlier,' said the Reverend. 'I said to my dear wife, Muriel, who was busy dusting her knick-knacks; I didn't think we'd be able to make it here today, given the snow. But Miss Duckworth called, most determined in her wellington boots and balaclava, looking like she was dressed for a trip to the Antarctic or the North Pole. She'd been tapping at her organ all morning, and although quite worn out, she insisted we make the journey here on foot.

The verger, Mr Nimmo, paused from his ecumenical work and called at the vicarage to tell me that Miss Duckworth had the church filled with joyous Christmas carols, which had put Mrs Mottershead, Miss Ryder, and Miss Bush in quite the festive mood. They had braved the weather and were at the church getting their meticulously planned

Christmas floral displays ready - I think the verger was happy to leave the church; he said Mrs Mottershead was getting giddy and carried away with the mistletoe.'

The Reverend cleared his throat and turned to a blushing Miss Duckworth. 'Miss Duckworth rightly said the good Lord would expect us to face adversity and come here today. After all, the concert is tomorrow evening, and it's all for a good cause, for the village, church, and the festive season. It's also an excellent opportunity for the whole town to come together, get into the festive spirit and remember the true meaning of Christmas.'

He continued, not drawing breath, 'The choir have been busy practising their Christmas carols; I'm told they're even going to do a rendition of Jingle Bells.' He smiled, 'As Miss Duckworth says, practice makes perfect, and after everyone else has made such an effort today at the church, I couldn't argue with that, so here we are. It must be God's will; sometimes, he works in mysterious ways.'

He glanced at the piano, 'I see you're ready for us. When I left the house, even my dear wife, Muriel, was practising 'Oh Little Town of Bethlehem' on her ukulele; she has such nimble fingers and is a big fan of the up-and-coming singer George Formby,' the Reverend looked bemused. 'She's even learning to play the banjolele. I've had to invest in some earplugs; she strums away at the strings night and day,' his expression dulled, and he stiffened. 'My wife's had to find an outlet for her exuberance since she gave up Scottish Country Dancing and the polka, due to her throbbing bunions and bumping bladder. She was a very accomplished dancer but now says she can't dance without wincing. Muriel's become a martyr to the articulated gusset,' he smiled. 'My dear wife constantly raves about it; I feel like I've become quite the gusset connoisseur. Muriel says they're best in a breathable fabric.'

Silence...

'Mind you, these days, even with the wonders of the articulated gusset, she insists on not being too far from a convenience,' the Reverend sighed and grimaced, turning to the four of us. 'My wife is known in the village for her dancing and dressmaking skills. I don't know why she can't just add to her dressmaking repertoire and take up knitting, crochet, or embroidery. We have a very active knitting circle in the parish, and it's a much quieter hobby and all for a good cause.'

Agnes and Clementine agreed, quickly steering the conversation away from undergarments and bodily functions. We left the four of them discussing the merits and complexities of knitting, with Miss Duckworth explaining the technicalities of the two-tone lattice, honeycomb cable, and lotus flower stitches.

Once we were all wrapped up against the elements and I'd found a spade in one of the outbuildings, we set off in the falling snow to find the family graves in the aptly named white garden and explore the grounds.

I'd borrowed, well, I call it borrowing, a collection of clothes from Anderson and Sheppard of Savile Row in London, not that I felt the cold or, for that matter, the heat. Of course, they'd all have to go back! I like to look the part when visiting a grand house. I always need to ensure I'm dressed for the period, one day, I'm 1530, and the next, I could be in 1760 or any period or, for that matter, country. I've never learned any foreign languages, yet somehow, I can speak and understand them fluently, even native languages; I'd grown to like Swahili!

As we walked out of the front entrance, the air was gelid, sharp, and crisp. I stepped back in the stark sunshine to admire the snow-covered Georgian country house and long sweeping tree-lined drive. It was quite the winter scene, grand, elegant, and pleasing to the eye. The house had rigid symmetry, large sash windows and honey-coloured stone. Yet, for all its charm, it held a dark mystery.

'Where should we start?' I asked, squinting in the sunshine.

'I'm strangely drawn this way,' said Jocasta moving towards one of the terraced gardens. 'The grounds here have a strong energy, a psychic force; I didn't notice it when we arrived.'

I didn't like the sound of that. 'What sort of psychic force?' I asked apprehensively. Detectable energies in our line of work were not uncommon or necessarily a good thing, particularly if they were strong. Spiritual energies held onto things they couldn't or wouldn't let go of - most often due to unresolved issues during life. You could call it unfinished business or the past whispering at you, trying to tell you or remind you of something it didn't want you to forget.

'I'm not sure,' said Jocasta pensively, her breath frosting in the cold air. 'I've never come across such a feeling before. Of course, I've sensed energies, but not like this one,' she glanced at Florence. 'What do you think?'

Florence stood rigid for a moment with her eyes closed, holding her arms out, rolling them in the air as if exercising; the three of us watched on... 'Yes - I know what you mean,' she shivered, looking pensive. 'Something is hanging over this place. Something that only becomes apparent at this time of year. It's strange - I'm sure ghosts visit this house from Christmas past to relive unhappy events; it's as if they're compelled to be here,' she opened her eyes. 'It's interesting that the energy is in the grounds and the house; in my experience, that's rare.'

Jocasta nodded musingly. 'I wonder if the house could sit on ancient ley lines? It's claimed they were recognised by early societies who deliberately erected structures along them. Ley lines are said to demarcate earth energies, and alignments between powerful magical places thought to be psychic in nature.'

'It's a fairly new idea,' said Winston. 'One put forward in the 1920s by the English antiquarian Alfred Watkins. He argues that straight lines can be drawn between various historic structures and sites established during different periods of the past. Watkin's claimed that magical energies may run through these ley lines.'

'Yes, he gave a lecture with Professor Wimble at The Society for Psychical Research,' said Jocasta glancing into the distance. 'We must keep his ideas and ley lines in mind.'

I looked back towards the house and the countryside beyond. 'Hmm, ley lines - whatever it is, it's like this place is holding onto a long-held grudge or punishment.'

'A punishment!' Exclaimed Jocasta pulling a face. 'That's an interesting way of putting it... but now you've said it; I fear you could be right.'

As the snow fluttered like dancing confetti, we walked through the gardens passing formal beds with box hedging, the snow crunching satisfyingly underfoot. The upper and lower terraces were separated by ornamental stone balustrades decorated with urns, covered in a thick layer of snow, as were the deep flower borders. The snow sculptured the shrubs and plants into different shapes and textures.

The sweeping lawns were a carpet of white which led to the park and freezing woodland beyond, the trees twisting into one another; it was quite a place. And while it looked magical in the snow, like a winter scene on a Christmas card, I could imagine it being the perfect setting during the summer with honey-coloured skies, the garden full of glorious flowers all blooming in colour, the air filled with redolent perfume, and the sound of buzzing insects.

'Is that a lilac tree?' Asked Jocasta pointing ahead of us as birds twittered frantically somewhere in the background. 'It's hard to tell in all this snow, but there's something about the bare branches; I have a lilac tree at home, in my garden in Folkstone - I'm sure that's lilac.'

'Yes, it's lilac,' agreed Florence assuredly. 'But I don't sense anything here,' she stared into the distance. 'These grounds are vast, and we can't afford to waste time. Let's find the graves; there could be some lilac bushes there. Otherwise, I fear it will be like looking for a needle in a haystack.'

We carefully wandered through the icy gardens, following what we could see of the snow-covered paths, the falling snow blowing around us in windy swirls, the others getting rosy-cheeked in the biting wind. As we walked through a magnificent snow-covered topiary arch, we entered a beautiful, yet isolated walled garden; I pointed to a memorial, 'This must be the white garden; that has to be the family grave.'

In the distance stood a neoclassical portico monument reminiscent of a Greek temple, the style defined by its symmetry. It stood on two steps with two columns on either side, all made from white marble. Engraved just below the apex was the family name *ROTHERY*. It stood in simple splendour with marble urns on either side; we could just see their tops in the drifted snow.

As we approached, we walked past a white marble statue of a heavenly angel pointing toward the monument. The monument appeared ideally situated, south-facing. And while the grounds, plants, and shrubs were covered in snow, it wasn't hard to imagine the place in the spring and summer sunshine, surrounded by a mass of fragrant white flowers and shiny green foliage.

The four of us stood for a moment getting our bearings, Jocasta trying to centre herself and detect any spiritual forces or ectoplasm. Due to the snow, no names were visible on the parts of the monument we could see.

'I sense all emotions here,' said Jocasta concentrating hard; she sounded overwhelmed. 'Love, joy, happiness, despair, and great sadness,' she did a 360-degree turn. 'Do you see a lilac tree anywhere?'

'Nothing jumps out,' said Winston pushing his gloved hands deep into his pockets, stamping his feet to keep warm. 'We probably need to take a closer look around.'

'All this snow isn't helping,' said Florence as she shivered in the cold. 'Let me try and cast an ancient revealing spell. I have one from a 15th-century book of magic by the Italian white witch Aurora Dorondonella. I'm the custodian of her covens work and keep it in my secret library at home for the Celestial Fellowship of Witches; I'm sure I can remember it.'

Florence stood back from us, closing her eyes, taking deep breaths, becoming at one with nature. She cast her arms out and slowly rotated on the spot, '*Stratum normeum corpus arantum relinctom - hear me wise sisters of Dorondonella. I seek the letter R; it's engraved on a stone and held here in the shadow of a lilac tree,*' she placed her hands together as if in prayer and held them up to the silver sky and falling snow. *'Carmina gadelica, atharvaveda merseburg, maqlû, zu-buru-dabbeda, kotodama zagovory, if the letter R be here in this park, I command for it to be revealed to me. Carmen lorica yajna slavica projanica - wise sisters of Dorondonella, I call upon you to reveal to me the letter R.'*

Florence stopped turning and opened her eyes, looking quite pleased with herself as she glanced around the snowy garden and nodded to herself, 'Yes, I think that should do it. I think I remembered it correctly - I've thrown the kitchen sink at it.'

The four of us stood waiting expectantly in the falling snow... 'Something is happening,' said Florence excitedly, holding out her hand. 'Don't anyone move; I sense ancient meridians of magic are at work.'

We stood motionless; there was a sound like a long breath as a gentle wind came from the east tinged with ancient whispers. The breeze caused the snow to swirl in pirouettes as it moved towards the monument, revealing something on the ground. We remained motionless, watching as the wind shifted to a recessed area in a hedge, something we hadn't noticed in the deep snow. The wind shook the snow from the bushes, bringing them to life as they magically burst into bloom, revealing fragrant white flowers of roses, peonies, jasmine, and a glorious lilac tree, all bathed in golden sunshine. It was as magnificent as it was incongruous. As the wind caused the snow to swirl gently, the swirl became faster, moving to the ground, exposing something. Then just as quickly as the wind arrived, it was gone, leaving no flowers, only the bare branches of the trees and shrubs catching the falling snow. It was quite a spell.

Intrigued, we moved forward to the recessed area. On the ground was a stone; beautifully carved into it was the letter R. Jocasta knelt, took off her glove and put her hand on the stone....

'Do you sense anything?' Asked Florence expectantly.

'I do,' said Jocasta sombrely, catching her breath. 'A child is buried here, a boy, but it's a child that had no life here on earth, a stillborn child.'

'Are you sure?' I asked.

'Absolutely,' said Jocasta, deep in thought; she looked lost and far away. 'This child was buried here many years ago, with great love, but also, great pain, terrible longing, grief, and suffering.'

'All the feelings trapped in the house,' said Florence.

'Yes,' agreed Jocasta standing up slowly. 'But I'm sure there's more; come, we must look at the monument.'

The four of us moved to the family grave; the spell had cleared a small area in front of the marble monument, which read, remembering Montague and Elspeth, the rest of the inscription remained covered in snow. 'Fascinating,' said Jocasta wiping a tear from her eye. 'I think I know what happened. R was the child of Montague and Elspeth and must have been their first child.'

'But why bury the child here with such secrecy?' I asked.

'Hmm, I know what you mean,' said Jocasta thoughtfully, her voice filled with sadness. 'I'm only making an educated guess, but I'd call it a coping mechanism; I've seen it happen before. At the time of the child's death, I suspect it was the only way Montague and Elspeth could cope with their loss. They wanted to acknowledge the child, but they also wanted to put the loss behind them - the fewer people who knew about it, the better. They didn't want people to talk about it or dwell on it; that would have been too painful and unbearable for them and a constant reminder of their loss. People cope with grief in their own way, and they were different times.'

'And you can sense all that from this place?' I asked.

Jocasta nodded, 'Yes, I can see it all so clearly, just like looking at the three of you - it's hard to explain. Of course, stillbirths are not and were not uncommon,' she shook her head. 'But I can't help thinking there was something different about this one.'

'Different in what way?' I asked, not sure I really wanted to know.

'Ah, good question, what do I mean?... Of course, for all intents and purposes, it was a natural stillbirth, but I think dark magic was at work,' Jocasta paused, listening to her vibrations. 'Dark magic caused by the pain and suffering of someone else, someone who wanted, no, wants revenge and is using the dark arts to achieve it.'

Jocasta turned to Florence, 'It ties in with what you said earlier. Something is hanging over this place. Something that only becomes apparent at this time of year when ghosts from Christmas past are forced to return here to relive unhappy events – I fear their pain feeds the magic; it gives it energy,' she shook her head again. 'I suspect it's been going on for years, becoming more apparent when Violet died in 1902. I wonder what poor Edmund made of it all?'

'And you can tell all this purely from this monument?' I asked doubtfully.

'In a way,' replied Jocasta. 'It's hard to explain; it's a combination of things - things my vibrations and presentiments have eventuated to me in my base chakra.'

'Have you any idea when the child R was born?' Asked Winston.

'No, well, not for certain, but obviously before Edmund, so sometime in the 1850s,' said Jocasta, deep in thought. 'But I suspect R was stillborn at 3 p.m. on Christmas day; that day and time appear to be part of whatever is happening here. Thankfully for Montague and Elspeth, they put the loss of R behind them and went on to have two healthy children, Beatrice, and Edmund. Everything here was perfectly normal, that is, until Thomas died, which triggered the pain and suffering of Violet and Edmund.

I don't know how it works, but I feel some sort of curse must hang over this place and the Rothery family – but why?' Jocasta stared at our blank faces. 'Of course, if it's with the family, it dies out with Agnes and Clementine. However, that won't stop the house hauntings at this time of year; they will continue, as will the curse if it's this estate, which is why we must stop it.'

'Do you think Agnes and Clementine could be in danger?' I asked. As I said this, the wind whipped around us; and apprehension ran through me.

'Hmm, I suppose they could be. Whatever is going on here seems to strike at the very core of love, family, and devotion, the sort of human emotions guaranteed to generate the strongest feelings of affection, protection, and concern for others.'

'And pain,' said Florence, as her senses tingled.

Chapter 7

It was getting colder, and the snow fell faster as we returned to the warmth and comfort of the house, not that I was ever cold or needed warmth, at least not in a physical sense. My mind was spinning with the notion of Christmas ghosts and a curse, although whatever ghosts resided here were not like me. I've often wondered if I was unique; I had no idea. Ghosts tend to have a bad reputation and are often mistaken for the devil. However, ghosts come in many forms, the good, the bad, the ugly, and everything in between!

Why would someone become so obsessed with this place and the Rothery family they wanted generations of the family to suffer pain, specifically at Christmas time. Yet it didn't stop there; those who had suffered appeared compelled to return to the house every Christmas to relive their suffering.

Clearly, there was a reason, revenge, or perhaps a punishment passing down the generations for forgotten events involving the sins or crimes of a person or personage's unknown. I've been involved with several cases involving curses; they went hand in hand with dark magic and witchcraft. Curses went back thousands of years, although, in my experience, active curses were quite rare. Most curses were nothing more than old wives' tales and folklore passed down the generations, a colourful story told during idle village gossip and tittle-tattle.

Many believe witchcraft ended in Britain during the 18th century when the laws against witchcraft were repealed in 1736. However, it has never stopped. Witches, warlocks, occultists, and others are still casting spells and searching for ancient books of alchemy and magic, believing they hold the secrets to ancient wisdom, wealth, power, and eternal youth. Of course, many witches, like Florence, work for the greater good.

Looking at the history of Rothery Hall and the family, we were mainly in the Victorian period; I felt sure dark witchcraft had to be at work here at the house; what else could it be?

During the 19th century, witchcraft and folklore continued to be an active and potent force in everyday life. And although hidden under the strict notions of Victorian respectability and morality, superstitious beliefs about witchcraft and things like gipsy curses remained throughout the country, particularly in rural towns and villages.

The eighteen hundreds also saw a growing interest in the supernatural and spiritualism, resulting in the birth of the spiritualist movement. Victorians delighted in ghost stories, fairy tales, and legends of strange gods, demons, and spirits. Victorian spiritualism was particularly attractive to women because they were regarded as more spiritual than men, with a better predisposition to spiritual perfectibility.

Jocasta had mixed views about it all and often referred to it as the dawn and age of the fake medium. She has spent years conducting detailed research to expose fake mediums, past and present, revealing all their tricks and techniques in her articles for Psychic Monthly Magazine and during her lecture tours. To her, a fake medium was like a red rag to a bull dishonouring the reputation of her unique profession, although I'd say Jocasta was a true original.

During the 19th century, both the rich and the poor believed in the power of witchcraft and curses, blaming their bad luck and misfortune on witchcraft; some cases even ended up in the courts and are well documented, should you wish to look. Vigilantism against witches in Britain was still commonplace throughout this period due to a highly superstitious public and few protective laws. Alleged witches often found themselves hectored, abused, attacked, and sometimes murdered by their accusers and apparent victims.

In terms of curses, you are perhaps familiar with those associated with the violation of Egyptian tombs. The ancient Egyptian priests were known to place curse inscriptions on markers protecting temples, tomb goods, and property; they used an evil elemental spirit to protect the mummy. They were effective and often gruesome; I witnessed some of them in action, but that's another story. Even in the Bible, curses appear. In various books of the Hebrew Bible, there are long lists of curses against transgressors of the Law. However, in my experience, finding an active curse on a house or family was rare.

We joined Agnes and Clementine in the drawing-room by the sparkling Christmas tree and warmth of the raging fire; the Reverend and Miss Duckworth were still with them, both fortified by a glass or three of brandy and sherry, the Reverend with a deepening ruby glow. Miss Duckworth sat at the piano with some tinsel draped around her neck playing and singing the Cole Porter song, 'You Do Something to Me'; it was an interesting rendition. She had certainly come to life and looked relaxed with more colour and, dare I say, vivacity!

Our arrival made the two of them acutely aware of the time. The Reverend remembered he had his bible reading group in the village library, telling us they were reading and discussing bible verses with a Christmas meaning. He quoted Isaiah 9:6-7 saying, 'For to us a child is born, to us a son is given; and the government shall be upon his shoulder, and his name shall be called Wonderful Counsellor, Mighty God, Everlasting Father, Prince of Peace'. I worried he was getting carried away in his religious fervour, but Agnes politely kept him focused, reminding him of his pressing bible class; I thought she'd make an excellent diplomat.

The Reverend thanked Clementine and Agnes for their hospitality, saying he would see them at the concert tomorrow, confident the inclement weather wouldn't deter the eager villagers. The four of them moved to the hall so the Reverend and Miss Duckworth could prepare for their journey in the ice and snow. Miss Duckworth struggled to put on her wellington boots and balaclava, having lost her balance and coordination. She blamed it on a sudden dizzy spell caused by the cold weather and the brightness of the snow! However, once they were well wrapped up in several layers, the two left feeling quite giddy, staggering merrily back to the village; I doubted they'd feel the cold!

When Clementine and Agnes returned to the drawing-room, Ethel was busy clearing the cups, plates, and glasses, humming the Christmas carol 'In the Bleak Mid-Winter' to herself. Clementine glanced at her, 'If the Reverend and Miss Duckworth become regular visitors, Ethel, we'll need to stock up on brandy and sherry.' She gave a wry smile, glancing at the drinks cart and then at Agnes, who was carefully putting her sheet music in her music case.

'Hmm,' replied Ethel with a tut in her tone and a sneer. 'As you know, I'm not one to gossip, but the verger, Mr Nimmo, a lovely man, he has immaculate cassocks, and his shoes are always well polished. He says they're constantly topping up their supplies of communion wine - I think I can guess why,' she sighed disapprovingly. 'Anyway, I'll leave you to it; I need to check on my steamed treacle pudding. I've found a lovely Mrs Beeton recipe - the puddings at a delicate stage; I need to make sure the water simmer and steam is just right.'

Ethel departed, humming her Christmas carol, leaving us wondering how one achieved the perfect steam!

'Now, did you find anything?' Asked Agnes eagerly, craning her neck as she glanced out of one of the windows. 'I'm sure the snow's getting worse - you four are certainly determined and must all be perished. But I do hope the Reverend and Miss Duckworth will be alright. I don't think I've ever seen the two of them so animated, particularly Miss Duckworth; she had quite a rosy glow.'

'Hmm, that's a polite way of putting it, sister dear,' said Clementine shaking her head and laughing. 'Although I don't think I've ever seen her so chatty and relaxed - she's grown on me.'

Agnes moved to sit next to Clementine near the blazing fire. 'I'm always polite, sister dear – Anyway, Miss Duckworth has been trying to persuade Clementine and me to appear in a musical she wants to produce in the village hall; it has a delightful little stage. It's quaint and quite charming.'

'What kind of stage musical?' Asked Jocasta tentatively. 'I must take care with musical productions; I've found that melodic arrangements in a theatre or concert hall can affect my vibrations,' she wrinkled her nose thoughtfully. 'It's strange because I'm never affected by music and songs in a religious setting like a church or cathedral.'

'Ah, you may well ask,' fluttered Agnes. 'Even we were surprised. Can you believe she wants to produce the show, 'No, No, Nanette'? If you don't know it, it's a musical comedy. Apparently, she saw the London production in 1925 at the Palace Theatre. It's a story involving three couples who find themselves at a cottage in Atlantic City in America amid a blackmail scheme. It focuses on a young, fun-loving Manhattan heiress who naughtily runs off for a weekend, leaving her unhappy fiancé. We told Miss Duckworth we thought it sounded far too racy for our little village. The Reverend agreed, needing another large brandy to calm himself - she's a dark horse that Miss Duckworth.'

'Well, it's as I always say, sister dear,' smiled Clementine knowingly. 'Still waters run deep. I'm reminded of the butter wouldn't melt, Solange Ottoline-Partridge; we've had a Christmas card from her and her husband, William, in the morning post. Do you remember James and Marjorie Condomine's summer soirée at their country estate?'

'Of course,' nodded Agnes blissfully. 'A delightful evening; I always look forward to it. It's one of the highlights of the social season. I'm always fascinated by their inquisitive peacocks,' she turned to the four of us, wanting to clarify. 'They wander freely around their gardens and grounds displaying their extravagant plumage; they're such show-offs, screaming at the tops of their voices.'

'They are,' agreed Clementine. 'But talking about showing off, if you remember, Solange was no better than she ought to be. There was no stopping her after a few champagne cocktails. She was terribly over the top when she sang, 'I Wanna Be Loved by You' to several men who were lapping it up,' Clementine raised her eyebrows. 'And some of the men were married. In fact, I don't think she knew where the top was with her vulgar shimmies and grotesque contortions – Oh dear, listen to me, I'm digressing, please forgive me – I know we have far more pressing things to think about with whatever is going on in this,' she lowered her voice. 'This haunted house,' she sighed. 'I'm trying to distract myself and not think about it.'

I was disappointed; I thought Solange sounded fascinating and wanted to hear more!

'Yes, we do,' agreed Agnes, lowering her voice to a whisper, 'Ethel's just told me that Mrs Pumphrey's reported hearing strange moans and groans on the landing again; she won't go into any of the bedrooms on her own, and I can't say I blame her,' she shook her head looking relieved. 'I'm pleased it's Mrs Emmerson and Mrs Shaw's days off,' Agnes turned to the four of us again. 'They help us with the house, but they only work here two days a week. Mrs Emmerson helps her husband with his little gin distillery, although she calls it 'mother's ruin' and says she can't stand it. She and her husband constantly bicker about it. Mrs Shaw helps her husband with his pickling - he rents one of the farms on the estate and is famous for his root vegetables, beetroot, and onions. He has a small pickling factory on the outskirts of the village, Shaw's Pickles – he's an expert in vinegar.'

Silence...

Clementine took a deep breath bobbing her head, 'I'm amazed we have any house staff left. Although if we don't sort out whatever is happening here in this house, I don't think we'll have them for much longer. Even Ethel's wavering and wandering around the house with her bible, crucifix, and some holy water. She says people in the village are starting to gossip and give her strange looks.'

'Ah, yes,' said Agnes with a note of caution. 'I think that's because she's been asking Mr Froggatt, the greengrocer, if he sells garlic. People are worried she's developing strange tastes and going all continental and foreign.'

'Have faith, ladies,' declared Jocasta grabbing her Gladstone bag. 'Talking about garlic, think of this mystery rather like an onion; we're peeling it away in layers, revealing clues until we find the root cause - Now, we really do need to focus and not allow ourselves to become distracted - we've made a discovery regarding R.'

Jocasta proceeded to explain to Clementine and Agnes our findings....

After a period of long silences and looks of disbelief, with Clementine and Agnes making several attempts to speak, trying to find the right words, Clementine uttered, 'Such a thing had never crossed our minds,' she glanced at Agnes. 'But then why would it? I'm sure our mother and Edmund didn't ever know they had an older brother - our poor grandparents; it must have been heartbreaking for them.'

'Yes,' agreed Jocasta. 'But sadly, not uncommon, although I believe Montague and Elspeth's sad misfortune was different and may have been caused by a curse that hangs over this place.'

'A curse!' Exclaimed Agnes with a look of horror, putting her hand over her mouth and grabbing her bag for her smelling salts. I was pleased she was sat down... 'In the newspapers,' she said breathlessly. 'You read about curses linked to the ancient Egyptians and their sacred tombs, but I never imagined we had them in England. Is it safe for us to stay here? Are we all in danger?'

Jocasta was about to explain as the windows rattled loudly, and a gust of wind howled outside, whipping clouds of powdery snow in every direction. The temperature in the room suddenly dropped, and the music box with the heavenly angels and baby Jesus started rotating and playing Oh Come All Ye Faithful. There was an awful scream from somewhere in the house; Agnes and Clementine jumped. We all froze, looking at each other before running out into the hall hearing another cry.

Undaunted, Ethel was flying up the stairs with a tea towel in one hand and her crucifix in the other. We all followed. When we arrived on the landing, Ethel was clutching onto Mrs Pumphrey, who looked agitated and light-headed.

'What is it?' I asked nervously, glancing in every direction; the others stood behind me, trying to get their breath.

'Mrs Pumphrey thought she saw something,' said Ethel

breathlessly with a shiver.

'Oh sir,' said Mrs Pumphrey trying to control her breathing and keep the lid on her emotions. She put her hand on one of the windowsills to steady herself, her breath frosting in the cold air. 'Something - something is happening here - I think the devil possesses this house. I was sure I saw the shadow of someone,' she glanced at the portraits on the wall and gulped hard, going pale, 'And I swear the people in those portraits were following me with their eyes looking at me like I was a - a heathen.' She shuddered, closed her eyes, crossed herself, fell to her knees, put her hands together like someone possessed, and began reciting the Lord's prayer.

We all glanced at the portraits but were distracted by the sound of awful whaling, sobbing, and a melodic rocking, the rocking getting faster and faster.

'I'm sure that's the rocking chair in the nursery,' said Agnes, nervously wringing her hands. 'I've heard it before,' she stiffened and lifted her chin, trying to find her resolve, looking at Ethel. 'You'd better take Mrs Pumphrey to the kitchen and make her a cup of sweet tea or get her something stronger,' her voice broke as she held her hands together tightly to stop them from shaking. 'God willing, Clementine and I will join you both shortly.'

Ethel nodded, looking ashen as she took Mrs Pumphrey firmly by the shoulders, uttering soothing words as she carefully raised her to her feet. She glanced knowingly at Agnes and Clementine, clutching her crucifix, and carefully escorted Mrs Pumphrey to the stairs and back down to the kitchen, singing the hymn, 'O God, our help in ages past'.

In a fluster, the six of us quickly made our way to the nursery, the others shivering as their breath frosted in the cold air. The sobbing stopped as we arrived at the door, which slowly creaked open like we were expected, letting out another blast of freezing air. I sensed the others holding their breath. The rocking chair was in the centre of the room, almost rocking off its feet but stopped abruptly; no one moved – silence...

The silence was broken by a child crying; at first, it sounded distant and far away but grew louder and louder, echoing all around the house. It was so disorientating and disturbing, a crying child that finds no comfort or relief. And then, just like the rocking chair, it stopped abruptly – silence... I could see the relief on the faces of the others, as they breathed sighs of relief without realising they were doing it.

Jocasta was sniffing the air and about to speak, but Winston put out his hand. 'Shh,' what's that?' he put his hand to his ear.

Somewhere in the house, we could hear the muffled sounds of sobbing, possibly a man. We stood motionless, listening for a moment, 'I think it's coming from downstairs,' offered Winston in a whisper. We moved back onto the landing and quickly descended the stairs. The six of us stood in the hall listening intently, trying to remain calm, which was easier said than done. Even I felt nervous, I kept telling myself I was a ghost, but it wasn't helping, although I found the steady tick-tock of the stately grandfather clock calming.

'It sounds like it's coming from the direction of the study,' said Winston.

'I can smell ectoplasm most strongly,' said Jocasta sniffing the air, looking severe. 'It's the same upstairs. Right now, this house is filled with a surge of psychic energy; it's appeared from nowhere - we need to take care. I fear dark forces could be at work.'

We moved to the study and stood apprehensively by the door; we could hear wailing and a man sobbing with grief. 'Should we go in?' I asked in a whisper; they all looked at me blank. I made an executive decision, turned the door handle, and pushed, but the door wouldn't budge; it didn't even rattle.

As I kept trying the door, the house echoed; it was alive with incoherent whispers; they seemed to be coming from everywhere. None of us had a clue what to do. Then, like upstairs, the whispers and sobbing stopped as quickly as it started – silence... As we stood in the stillness, we quickly stepped back as the door to the study slowly creaked open; I could tell the others were holding their breath again...

While everyone stayed back, I quickly glanced inside. Of course, the room was empty - no one was there, not even a ghost! However, the diary with the symbol was another matter. It sat open on the side table with its pages flicking backwards and forwards in a cascade with words and audible mumbling flying from the pages. We stood mesmerized until the pages finally came to rest, and the book slammed shut with a loud thump – silence…

'What should we do?' I asked in a whisper.

Jocasta moved forward, pulling her shoulders back and pushing me out of the way, 'Investigate, of course.'

We nervously entered the study, all on high alert, wondering what might happen next; Jocasta sniffed the air loudly. 'The ectoplasm is strong here,' she moved to the desk. 'And more so here just like before,' she touched the desk chair and shuddered. 'Someone has been sitting here, someone in deep distress.'

Throwing caution to the wind, I picked up the diary and began flicking through the blank pages feeling bewildered, 'Tell me; you did all hear voices and see words flying from these pages?'

'Oh, be careful with that,' said Jocasta with a warning in her tone. 'It needs handling with great care; we don't know what dangers it might hold.'

Florence looked over my shoulder, 'Yes, I did.'

'We all did,' said Jocasta casually, still sniffing the air. 'But it's not the first time we've seen it happen with a book, although never a diary.'

Which was true.

'I think it's – oh, I was going to say a book of magic,' said Florence standing beside me. 'But that's not what I mean. As I said before, I feel the diary is infused with some sort of magic; it must be. It's not uncommon for books of magic to have spells on the pages that are invisible to the naked eye. I have some back at my cottage in Pluckley, hidden away in my secret library. Only the initiated can see the writing and drawings on the books' pages.'

I put the diary back on the table, disappointed to find that all the pages were blank, 'I know diaries are personal, but this takes privacy to a different level,' I said. 'Unless....'

'Unless what?' Asked Jocasta.

'Unless it holds a warning or clues that someone doesn't want anyone to see.'

Clementine looked weary and perplexed, 'With it saying 1861, I wonder if it was Bernard's diary or is connected to him in some way – to me, it's the only logical explanation, not that there is anything logical about this house. That diary is an example; it just appeared from nowhere. I asked Ethel and the house staff if they'd found it by chance, but just like the music box, no one knows anything about it.'

'Perhaps someone wanted us to find it,' I said. 'Not that it tells us anything.'

'No,' interjected Jocasta shaking her head. 'No, that's not it at all. The diary is linked to whatever misfortune has been cast on the Rothery family. As Florence said, it holds magic; I'm sure the diary only appears at this time of year. I can feel it strongly in my base chakra; you could even call it a presentiment.'

'Should we burn it?' Asked Agnes. 'Isn't that what they do?'

'I think you're confusing magic with diseases and infections like Black Death known as the plague,' said Winston. 'Which created religious, social and economic upheavals, with profound effects on the course of European history.'

Jocasta looked at Agnes, horrified, 'Certainly not,' she said sharply. 'It may hold dark magic, but it's also a clue and could hold the answer to our problem or be part of the resolution.'

'If we burnt it, I suspect it would just reappear,' said Florence thoughtfully. 'This type of magic can only be destroyed by overcoming the magic at its source. If this house is cursed, we need to deal with whoever or whatever cursed the house and family; I'm afraid that's the only way you can be rid of it.'

I could tell that wasn't what Clementine and Agnes wanted to hear. Nor me, for that matter!

'Don't lose faith, ladies,' said Jocasta trying her best to sound upbeat. 'Tomorrow morning, the four of us will brave the weather and visit Bernard and Dora's grave at the church. You never know, I may get a presentiment, which could lead to an eventuation that might help us. In the meantime, I'll consult my crystal; it may guide me and point us in the right direction,' she turned to me. 'Oh, and Jasper, remind me to phone the Reverend; Winston's had an idea; he feels we need to look through the church land registry records.'

I was about to ask why when the doorbell rang.

Clementine glanced at the mantel clock, 'Oh, look at the time; I wonder if that's Mr Ingleton from the bank? I telephoned him earlier; he said he'd brave the weather and bring Edmund's pocket watch to the house - I know you wanted to look at it, Jocasta,' Clementine laughed to herself. 'He thought I was contacting him because we wanted the family diamonds and tiaras to wear at various Christmas parties and balls.'

Agnes looked at her with disbelief and laughed, 'Sister dear, you and I in tiaras, goodness, the very idea. We don't have the right-shaped head for a tiara; you really need to be royalty. People will think we've developed delusions of grandeur.'

***

'It was just as I expected and had seen in my crystal,' said Jocasta with a note of self-satisfaction, as the four of us headed on foot in the fluttering snow towards the village church. We were well wrapped up against the cold, not that I needed it, but I had to keep up appearances and dress for the weather. Winston decided the ice and snow on the narrow roads were far too deep and treacherous to risk driving into town in his much-loved Rover. We all agreed, Jocasta saying the fresh winter air would help to keep her energy centres flowing and keep her in tune with the spiritual highway. Not that I minded walking; the freezing weather made me feel strangely alive.

'The moment I saw the pocket watch, before I'd even touched it, I had a presentiment and felt a vigorous stirring in my base chakra,' continued Jocasta. 'Of course, when we get back to the hall, I'll need to examine the watch in detail looking at the minutiae. I didn't have sufficient time yesterday due to problems with my crystal,' she sighed jadedly. 'Like most things involving the Astral Plane and the spirit world - it can be temperamental - this bitterly cold weather doesn't help. It's full of troublesome elementals.'

Jocasta shivered, pulling her coat and thick wool scarf closer to her with a gloved hand, her breath frosting in the air like diamond dust. 'However, just like the music box and diary, Edmund's pocket watch is somehow connected to whatever is happening at the house. It looks innocent enough, but I'm sure it holds more than a simple clue,' she sighed again, shaking her head in despair. 'I can't help feeling we're missing something – something important.'

It was more food for thought as we made our way along the narrow, snow-covered paths and quiet country lanes. I'd come prepared with a spade in hand, thinking we might need it to clear our way in the snow, and felt sure we'd need to remove some from Bernard and Dora's grave.

As we walked, I found myself enjoying the icy scene of white and silver. I was unsure if the others felt the same due to the biting wind and freezing temperature. Although the seasonal sun offered moments of comforting warmth and respite as it made everything sparkle.

While bathed in the sun's pale-yellow rays, Florence described the cold air as invigorating and an elixir to the mind, circulation, and lungs, making one glad to be alive. I didn't comment!

Coils of twisting smoke drifted up from the farm cottage chimneys, leisurely making its acquaintance with the icy morning sky. For miles, random stone cottages mingled with farm buildings in tiny hamlets, set in snow-covered fields dotted with stately trees; their gnarled branches groaning under the weight of the snow, the ice glistening on their course knotted bark.

As we walked, the snow crunched satisfyingly underfoot; the bitter cold made any moisture in the air sparkle, turning it into ice crystals. As far as the eye could see, a glare of white surrounded us. We could hear the sharp, repetitive thud of an axe as someone chopped wood for the fire; the sound seemed to echo from every direction.

We moved with purpose, stepping hastily through the powdery snow taking in the winter scene, occasionally finding ourselves knee-deep in snow. In the distance, the stark yellow sun looked majestic as it rose above the freezing woodland, warming the air with its shimmering, translucent beams as they slowly mingled with the silver sky. An inner heat seemed to warm and energise the others as we admired nature in all its purity and glory, the snow draping everything in a clean napkin of white.

Even I found it invigorating; everywhere you looked, the freezing air created a winter wonderland of snow-bound meadows and forests. The trees, hedgerows, and mature shrubs drooped under the weight of their snowy burden. The only thing punctuating this midwinter scene was the sharp spined, dark green leaves and abundant red berries of holly – the berries cutting through the glare of whiteness like sparkling gemstones.

As we carefully made our way around a patch of deep snow, we found a recess next to an old rickety gate framed by two well-weathered stone pillars covered in snow and ice. We stopped; the others needed time to get their breath in the bitingly cold air. It gave us a moment to appreciate nature and the sparkling winter scenes around us. Our reverie was broken by an annoying unseen dog barking loudly. The jarring sound triggered alarm calls from the ever-vigilant birds tucked away in the thorny hedgerows and snow-covered shrubbery.

A thin column of smoke twisted and curled into the inauspicious sky from the chimney of a farmhouse hidden behind a dense cluster of snow-covered trees. The pale-yellow sun caused a vapour to develop like a cloud above them, exposing the tops of their bare gnarled, crusty branches. All around us, the snow concealed nature's bounty of curiosities, except where the gusting wind had swept the snow and ice away, exposing the bare frozen land, icy twigs, and sere leaves. The few exposed areas attracted foraging birds looking for scraps of food.

'It's good to get out in nature,' said Winston with a look of satisfaction, his breath dancing merrily in the icy air. 'In the winter months, I think we lead a more inward and isolated life. Although I find the cold helps me focus, there are fewer distractions; it inspires my historical research and writing,' he paused, taking in the winter countryside. 'I like to think that despite the short days, long dark nights, and cold weather, our hearts are warm and cheery – that we are content to sit by the hearth and see the icy sky and winter scenes from draped windows,' he smiled inwardly. 'At such times, we should all count our blessings enjoying the quiet and serene life that may be had in a warm corner by the chimney side or while sitting around a warm stove or fireplace.'

It all sounded philosophical, even poetic, but we all agreed. Jocasta and Florence smiled, accusing Winston of being a slipper and pipe man, as well as an old romantic lost in literature and his library of books, which he was. None of us would want him any other way.

We continued along twisting country lanes framed by more hedgerows and dry-stone walls, most of them hidden beneath the snow. Eventually, the scene changed; the snow-covered fields, farmhouses, and woodland gave way to narrow streets and snow-covered buildings, all charmingly clustered together. It was the start of Brenchley village with its quaint rows of half-timbered cottages and smoking chimney pots, which tinged the cold, musty air a sombre grey accompanied by the smell of charcoal and creosote.

I could see sparkling Christmas trees through some of the cottage windows; you couldn't miss them - they were meant to be seen! Some houses had wreaths or 'welcome rings' hanging on the front door made from holly, ivy, pinecones, and colourful ribbons, reminding us we were in the festive season.

The narrow, cobbled streets snaked through the town like a frozen river, which we carefully followed. Jocasta stopped as she came across a black meowing cat sitting on top of a gate post, which filled her with delight as it reminded her of Cassiel, her black cat at home. She couldn't resist stroking it and said black cats not only bring good luck, but they frighten away demons and evil energy. She felt the cat was a good omen. I hoped she was right; I was tempted to take the purring bundle of black fur with us!

I could tell the others were heartened to finally see our destination, All Saints Church, standing prominently in the snowy distance. The church occupied a commanding position in the centre of the village. It was built from local sandstone with a square tower, just as Clementine had described. Its appearance encouraged us on as dense white clouds gathered above us, and more fluttering snowflakes began to descend, getting faster and faster, quickly shutting out distant objects.

The snow settled on every exposed surface, leaving no crevice untouched or forgotten. Icicles hung from roofs and windows, glistening like sparkling stalactites. Any sere leaves or detritus not buried before were quickly concealed, as were the tracks of men and beasts. There was an airy silence in this sleepy hamlet, with every sound muffled as we walked along slippery paths, passing the village pub, timber-framed shops, a bright red post-box, and more snow-covered gardens, charming cottages, and houses.

I smiled to myself, thinking how nature reasserted her rule, blotting out all traces of man with such little effort, the snowflakes falling thick and fast. The biting wind seemed to lull as the snow fell incessantly, covering and levelling all things as it folded them deeper into the bosom of nature.

Finally, we approached the hallowed church gates. I could tell the others were relieved, but the journey had certainly brought more than a flush of colour to their cheeks.

Winston glanced at the timber-framed vicarage to our right; it sat right on the edge of the churchyard, 'I'm pleased we're calling at the vicarage before we return to the Hall,' he said, stamping his feet to keep warm, trying to get his breath. 'Hopefully, we'll be offered a warming cup of tea. Otherwise, we'll have to try and find a delightful little tearoom somewhere in the village; Agnes did mention one aptly called Tea & Cake; she said they were famous for their afternoon teas, date scones, and coffee and walnut cake.'

'Oh, I do like a nice crunchy walnut,' replied Jocasta dreamily. 'I'm sure the Reverend or his dear wife will offer tea and all the necessary accompaniments. I'll remind them of Christian kindness to the weary traveller if they don't. I'll be expecting Christmas cake, a mince pie or three, and an assortment of delicious biscuits. And depending on how cold we are, we may require a warming brandy or stiff whisky to get our circulation going, and I won't be settling for anything less. Paranormal investigation is thirsty work and gives one an appetite.'

This lot and food! I smiled to myself as I opened the wooden gate to the churchyard; it had a satisfying click.

'This ornate lychgate,' said Winston putting on his glasses to examine the wooden structure and roof, 'was erected to commemorate Queen Victoria's sixty years as Queen.'

It created an impressive entrance, but due to the cold, we didn't linger. In the falling snow, we walked up the tree-lined path, past stately yew trees and ancient gravestones, towards the imposing church entrance with its arched porch and heavy oak doors.

Winston continued, 'I found a book in the study at the Hall which mentions this church,' he shivered, pushing his hands deep into his pockets. 'Apparently, major restoration work was completed here by the Victorian architect Joseph Clark in 1849. Some parts of it go way back to the 12th century; it's a historical place like most churches. It's a pity it's not a better day; like the lychgate, I'd like to study those stained-glass windows Clementine mentioned,' he slowly did a 360-degree turn. 'On a clear day, you must be able to see the surrounding countryside for miles. I don't think I've ever seen a village church with a more pleasing aspect.'

'Hmm, but I hope I don't feel overwhelmed,' declared Jocasta uneasily. 'Graveyards are always full of waiting spirits hoping to chat or pass a message to someone. Oh, hang on, I spoke too soon,' she turned, rubbing her shoulder. 'What was that my dear?... You haven't seen us here before... No, it's our first visit... Yes, I suppose we are determined coming out in this weather... Oh, it's Jocasta Bradman, and you are? ... Imogen Monserrat, what a delightful name it suits you... And I'm delighted to meet you too... You've been here since 1848, I see... I'm pleased you find it peaceful... Yes, graveyards can be very serene, and this one is in a lovely setting... That's most kind of you... Yes, I hope you have a lovely day and Merry Christmas to you....'

'What was she saying?' I asked in a whisper. I could tell the place was alive with ghosts; thankfully, they appeared friendly.

'Oh, nothing really; graveyard spirits tend to be caught in their own little world between the past and present. She was a fine young lady and must have been quite beautiful when alive. Imogen was her name; she had straw-blond hair and piercing blue eyes and wore a beautiful velvet, lace, and silk gown; it matched the colour of her eyes; she told me it was her favourite dress.

She wished us luck with our visit hoping we find the grave we are looking for given the deep snow and inclement weather, which I thought was most kind and thoughtful of her,' Jocasta cast her gaze around the graveyard. 'I always try to be polite with the dear departed, and clearly, they're sociable and highly observant here.'

'I hope you don't get too overwhelmed,' said Florence sympathetically. 'The sooner we find the grave, the sooner we'll be finished and out of here, and you can find some peace. Now, from what Clementine and Agnes told us, I think the grave must be this way; follow me....'

As we followed Florence, Jocasta continued to be interrupted by eager spirits wanting her attention. She tried her best to acknowledge them all, wishing them a good morning and the season's greetings, politely advising them that she couldn't take any messages.

We carefully made our way along an icy path around the side of the church, and then moved towards the back of the snow-covered graveyard to a sheltered corner. The shelter came from several mature trees, their gnarled branches bending and groaning under the weight of the snow. Despite the wintery scene, I could tell the churchyard was well-tended.

'Thankfully, it isn't a big graveyard,' said Winston, quickly glancing around. 'I'd estimate there are only around three to four hundred graves here, some probably dating back hundreds of years.'

I didn't know how he could tell other than by the size of the church grounds; most graves were hidden under the snow. However, some were half-hidden; the grave monuments differed widely in style and shape, with chests, truncated pyramids, obelisks, standing crosses, sculpted figures, and carved headstones peeping out through the undulating snow.

Some looked pristine, while others looked old, weathered, crooked, and neglected; some were crumbling. That's the problem with graves; once the person is forgotten, their grave becomes neglected. I suddenly thought about mine; I was in an unmarked pauper's grave with several others at the now-demolished Newgate prison. I shuddered just thinking about it, trying to block all the horrors and injustices of Newgate prison out of my mind.

Jocasta was diverted, discussing the cold weather with a spirit, an older gentleman; for some reason, I could see him. He looked like he'd had a hard life. He said winters were not like they used to be in his day and were getting milder. In his opinion, people today had it far too free and easy. He blamed the milder winters on the Industrial Revolution - the machines, iron production processes, railways, and the preponderance of smoking chimneys choking the air. Given the extreme freezing conditions, he must have lived during the ice age!

'Could that be the grave there?' Asked Florence, stepping back. 'The one with the,' she stopped mid-sentence with surprise. 'Oh, I say, how odd - the one with the fresh bouquet of flowers,' she hesitated, looking bewildered. 'How on earth can fresh foliage and delicate blossoms survive in this freezing weather?' She looked up to the heavens. 'And why hasn't the bouquet been buried under all this falling snow?'

It was a good point; the snow seemed to fall around it, not on it. I followed her gaze, 'Perhaps it's just been put there,' I said, trying to think rationally. 'That said, I don't know how because we haven't seen anyone,' I glanced around us; I couldn't see any footsteps in the snow other than ours, and they were quickly disappearing in the falling snow. If you are wondering, I leave footsteps, but only when necessary. I had to appear as normal and alive as possible. It's a long story, one that I can't go into now!

Like a skilled surgeon, Florence checked her gloves finger by finger, pushed up her coat sleeves, and moved forward to study the bouquet more closely; she was a woman on a mission. I noticed she didn't touch the flowers and foliage with her gloved hand.

Before us stood the top of an elaborately carved headstone, most of it buried under the falling snow. Completely untouched by the snow lay a fresh bouquet of flowers, berries, foliage, and herbs carefully tied together with string in the nosegay style. I brushed some of the snow away with my hand to get a better look at the headstone's inscription, revealing the letters *RIP* and the family name *ROTHERY*. 'Ah, you were right, Florence, this is it,' I announced, feeling very pleased with myself.

My discovery snapped Jocasta back into the moment and away from her spiritual socialising. 'Is this it?' She asked, touching the headstone, immediately appearing lost to something.

Florence looked at the three of us with disbelief as her witchy suspicions were realised. 'Goodness, this colourful bouquet may look charming, particularly against all this freezing snow, but it's a deadly mixture of highly poisonous plants,' she stared at the bouquet for a long moment. 'It's most peculiar, normally, none of these plants grow at this time of year, and most are not even native to this country. I can see Water Hemlock, which is closely related to poison hemlock, which famously killed the Greek philosopher Socrates. It's infused with a deadly toxin. Then there's deadly nightshade; those black berries cause paralysis to the heart.'

She shuddered as she pointed at some charming white flowers. 'That is White Snakeroot, a North American herb - what is it doing here? It contains a deadly toxic alcohol,' she pointed to a glossy green leaf. 'That's Castor Bean, a plant native to Africa; it contains the poison ricin. And then we have the striking pink flowers of the Oleander; they look delightful, don't they, but all parts of the Oleander plant are deadly; they also contain lethal poisons to the heart. The toxins in Oleander are so potent that people have become ill after eating honey made by bees that have visited the flowers.'

The wind suddenly picked up, scattering the swirling snow in different directions. As it did, I spotted something, 'Look, there's a card attached to the back of the bouquet with a piece of string.' I bent down to see if there was a message.

'Careful with that, Jasper,' said Florence severely. 'If you touch anything, don't put your hands near your mouth.'

I nodded, not worried for obvious reasons, and turned the card over, 'Ah, there is a message written in red ink - it says, Bernard, gone but never forgotten. ML.' I curled my lip, 'Hmm, interesting; there's no mention of Dora; I wonder who ML could be?'

'Hmm, ML - I suppose Clementine and Agnes might know,' said Florence with a shiver. 'But whoever ML is, they can't think fondly of Bernard leaving him a bunch of highly poisonous and deadly flowers. But if that's the case, why leave them at all? And why the red ink? To me, it suggests whoever ML is, they still have a score to settle about something. It makes me think Bernard might have been poisoned.'

'Whoever ML is,' I said. 'They have gone to a great deal of trouble to source such a specific bouquet of highly poisonous plants, and they must be quite elderly; remember Bernard died in 1861.'

'What date did he die?' Asked Winston.

'Ah, good point,' I said, quickly brushing more snow from the headstone... '25th December.'

Silence...

'I sense torment,' muttered Jocasta coming back into the moment; she looked drained like she might faint; I quickly took her arm to steady her... 'Oh, thank you, dear boy,' she said breathlessly. 'I was having a moment; my vibrations were swimming,' she took a deep breath, trying to steady and centre herself. 'For some reason, this grave is held in torment. Give me a moment, and I'll try to make a better connection,' she stiffened, taking off her gloves, putting both her hands on the headstone, concentrating hard, trying to centre her core chakras... 'Hmm, fascinating - I can't explain it, but I sense it's Bernard who may be in torment, not Dora. I feel Dora is at peace and has transcended to the Astral Plane, but not Bernard - now why would that be?'

The wind picked up again; it came from nowhere, whipping the powdery snow into a whirling vortex around us; we could hear whispers like those we heard back at the Hall. *Be gone, be gone...* And I was sure I could see dark shadows, but they were not the shadows of ghosts. The shadows flickered where they shouldn't, twisting and shifting on the ground and gravestones, but there was no object there to cast a shadow; I couldn't explain it, yet it felt wrong and out of kilter with the natural order of things.

Sometimes I feel like I've lived a thousand lives and seen long forgotten times, ancient wonders, and future ones. Yet I was reminded there is far more to this world and the spirit world than I knew. As I glanced across the graveyard, I had another thought about light attracting darkness; Jocasta always said the brighter the light, the more it attracts darkness but not in a good way. Was our light shining too bright? Were we getting too close to something and attracting darkness?

I opened my mouth to speak, but Jocasta started talking to someone. 'Oh, what's that, my dear?' She asked, quickly putting on her gloves. We all looked at her as the snow swirled and danced wildly around us, the wind getting stronger. 'It's Imogen, the lady I talked to earlier; she's returned... Jocasta nodded, listening intently... She is concerned for our safety... Imogen says ghosts, vampires, and devils don't scare her. But a cruel heart devoid of love and compassion is truly terrifying... She says the spirits, the residents here, always avoid this grave... they believe evil holds onto someone heartless... Apparently, its occupants are never seen... No, my dear, please don't apologise; you have not offended me at all... No, they are not my relatives,' Jocasta glanced at the three of us. 'We are here on behalf of people connected to them through their family history, but what you say is most interesting and helpful.'

While Jocasta was talking to Imogen, the wind continued to strengthen, the snow swirling around us as something caught my ghostly eye - a tiny, faded symbol carved onto the back of the headstone. I immediately recognised it, 'Uh-oh, I think I've found something,' I pointed. 'Look at this.'

Battling the wind and snow, the others moved closer to look at the tiny mark; Winston putting on his glasses...

'Good grief, well done, dear boy,' said Jocasta, wide-eyed looking stunned as the wind howled around us. 'Well spotted, you have a sharp eye; this case is getting curiouser and curiouser.'

I looked at Winston in his snow-covered glasses, 'I think we can conclude this symbol isn't a makers mark but something far more sinister.'

Be gone, whispered on the air. *Be gone- be gone*...

'Can you all hear that?' I asked as we stood by the grave, being blasted by the wind and snow.

Jocasta sniffed the air, 'Yes, and I can smell ectoplasm flying in on the wind; it's getting stronger.'

'Darkness is around us,' said Florence breathlessly, grabbing hold of the headstone to stop herself from being blown off her feet. The tree branches swayed wildly, buffeted in the extreme turbulence. Their snowy branches lay bare in the chaotic flurry of the whipping wind. Florence glanced at the three of us uneasily, holding on to her woolly scarf to stop it from blowing away. 'It proves we're onto something,' she said nervously, shouting so we could hear her over the howling wind, which was almost screaming. 'But I think we've outstayed our welcome here; I sense the undead, dark shadows are pushing down upon us, joining other dark shadows that hide here. Whatever haunts or watches the Hall is also somehow connected to this grave. Come, we must leave and get out of here while we still can.'

Chapter 8

As the wind howled and the snow swirled fiercely around us, we held onto our hats, pulling our coats tightly to us, desperately clinging to the trees, gravestones, and anything we could find to help pull us forward as we battled to stay upright and on two feet. The four of us followed what we could see of the ragged, snow-covered path towards the church, twisting our way sideways, backwards, and forwards to get through the extreme elemental forces trying to overwhelm us.

As we tried to push forward, we could hear those sinister whispers as they echoed and lingered on the gusting wind - *be gone – be gone...* I sensed a surge of dark energy around us; Florence was right; we needed to get out of here.

Given the force of the wind and snow, I deliberately stayed at the back, bringing up the rear. Unbeknown to the others, I was pushing the three of them forward using psychic energy. With much effort and determination, we finally made it to the church and clung closely to its ancient stone walls.

As the snowstorm whipped around us, we rested for a moment; the others needed to get their breath. Once they were ready, we clung to the church walls, slowly making our way towards the church entrance buffeted by the wind and snow until we reached the shelter of the porch. Once there, the four of us huddled together by the heavy oak doors for a long moment as Jocasta, Winston, and Florence tried to calm their breathing and rapidly beating hearts, building their resolve to get out of this possessed graveyard. Our visit had awoken something sinister from its ghostly slumber.

As we watched from the shelter of the porch, the wind raged, picking up more speed, ripping plants and shrubs up by their roots, sending anything not bolted down flying across the churchyard like feathers. I felt sure it would rip the roof off the porch, if not the church, and blow out all the ancient stained-glass windows. In all the chaos and turmoil, I could still see dark shadows; they were unaffected by the raging wind moving among the snow-covered gravestones in a gentle rolling mist.

Once the others had their breath and felt ready to make the final sprint, on the count of three, we dashed for the lychgate. Again, I stayed at the back, pushing them forward against the raging wind using psychic energy; I was determined we'd get out in one piece. As we battled ahead, our senses were overwhelmed; everything became a blur as we wrestled through turbulent gusts, ice, and biting snow, the four of us blown in every direction in a raging blizzard until we reached the lychgate and were finally out of the churchyard looking like we'd been dragged through a hedge backwards.

The extreme weather was otherworldly; the others stood frozen and exhausted, relieved to be out of the churchyard, trying to calm their ragged breathing and thumping hearts. They quickly glanced in every direction, attempting to get their bearings and find some semblance of reality, hoping they were safe.

As soon as I closed the gate and we were on the street, the rolling shadows disappeared from around the gravestones, the whipping wind mysteriously dropped, and the snow turned to a gentle flutter of white, lacy petals falling like confetti. The silence was almost deafening.

In the stillness, the snowy graveyard looked as it should, calm, peaceful, and serene. It had seemed normal enough early on, but something dark lingered over Bernard and Dora's grave, making it known it didn't want us there - even the graveyard ghosts avoided it. For the moment, I was relieved to be out of there. If we decided to return, we needed to understand who or what we were dealing with, making sure we had a plan and the right magic to deal with whatever might be thrown at us.

'Most bracing,' declared Jocasta; still getting her breath, she looked shaken as she sniffed the air. 'Ah, good, that's reassuring; I can't smell any troublesome ectoplasm - I don't know why I'm always surprised by supernatural events - I find it best to always expect the unexpected in a graveyard, ancient tomb, or historic burial site. After all the years we've spent investigating and exploring them, along with old houses and ruins, you'd think we'd be used to it by now.'

'Hmm, well, this one didn't disappoint,' I said. 'It was extraordinary; I think it's the most haunted graveyard I've ever come across. Whatever that was back there, it was all aimed at us, and I'm in no rush to return to Bernard and Dora's grave for a repeat performance.'

'Nonsense,' said Jocasta with a tut and a shiver, adjusting her long wool scarf as her breath frosted in the air. 'Where's your sense of adventure, dear boy? It's all in a day's work for us. We won't let unseen forces and a bit of dark magic deter us. It's our duty to go where we're not wanted and journey into the unknown.'

Florence laughed nervously, still trying to regain her composure, 'That was more than a bit of dark magic, Jocasta,' she shuddered, shaking her head. 'Powerful elemental magic was at work back there - I'm fascinated to know why someone, or something wants to haunt the long-dead; they're hardly likely to return - at least not as flesh and blood.'

I could tell Florence was unsettled, her mind full of unanswered questions, her instincts telling her there was far more to this case than we knew.

'Nor I fear as ghosts,' said Jocasta warily. 'At least not Bernard; for some reason, something wants to keep him in a state of torment and purgatory and has gone to a lot of trouble to do so,' she curled her lip, chewing on it. 'But why?'

We stood for a long moment by the perimeter wall staring into the graveyard, trying to comprehend everything that had just happened, searching for answers to the inexplicable, but we didn't have any. Once the others had regained their composure, we slowly headed towards the warmth and shelter of the vicarage. I could tell Jocasta, Winston, and

Florence were looking forward to getting out of the cold; they needed an opportunity to rest before our return journey to the Hall.

In the distance, I could see a woman leaving the vicarage and rushing in our direction. It turned out to be Miss Duckworth looking flustered in her balaclava, wellington boots, and Antarctic attire. She looked like she was heading for the North Pole. We could only see her eyes; she looked like a startled mouse. Given the inclement weather, Miss Duckworth was surprised to see us. She was dashing to the church to greet the church ladies, Miss Lovage, and the choir in the nave. They were in the final countdown, making the last-minute preparations for this evening's carol concert.

As she stood fidgeting with her music case, I felt confident she wouldn't receive the same reception we'd just had in the churchyard. I was disappointed to see that she'd returned to her rather dull grey self; bring on the sherry, I say. Not, you understand, that I encourage excessive drinking! Miss Duckworth didn't linger in the cold, rushing off saying something about the Concerto grosso in G minor, commonly known as the Christmas Concerto. She hoped to perform it at tonight's concert on the church organ; she said it was all terribly fussing.

After she'd gone, Winston looked doubtful, 'Hmm, I think Miss Duckworth is being overly ambitious with her musical repertoire. I'm not aware of the Christmas Concerto having ever been played on the organ. It's a famous ensemble piece written by the Italian composer Arcangelo Corelli. If my memory serves me right, it was first performed in 1690.'

As I didn't know it, I was none the wiser. It was even before my time! And anyway, my mind was far too preoccupied with the events in the graveyard. As we walked towards the vicarage, I turned to Florence; I'd been eager to speak to her following the incident by the grave; like me, she was lost in thought, looking troubled. 'Back in the churchyard, you mentioned dark shadows. What exactly did you mean? What did you see?'

She hesitated, pulling her thoughts together, thinking how best to answer, 'I could see them clearly,' she shook her head. 'It was some sort of black magic, unlike anything I've seen before; as you know, magic takes many forms,' she shivered, pushing her gloved hands deep into her pockets. 'I saw tendrils of darkness, shadows of dark energy rolling like a mist around the four of us and the graves. Rather like dark clouds forming and moving in the sky... Shadowseers tell me they're not as uncommon as we might think.'

That was a new one on me; I looked at her blank, 'Shadowseers? What are they people who can see the devil?'

Florence looked at me surprised, 'You've not heard of them?'

I shook my head.

'Hmm, I suppose the shadows could be connected to the devil; it's the most logical explanation. Darkness attracts monsters in all forms; that's where they hide.'

That was not what I wanted to hear, 'I saw dark shadows in the graveyard, moving like a rolling mist among the graves; I instinctively knew they were dangerous.'

Florence looked relieved and nodded, 'Good, I thought it was just me – some psychics have the gift of shadowseeing - I'm not normally one of them, but I could see shadows as they gathered by Bernard and Dora's grave. They're obviously part of an elaborate spell; the shadows are dangerous and can manipulate things. In some cases, they can even take control of a person, and like ghosts, they can haunt places. However, more worryingly, if the spell was cast before or at the point of Bernard's death and burial, it has retained its power, transcending time, making our job much harder.'

Just what I wanted to hear!

Florence stopped walking and glanced across the graveyard in the falling snow, narrowing her eyes... 'I can't see the shadows now.'

'No, they've gone,' I said, shaking my head, trying to make sense of it all. 'The shadows disappeared as soon as we left the graveyard, and I closed the gate; I saw them vanish.'

'Yes,' agreed Florence reflectively. 'For the time being, they've done their job; I don't know if the shadows intended to bury us under piles of snow, to push us away from Bernard and Dora's grave, or out of the graveyard; I'm pleased we didn't hang around to find out.' We continued walking towards the vicarage catching up with Jocasta and Winston, 'Clearly, Bernard is, or was, involved with something that has followed him to the grave and the Rothery family to the Hall. Jocasta thinks it's a curse, and although they're rare, I'm beginning to think it's a possibility. Maybe the shadows are a part of that.'

We were nearing the vicarage; I stopped walking, 'And if it is a curse, do you think it will affect Agnes and Clementine?'

Florence gave a shrug, one that seemed like a long story, 'Ah, good question. Whatever it is, it's hard to say; it doesn't appear to have done so to date; I'm sure we'd know if it had. But even if they're not directly affected, the house and estate are, so they can't escape whatever haunts the place at this time of year,' she pursed her lips, shaking her head. 'We know of the tragic family deaths at Christmas, but something happened to make Christmas and the 25th of December so significant?'

'It's key to everything,' I said as a chill ran through me. 'It must be. Someone messed with the wrong person or persons, and whatever they did has had far-reaching consequences, particularly if it's followed Bernard Rothery to his grave. The symbol is a clue. I think it must be part of the magic or spell; if we can identify its origins, it might point us in the right direction.'

Florence agreed, 'Yes, symbols and magic go hand in hand; they're used for protection and evil in equal measure. I fear ours will be for the latter.'

'What a charming house,' declared Jocasta as we arrived at the small wooden gate to the vicarage; she stood motionless admiring the house, her breath dancing in the icy air. 'This is just my cup of tea, and unlike any vicarage I've seen before - it's not quite the grand status symbol, and, in my opinion, all the better for it. To me, it looks more homely,' she smiled, looking pleased with herself. 'It really is quite delightful; I could see a picture of it on a chocolate box,' she glanced around, looking back at the church. 'There's something approachable about this house,' she wrinkled her nose approvingly. 'Like churches, vicarages can be rather imposing, but this is charming and blends into the street scene perfectly; it looks part of the village, like it belongs here.'

Winston concurred, 'Originally, vicarages were built to illustrate the importance of the Church. Their occupants regarded as the pillar of society, held in the highest regard. The vicarage was seen as a building that should command respect, which is why they're normally quite grand and well situated.'

How could it not belong here, I thought to myself. The timber-framed property sat back from the road behind a mature garden surrounded by a low brick wall with iron railings and a timber gate. The gate provided access to a snow-covered lawned area and a stone path leading from the road to the front entrance. As we approached the oak front door with its polished brass furniture, it opened, and the Reverend greeted us in his religious robes, his complexion glowing like a beacon. We could hear muted twanging sounds from upstairs; someone playing the banjolele while singing the Christmas carol, God Rest Ye Merry, Gentleman. It was an interesting rendition, one I feared only for the banjolele enthusiast. I assumed it must be Muriel, the Reverend's wife.

'Do come in and let me take your coats,' said the Reverend. 'You all look perished, and I'm not surprised,' he glanced out of the door, looking up at the sky. 'It's like Siberia; this cold spell shows no sign of abating; I can't remember a winter like it,' I handed him my coat, hat, and scarf. 'You've just missed Miss Duckworth,' he paused, looking bemused. 'I'm afraid she's worked herself into quite a state about this evening's carol concert. I had to pour her a fortifying glass of sherry to calm her. She has what I call a nervous disposition – Miss Duckworth protested about the sherry, but it seemed to do the trick; well, it must have done; she asked for another and then another before she left to warm her against the cold.

I find nerves are common with the musically minded. Miss

Duckworth hasn't been the same since she saw the bishop's organ – I think she found it overwhelming... These days I fear our humble church organ isn't good enough for her musical tastes and ambitions as a chorister and organist. Like my dear wife, she takes on too much and sits on various committees; one of them, her botany group, takes up a lot of her time,' he looked vacant, curling his lip. 'However, I fear Miss Duckworth overstretches herself. Did I tell you she's working on a book about sublime organ transcriptions?"

Why wasn't I surprised!

'The book sales will be donated to the church to support our good works. Although I do wonder if there will be a market for such a book here in the village.'

'No, you didn't,' replied Jocasta smoothing down her hair. 'But the ability to play an instrument is a wonderful skill to have. Even if it's only a hobby, I think it helps one find the rhythm of life; by that, I mean our legitimate needs, deepest desires, and unique talents, bringing them all into harmony,' she smiled reflectively. 'Oh dear, listen to me; I sound terribly deep.'

The Reverend shook his head warmly, 'Not at all; my dear wife has become quite musically minded and is just the same. She's always striving for musical perfection,' he hesitated. 'Sadly, she never quite manages to achieve it,' he lowered his voice to a whisper. 'As you can probably hear,' he forced a smile. 'But God willing, she'll get there one day; as they say, practice makes perfect, and my dear wife is certainly doing plenty of that. As I think I mentioned when I was at the Hall, I've invested in some earplugs; after a while, I find her musical aspirations distract me from my bible and lengthy sermon preparations.'

The Reverend moved to the bottom of the stairs and called his wife. I detected a note of irritation in his tone. He had to shout to be heard over the sound of the banjolele, advising Muriel we'd arrived; she didn't answer. Once he'd taken all our coats, hats, gloves, and scarves, we moved to the quaint drawing room with its roaring fire and sparkling Christmas tree; every surface was adorned with colourful nick-nacks and

Christmas cards.

'What a charming room,' declared Jocasta admiring the beamed ceiling and fireplace. 'I've never seen such a homely vicarage before; it's just as I imagined from seeing the outside. It makes me feel homesick for my little cottage in Folkstone, with its beamed ceilings and quirky little details. I like a house with uneven walls and imperfections, a house with a lived-in feel, a bit of soul and history.'

'Well, this house certainly has that,' agreed the Reverend smiling. 'We always strive to welcome our visitors and parishioners and be the hub of our little community here in Brenchley. Now please sit down and make yourselves comfortable, do gather around the fire and try to thaw out. You look positively frozen to the core, and I'd hate for you to catch a cold.'

'I don't mind if I do,' said Winston moving towards the raging fire. 'I can't feel my toes; it's so cold it gets into one's limbs,' he glanced around the room. 'Tell me, how old is this house?'

The Reverend followed his gaze, 'Oh, it dates to the 16th century,' he announced proudly. 'The house has retained a wealth of period features throughout, yet it manages to feel light and spacious for a property of its age, benefitting from the unusually high ceilings. I like to think my dear wife and I have sympathetically updated and modernised the house with 16th-century carpentry, and this wonderful late 17th-century parlour with its wood panelling. The painted decoration in the house remains almost perfectly intact, as do the exposed beams, the wide inglenook fireplaces, and this attractive 18th century fitted corner cupboard.'

He moved to one of the windows with its oak sills and folding shutters. 'And as you can see, we have a delightful outlook over the village centre and the church. My wife sits at this window for hours watching the comings and goings in the village,' he smiled. 'She's like the all-seeing eye - not that she's one for village gossip.'

The door opened, and Muriel appeared carrying a tray of her best tea china; she wasn't at all what I expected. She was a tall slim woman, probably in her mid-forties, with striking green eyes, porcelain skin, and auburn hair styled in an elaborate updo with not a hair out of place. Dressed in the latest fashions, she wore T- ankle strap shoes in green with medium-high heels, a long-sleeved fitted wool dress in a brighter shade of green, with button details and gathered shoulders; the dress emphasised her slim figure. Her elegant jewellery included diamond and emerald earrings with a matching broach.

Her delicate features were enhanced with a light touch of makeup, and she smelled delightful of roses and bergamot. She put the tea tray on an inlaid side table and twinkled, 'Hello everyone, I'm sorry I wasn't here to greet you when you arrived. Please excuse me; I'll be back in just a moment.' Muriel returned to the kitchen, coming back with another tray full of cakes and biscuits putting it next to the tea tray; she must have read Jocasta's mind or received a telepathic message!

'Ah, that's better,' she said, rubbing the palms of her hand several times as if wiping something away. 'I'm Muriel.'

The Reverend quickly did the introductions. I immediately liked Muriel but sensed she was bored and unfulfilled; call it ghostly intuition.

'I'm delighted to meet you all,' she said with a beaming smile. 'My husband tells me you're staying with Agnes and Clementine at the Hall, helping them with the house and interior decoration,' Muriel didn't give us a chance to answer, arranging cups and saucers with a clatter. 'Personally, I love the Hall just the way it is, it must be wonderful to live in such grandeur, and then there are all the spectacular views across the Kent countryside,' she pulled open a drawer taking out some silver teaspoons and napkins. 'I'd love to hear all your ideas and decorating and design tips. I try to keep up with all the latest trends and fashion modes,' she moved to a large mirror with an elaborately carved frame and quickly smoothed down her hair and patted her lip line.

'Now, before you tell us everything you have planned for the Hall, let's have tea. You must all be desperate for a hot drink; of course, we have sherry, brandy, or whisky if you'd prefer something stronger. Personally, I'm always ready for a nice dry martini,' she glanced at the ornate grandfather clock standing in a corner, ticking away with a steady rhythm. 'But I suppose it's a little early,' she winked and smiled mischievously. 'Although I'm game if you are?' She laughed, then hiccuped loudly. 'Oh, do excuse me; I had some beef tea earlier; I think it may have disagreed with me; I have a delicate stomach. Now, I hope you don't think I'm terribly fast suggesting a little dry martini, but it is nearly Christmas, and if we can't have a nice martini at Christmas time, when can we have one? I always have my cocktail shaker ready for a special occasion or celebration.'

I suspected any occasion or minor achievement was a reason for a dry martini or three for Muriel! I could tell she tippled, probably out of boredom.

'Muriel dearest, really, martinis at this time of day, let's not get carried away,' said the Reverend trying to sound jovial as he glanced at the clock, eager to create the right impression. 'I'm sure tea will be fine for our guests, and those cakes look delicious.'

Muriel agreed, 'Hmm, they do, don't they, although it's no thanks to me,' she turned to the four of us. 'Mrs Gunnerson from the dairy has made them; she helps me with the house. She's a treasure; I'd be lost without her. She's so good with anything requiring butter, eggs, and cream - well, any animal product really, she's known for her offal. We've told her she should open her own bakery; Mrs Gunnerson's an expert in sugar. My dear husband raves about her Bundt.'

Silence...

'In the summer, she makes her famous Bundt cake with fresh raspberries and blackberries; it's delicious, not that I eat a lot of cake having a delicate stomach, I find anything solid can set it off.' She hiccuped again. 'Oh, pardon me, it's that beef tea - I wonder if they've changed the recipe?' She pondered for a moment and started pouring tea for everyone with another clatter.

'The Bundt cake sounds delicious,' said Jocasta, her mouth-watering. 'I've never found a cake I didn't like.'

I could vouch for that!

'But I must admit, I've never heard of it.'

'No, I hadn't either,' agreed Muriel. 'It was quite a delicious discovery at a summer soirée we had here a few years ago to help raise funds for the church roof; the bishop came,' she paused, passing a cup of tea in a battered mug to the Reverend, hardly looking at him. 'I think Mrs Gunnerson may have foreign connections, not that she admits to them, nor do I blame her. I know the war was twelve years ago, but everyone in the village is still suspicious of anyone foreign or with foreign connections. I find it's best to keep quiet about such things. Well, anything that might be controversial - the villagers still haven't quite forgiven poor Dolly Bellfield.'

We glanced at each other, 'What did she do?' I asked hesitantly, thinking she must have collaborated with the Germans.

'Dyed her hair blond, that's what,' said Muriel raising a perfectly plucked eyebrow. 'Dolly said she wanted to have allure and be like one of those film starlets. I quite liked it myself, but from how the villagers reacted, you'd have thought Dolly had killed somebody. Miss Duckworth, the church organist, fainted when she saw her, causing quite a commotion in the village hall; she had to be revived. Luckily, Miss Urquhart from the haberdashery had her smelling salts in her handbag. Miss Urquhart gets the vapours since she nearly choked on a mint imperial in the post office when she saw Mr Biggar's package; she never leaves the house without them – I believe you've met Miss Duckworth?'

We nodded, thinking what to say...

'Hmm, yes, she does have that effect on people – I find Miss Duckworth to be an acquired taste. I think she's infatuated with my husband. She's always hammering on our knocker with a query.' Muriel sighed wearily, passing around cups of tea in elegant china cups with matching saucers, suddenly craving a drink with a bit more of a bite and kick. 'Are you sure you don't all want a nice dry martini? I assure you it's no trouble.'

'Please don't go to any trouble,' said Winston, glancing at the three of us. 'Tea's fine and much appreciated.'

Muriel nodded and forced a half-smile, 'Do help yourselves to milk and sugar; I'm from the 'adding milk after pouring tea school',' she yawned loudly. 'Oh, please excuse me; I'm quite worn out; I've been busy working on my musical repertoire for the banjolele and ukulele. I've been practising Christmas carols and doing my vocal exercises for tonight's concert; I've been at it night and day,' she put her hand over her mouth, stifling another yawn. 'Oh, there I go again; it must be this weather. Since I had to give up dancing, I've been trying to find other outlets for my artistic interests. I had musical ambitions when I was younger,' she paused, sighed longingly, and gave a withering look at the Reverend. 'But life takes over, and childhood dreams go out of the window.'

'We heard you practising, my dear,' said the Reverend under his breath, his nerves clearly on edge. 'I'm sure the whole street did.'

Muriel exhaled loudly, staring at the teapot, 'Tea, where would we be without it?... Like sponge cakes, it's a subject debated socially for hours at our local branch of the WI; you know, China or Indian, milk in first or after, sugar cubes or granules. To me, it's about as interesting as watching paint dry,' she laughed. 'The things we vicars' wives must endure, I sometimes think we deserve our own union, or perhaps a school where you can be taught the job and the right facial expressions and things to say,' she rolled her eyes. 'I just nod in the right places, smile, and talk about the weather; it seems to do the trick.'

'Muriel!' Exclaimed the Reverend, almost choking on his tea, going a deeper shade of crimson.

Muriel hiccuped and ignored him as she passed a cup of tea to Florence.

'Err, the Bundt does have European origins,' said Winston clearing his throat, wanting to change the subject. 'I believe it's made in a special pan with fluted or grooved sides and a central tube or chimney which leaves a cylindrical hole through the centre of the cake. I'm far from a baking expert, but I don't think the pans are easy to come by in this country. I believe the cake is quite popular in America.'

'Yes, that's it, how clever of you to know,' said Muriel with another twinkle. 'Now do take a plate and napkin and help yourself to cakes and biscuits, you must be ravenous, and I know you won't be disappointed. We've Christmas cake, mince pies, shortbread biscuits, and some Madeira cake, we always have that, oh, and some stollen, thanks again to Mrs Gunnerson. It's delicious and full of dried fruits, almonds, various spices, vanilla, and marzipan. The dried fruits are macerated in brandy. I love it, but it goes straight to my hips.'

The others didn't need any encouragement as they helped themselves to an assortment of cakes and biscuits. I could see Jocasta had hoped for a bigger plate!

'Now, do make yourself comfortable and thaw out by the fire,' fluttered Muriel waving the china teapot in the air. 'I'll just pop to the kitchen and top up the tea; I think I left the kettle on the boil,' she hiccuped, 'Oh dear, excuse me, there I go again; I swear it's that beef-tea; I think they've put too much beef in it. Now, don't have any fun without me,' she twinkled. 'When I get back, you can tell me all about your decorating plans for the Hall,' she smiled wistfully. 'It must be such a fulfilling job, particularly when you get a grand house like Rothery Hall - I wouldn't know where to start.'

As she approached the door, she stopped and turned, 'Mind you, I always say that just because people have money doesn't mean they have good taste or decorum. I have an acquaintance, a theatrical, who lives in London. She tells me she's huge in the West End and can do it all, tragedy, drama, comedy, singing, and dancing. You may have heard of her, Adeline Del Ray; although her real name is Edie Waters, she has a look of the film star Tallulah Bankhead. She's originally from the wealthy industrial town of Huddersfield in the West Riding of Yorkshire, but you'd never know - she has no trace of a Yorkshire accent. Her father and mother were weavers,' she raised her eyebrows. 'But Adeline has social ambitions and tells everyone her father was an affluent mill owner.'

She paused, chewing on her lip, lost in a memory, 'I saw her

Rosalind in Shakespeare's 'As You Like It' at the Old Vic in London. It was... unusual; the theatre critics said they'd never seen anything like it... Adeline says it can be bitter and brutal in the theatre. However, she's regularly featured in the gossip columns, not that I read them, of course... Oh, and the News of the World.'

Muriel wavered for a moment, 'That paper seems fascinated with her life; they're always running front-page articles saying how accomplished and versatile she is in several areas. Although she's not quite as colourful as they describe her to be,' she shook her head reflectively. 'Realistically speaking, I don't know how anyone could be – it's true that she worked in a touring circus early in her career, but she was never a contortionist,' she smiled. 'Anyway, I digress. Adeline decided to redecorate her small flat in Piccadilly; she was enthused after a summer holiday with one of her gentleman friends in cosmopolitan Marrakesh.'

'Gentleman friends!' Exclaimed Jocasta disapprovingly, her eyebrows shooting to the top of her head.

Muriel nodded, 'Yes, Adeline's gentleman friends are all philanthropic, artistic, and deeply probing; they're interested in supporting those working in the performing arts. Adeline says it's all purely professional and platonic... Now, where was I?... Oh, yes, her flat. She took inspiration from the vibrancy of Marrakesh, the street markets, architecture, bold colours, and exotic smells. She hired a well-known interior designer from London's swanky Mayfair; she'd read about him in Vogue magazine. Apparently, he's a friend of the society photographer Cecil Beaton and the socialite Stephen Tennant - I can't remember his name, but you probably know him being in the profession. I believe another one of Adeline's gentleman friends paid for it all.'

Muriel laughed, 'By the time he'd finished, her flat couldn't have been more different to the facade of her building and the grey streets of London. It looked and smelt like a bordello in an Arab souk or medina,' she held up her hand. 'I couldn't have lived there; the colourful, garish decor and smell of incense and exotic spices gave me a terrible headache. The first time I visited, I had to go and lie down in a darkened room with a cold cloth over my head,' she smiled mischievously. 'Mind you, that could have been all the vodka martinis we drank - Adeline likes her cocktails; she's quite the party girl.'

The Reverend cleared his throat, 'Err, yes, thank you, my dear. I'll come and help you with the tea,' he said, trying to sound charming. 'Do help yourselves to more cakes and biscuits; we won't be a moment.'

Muriel glared at the Reverend, bristling, 'I don't need any help, thank you,' she spat sharply. 'I'm fine. I can manage,' she glanced at Jocasta and Florence with a conspiratorial smile. 'Men, they do like to interfere and be in charge.'

'Oh, but I insist, my dear,' said the Reverend forcing a polite smile. 'We can't have you all worn out before tonight's concert, particularly after all those hours spent practising on your ukulele and banjolele.'

He gently guided Muriel out of the room, much to her annoyance and protest. 'You make me sound like some delicate fainting flower who needs to lie down after every little thing...'

I could sense some tension in the air. After they'd gone, we all looked at each other, 'I think Muriel might tipple,' I said in a low whisper. The others nodded, unable to speak as their mouths were full of cake and biscuits. 'Out of interest, have you heard of this Adeline Del Ray? She sounds colourful.'

They looked at each other blankly, 'I've never heard of her,' said Jocasta disapprovingly, quickly finishing a mince pie. 'I've no time for starlets, gossip, and celebrity tittle-tattle. Although I am interested in our local amateur dramatics group, the Folkstone Players,' she took a sip of tea before moving on to her Christmas cake. 'Ah yes, dear Mr Prendergast, he was the founder of the Players; I may have mentioned him before.

Sadly, he's no longer with us, a wonderful man. Mr Prendergast ran a gentleman's outfitters with his friend Mr Humphries; they shared a lovely house together and collected the finest porcelain and had wonderful little soirées with their theatrical friends. You could always guarantee impromptu performances, lots of laughter, and delicious finger food, all served on the finest china,' she hesitated and nodded. 'Probably Minton or Spode.'

Jocasta lowered her voice, 'But on a different note, I've just had a presentiment and think Muriel would make an excellent subject for psychic hypnotic regression; she has the right kind of aura. I can sense it in my base chakra. I feel she could have been a female warrior in a past life; she may have a distant connection to the warrior Queen Boudicea.'

While the others finished their tea and cakes, we sat uneasily and could hear clattering, banging, raised voices, accusations, and long-held resentments coming from the kitchen. Eventually, the Reverend returned with a pot of fresh tea rubbing his cheek, 'Here we are,' he said, trying to sound bright and breezy. 'I'm sorry to keep you waiting; please help yourself to more tea... I'm afraid my dear wife has had to excuse herself; she's suddenly developed one of her headaches and has taken an aspirin and gone to lie down; she's hoping it will pass in time for her performance at this evening's carol concert. After all her preparations, it would be a shame if she had to miss it.'

I don't think any of us was surprised. Florence stood up, 'Oh, I'm sorry to hear that; I fear we're being a burden, causing extra work for you and Muriel, adding to your busy schedule.' She moved to the side table, took the teapot, and began pouring tea for everyone. 'The Christmas season must be a hectic time for you both. The church is central to many village festivities.'

'It is,' replied the Reverend in soothing tones trying to sound assuring. 'But please don't reproach yourselves; Muriel and I are always keen to help visitors to our little village and this neck of the woods; we don't get that many. But I must admit to being curious; tell me, why are you so interested in the land registry records? You're lucky we still have them here as a civil parish. Many church records are now held centrally by district or county councils.'

Jocasta quickly finished her second slice of Christmas cake, eyeing a third, 'Yum, this cake is delicious; I can tell the dried fruits were well soaked in brandy, and it's been allowed to mature, which is so essential with a fruit cake, pass on my compliments to Mrs Gunnerson. But to answer your question, it's Winston here; he's interested in the history of Rothery Hall and this area; it's his hobby.'

'Ah, I see, and a fine hobby to have, history has always fascinated me,' he glanced at the grandfather clock. 'Goodness, look at the time, if you want to follow me, I'll take you through to my study, do bring your tea and cakes. I've had the verger, Mr Nimmo, light the fire in there. He's dug out the things he could find from the church records and left them on my desk - Oh, and while I think on, with all this snow, Mr Jenkin, the farrier, is collecting Clementine and Agnes from the Hall in his horse-drawn sleigh and bringing them to the church for this evening's carol concert. His sleigh comes in handy; it's proved to be a lifeline in the village when we have a lot of snow. I could telephone and ask him to collect you here and take you back to the Hall unless you're staying for our little concert.'

'That's most kind and thoughtful of you,' said Jocasta sounding relieved, glancing out of the window as we moved to the downstairs study. 'We'd certainly appreciate that. It's treacherous out, and the snow shows no sign of abating. Agnes and Clementine are keen for us to attend the concert, but given the weather, I think it's best we get back to the Hall while we still can.'

The study wasn't a large room and felt warm and cosy thanks to the beamed ceiling and decorative carved wooden fireplace with its raging fire; we could smell the natural oils in the burning wood. A heavy-looking leather-bound bible with gold edge gilding sat proudly on a mahogany table in the corner with bookmarkers left between certain pages. Oak shelves were groaning with other leather-bound books. I quickly scanned them; they looked to be mostly on theology and philosophy, although I did spot a few works of historical military fiction.

I moved to the window; it had views over the rear of the house, across the extensive snow-covered gardens and part of the church graveyard. The snow continued to fall in a steady flutter, settling on the tall conifers, mature trees, on everything it touched, creating a charming winter scene of undulating softness and sparkling purity; the pale-yellow sun peeked out from behind the thick clouds.

Once the Reverend left, Jocasta and Winston quickly finished their tea, moved to the desk, and sat down; Florence and I pulled up two chairs to join them. Winston put on his glasses and eagerly opened one of the files, and started scanning through the handwritten records. They weren't the easiest to read, but he was used to it and quite the handwriting expert.

'What exactly do you hope to find?' I asked as the fire crackled loudly, making the others jump...

'Goodness, we are jumpy,' said Florence clutching her chest and taking a deep breath to steady herself.

Winston nodded in agreement, joining Florence, and taking a steadying breath, trying to focus, 'A motive for everything happening back at the Hall. Historically speaking, I think someone must have had a grievance or grudge against a member of the Rothery family.'

'Hmm, it must be a deep festering grudge,' I said pensively. 'You know, to put a curse on generations of the family.' I don't know why I was surprised; we'd seen it happen before. I shuddered, 'But if you're right, whatever someone did must have been dire to warrant such long-term vengeance.'

'Indeed,' agreed Jocasta brushing her hair off her face. 'Of course, whoever the aggrieved are, may have paid someone to curse the family. It's also possible that something was on the land before the Hall was built or before the land registry records began. So, whatever is happening at the Hall could have nothing to do with the Rothery family; they might be innocent bystanders caught up in something.'

Winston didn't look convinced and continued, 'We know both Bernard and Montague Rothery held positions of power as town magistrates, so it's quite plausible to think someone could seek revenge on one of them. But that's not why I wanted to see these records. I had a thought about the Hall and the estate; it sits in such a perfect location, and that's what gave me the idea,' he patted the land registry records. 'Now, not that long ago, if areas of land became desirable, some unscrupulous people in positions of authority or with wealth could assert plausible claims to the proprietorship of the land on the strength of a grant from the legislature. In other words, they could take land off people. We know Bernard Rothery gave the land to Montague so he could build the Hall. I'm interested in how he acquired it.'

Florence and I sat patiently waiting while Winston and Jocasta worked through the records... 'Hmm, looking at this,' said Winston. 'Bernard Rothery started buying up land in this area in the 1830s, but I can't see anything untoward... Oh, but hang on a minute, what's this?'

'What is it?' Asked Jocasta eagerly, standing up to look over Winston's shoulder.

'The Sisters of Listan,' muttered Winston looking bewildered.

Chapter 9

The door flew open, and Muriel fragrantly swished in, looking very chic, her eyes bright with excitement and, dare I say, mischief. She wore vertiginous heels in black patent leather, a black, bias cut, silk velvet cocktail dress with silver buttons and short puff sleeves. Her look was accessorised with lots of jewellery, clearly inspired by the latest French fashions of Coco Chanel. She carried a highly polished silver tray with five dry martinis.

'Here we are,' she said breezily, carefully putting the tray on top of the old land registry records on the desk, much to Winston's horror. 'As it's the festive season, I couldn't let you leave without a convivial drink to wish you a Merry Christmas and all the best for the coming new year,' Muriel glanced at the silver tray. 'Now, although I say so myself, these martinis are rather good; I've just had one,' she smiled playfully and hiccuped loudly. 'Oh, excuse me, I swear it's that beef tea. I think I may have developed an allergy - although I did have a boiled egg for breakfast last Tuesday; I normally stick to a liquid diet,' she smiled, carefully taking a glass from the tray. 'This should help to make me feel better. Please take a glass, and I'll make a toast.'

Oh, 'I don't mind if I do,' said Jocasta warmly. 'I must admit a dry martini is one of the few alcoholic beverages which doesn't interfere with my chakras.'

Muriel looked at her bewildered and proffered a nod, probably thinking it was an interior design term, but didn't say anything. We all took a glass, not that I could drink mine.

'Will the Reverend be joining us?' Asked Florence, holding her breath - well, we all did!

'No,' said Muriel flatly, her expression turning morose. 'My husband has put on his winter coat, gloves, hat, and goloshes and popped over to the church to check on the needy Miss Duckworth,' she sighed despairingly. 'Why am I not surprised?... She only has to flutter a bible reading or organ recital at him, and he goes running like a lovesick puppy. Mind you, Mintie Clinch from the local tearoom is no better; she's always trying to tempt him with her big baps and sweet delights,' she sighed again. 'But anyway, now he's gone, we can take a moment to relax and enjoy ourselves; in my experience, dry martinis, having a little fun, and the clergy don't mix,' she raised her glass, smiling. 'Anyway, cheers everyone, Merry Christmas. It's lovely to meet you all.'

We all raised our glasses out of politeness, 'Cheers, Merry Christmas.'

Muriel drained her glass, 'Ahh, nectar,' she said blissfully, leaving bright red lipstick marks on her glass. 'Now, I hope I'm not interrupting your research. I never knew interior design could be so demanding. I'm amazed by how much preparation you're doing and your attention to detail - how are you getting on?'

Winston played along, 'Oh, it's too early to say,' he replied gingerly, sipping his cocktail. 'Tell me, how long have you and your husband been here in Brenchley?'

'I was born here,' replied Muriel like it was a punishment or jail sentence. 'My family have been here for generations; although not many are left now - we were a big family once. Donald, my husband, was assigned here by the clergy about twenty years ago. We came from the parish in Chilham, a delightful little town about forty miles from here; I loved it there; they had regular dances and sophisticated little soirées,' she smiled reflectively. 'It didn't feel like we were in the provinces, and I never thought I'd end up coming back here.

When I was younger, I attended Nora Bray's dancing school. Nora was a bit of a local legend, winning many dance awards and competitions; I took all my dancing exams, tap, ballet, and ballroom. It was one of the few things I was good at. I dreamed of going to London and working in the theatre or cabaret as a dancer, but that never happened, and I became too tall for the ballet,' she shook her head wistfully. 'Fates a funny thing... why do we get all this life if we don't do anything with it?' Her mouth and chin trembled as she wiped the corner of her eye, quickly regaining her composure and smiling... 'I never imagined I'd end up as a vicar's wife.'

There it was again; I could feel Muriel's sense of unfulfillment. I could tell the others sensed it too. She desperately wanted to find some meaning in her existence.

'Life is a mystery, a journey into the unknown,' said Florence philosophically, sipping her martini; it brought a flush of colour to her cheeks. 'Tell me, how did you and Donald meet?'

Muriel smiled, drawing on the memory, 'Gosh, I haven't thought about it in years. We met at the annual summer gala in the village of Horsmonden, a few miles from here. I went with a group of friends from the village; Donald was giving out church pamphlets, so no surprises there,' Muriel sighed nostalgically. 'He was different back then; I suppose we both were. He was full of life and such fun,' she laughed. 'Aha, Donald, full of fun, I know it's hard to believe now, but it's true,' she groaned, shaking her head. 'Where did that man go? Where did we go?'

Silence...

'Life changes us,' said Jocasta thoughtfully, sensing Muriel's unhappiness. 'Everything changes, yet somehow, everything stays the same, certainly our basic needs and desires. We need to count our blessings; we have a lot to be thankful for, particularly after the war.'

Muriel nodded, slowly curling her lip; she had a resigned faraway look, 'Yes - yes, of course – I do try to tell myself that.'

'Hmm,' said Winston, carefully moving the land registry records from under the silver tray. 'Muriel, do you know anything about the history of this area?'

She looked at him bemused, sitting in an armchair next to a colourful jardinière, which held a mature aspidistra, 'How do you mean?'

'Well, I'm specifically thinking of Rothery Hall, which you said you admired,' replied Winston finishing his martini and sitting behind the desk. 'Do you know anything about the land the Hall is built on, or what might have been there in the past?'

Muriel wasn't listening; she looked at me with disbelief, 'Jasper, don't you want your martini?'

I smiled, feeling awkward; in truth, I would have liked to try it, 'Um, I'm sure it's as delicious as you say, but I'm afraid I don't drink, but it was kind of you to offer and think of me.'

'Jasper's a paragon of virtue,' said Jocasta with a wry smile. 'I don't know how he survives. He lives on nothing but fresh air,' she looked me up and down. 'But I suppose he looks well enough on it.'

Muriel's expression turned to astonishment, 'You don't drink! Goodness, you're as angelic as you look, I don't think I've ever seen anyone with such vibrant blue eyes, and your hair is the perfect shade of blond,' she smiled wryly. 'Just the shade Dolly Bellfield was going for. You look like you should be in a painting by that artist - he's Italian... oh, what's his name?... Ah, I have it, Botticelli. Yes, you look like an angel from a painting by Botticelli.'

If I could have blushed, I would have been glowing!

'My husband is a lover of Italian renaissance art, thanks to its religious interpretations – personally, I'm not a fan; I find it all a bit over dramatic. I've never understood all the grand palaces built in the name of God; after all, Jesus was born in a stable... Anyway, your body may be a temple, but trust me, you don't know what you're missing,' Muriel stood up and took the glass out of my hand. 'We mustn't let this go to waste,' she drained the glass. 'Ahh, that's better, so reviving,' she moved to the armchair and sat down gracefully, crossing her legs, looking at Winston. 'Now, what were you saying?'

'Err, I'm interested to know about Rothery Hall, who owned the land, or if there was anything on the land before the house was built. Does the name Listan mean anything to you?'

Muriel pulled a face, 'Listan, hmm, I don't know why, but that name does sound vaguely familiar; it's certainly not a common name in these parts, that should make it easier to remember... Listan...'

''Yes, it is unusual,' agreed Winston. 'Do you know anything about the history of the land the Hall is built on?'

Muriel shook her head, 'No, I can't say I do; to be honest, I've never given it any thought; of course, it's way before my time,' she smiled. 'When I was a child, people said the woods around there were enchanted. They were known as fairy woods - I think they still are. I used to go there with my friends from school looking for fairies,' she laughed. 'Not that we ever found any. My grandmother, God rest her, used to say a group of wise women once lived by those woods; of course, most people called them witches. The older children used to say, don't go near the woods; the witches will get you, making us want to go there even more,' she shrugged and smiled. 'Not that I believe in such things, but it all adds to local folklore giving it more colour. Perhaps that's how the wood became known as 'fairy wood',' she shook her head. 'I don't know; I'm only guessing; it was a long time ago.'

'Hmm, I see, interesting,' said Winston, the cogs turning in his brain. 'Of course, in the past, the woods may have covered more of the land and encroached onto the areas where Rothery Hall now stands.'

Muriel nodded, craving another martini, 'Yes, it's possible; you need to speak with old mother Frobisher; I'll give you her address. Funnily enough, she lives in one of the farm cottages on the Rothery estate; she worked at the Hall years ago, before she was married,' she paused, looking at her empty martini glass. 'Although, on second thought, I think it would be better if I went with you. She's in her mid-nineties now and a bit deaf; she takes great pride in being the oldest person in the village.'

Muriel glanced out of the window at the snowy landscape. 'She remembers the area as it used to be, although I don't think it's changed that much over the years. Mother, as she likes to be known, tends to live in the past and is always talking about the good old days, which I'm sure never existed; she loves to reminisce and has a sharp memory - nothing gets past her.' Muriel glanced at the wall clock, stood up, smoothed down her dress, grabbed the silver tray, and began collecting the glasses. 'She's supposed to be coming to this evening's carol concert. Mother's stoic, so I doubt she'll be put off by all this snow. She loves Christmas and never misses the concert; one of her sons will bring her, he lives in the cottage next to hers. I'll see what she says and phone you at the Hall in the morning.'

'We would be most grateful,' said Winston, with a sense of anticipation. 'But ideally, we need to see her tomorrow; the sooner, the better.'

'Oh, you make it sound like life or death,' twinkled Muriel jokingly.

Little did she know!

***

Once the others had finished a hearty breakfast of porridge, kippers, bacon, eggs, mushrooms, hot buttered toast, jam, marmalade, honey, and, of course, lots of tea, we headed on foot in the crisp snow towards old mother Frobisher's farm cottage. Thankfully, it had stopped snowing for the moment, although the roads were still treacherous. The countryside remained a winter wonderland of white and silver, the morning sky clear and fresh with a sharp icy bite.

'Ahh, just take in this bracing air,' said Jocasta breathing deeply and then exhaling loudly, sounding like a set of old bellows as her breath frosted in the air... 'It energises the lungs and stimulates the circulation making one feel quite invigorated. I also feel it's good for my chakras - having alert chakras can lead to a sudden presentiment which may lead to an eventuation.'

Florence and Winston pulled up their coat collars and shivered, not looking convinced.

'It's certainly bracing,' I'll give you that,' said Winston. 'Now, from what Clementine and Agnes said, I think it's this way,' he pointed his expensive walking stick towards a small hamlet in the far distance with smoking chimneys. 'Muriel said she would meet us there.'

'Is she really coming?' I asked doubtfully. 'She didn't strike me as the sort of person to trudge down country lanes, particularly in such harsh weather. Do you think she'll turn up?'

Winston nodded, pulling his leather glove back to look at his wristwatch, 'Yes, Muriel said the fresh air and exercise would do her good. She also wants to avoid the church ladies; she said they would be full of gossip after last night's carol concert. Apparently, there was a bit of a to-do at the church.'

'Oh yes, Agnes and Clementine mentioned it,' said Jocasta, raising an eyebrow. 'Someone brought a real donkey – and another a goat into the church for the nativity. Others brought pet rabbits, guinea pigs, and hamsters; someone even brought some hens. Can you imagine what they might have brought had we been living in the tropics!'

'They brought a real donkey and goat!' Exclaimed Florence. 'No wonder Agnes and Clementine looked flustered this morning. Mind you, it sounded like they'd had quite a hair-raising journey home in Mr Jenkin's sleigh. Apparently, he'd greatly overindulged on the mulled wine and mead and made suggestive comments to Miss Lovage, the choir mistress in the church vestry. Agnes said Miss Lovage has a delicate nature and isn't used to men, so nearly fainted. She said on their way home, Mr Jenkin repeatedly sang God Save the King while saluting and the Christmas carol, Good King Wenceslas. He couldn't remember all the words, so he made them up as he went along.'

'Yes, so I believe,' said Winston trying not to laugh. 'Luckily for Agnes and Clementine, Mr Jenkin's horse seemed to know its way to the Hall; let's hope he arrived home in one piece... Clementine told me the Sunday school children were asked to make a toy animal representing the nativity and bring it to the concert to add to the church nativity scene. No one expected the children to bring living animals - but I suppose we are all God's creatures - they caused quite a commotion.

The Reverend told Muriel the donkey and goat ran amok, eating the nativity scene and church lady's floral displays. The donkey hee-hawed all the way through Miss Duckworth's Christmas Concerto, much to Muriel's amusement. And the goat attempted to eat one of the church ladies' hats. A floral confection owned by a Miss Prothero, apparently the goat chased her around the chancel; people were in hysterics. In the end, the beasts had to be pulled out of the church, with both animals protesting loudly. Three people had to follow behind with a shovel, mop, and buckets. For a while, it sounded like complete mayhem.'

'It must have been,' said Jocasta, picturing the scene and trying her best not to laugh. 'It must have brought the nativity and idea of a stable to life.'

'Well, I think it all sounds charming and part of rural village life,' said Florence romanticising. 'I'm sorry we missed it. Agnes told me the evening began with an eloquent reading by candlelight - someone talking about their memorable Christmases in the village. They described twinkling Christmas trees, delicious food, carols around the fire, and a lively snowy scene. The evening continued with the choir's rendition of Jingle Bells, led by Miss Lovage. They also performed Silent Night, Holy Night, and someone did a couple of readings from Charles Dickens, 'A Christmas Carol', which was interspersed between the other musical performances and the Reverend's lengthy bible readings. Lengthy being the operative word from what Clementine said - people in the congregation could be heard snoring,' she smiled, raising an eyebrow. 'Although I suppose that could have been the mulled wine and mead.'

'It sounds to me like the Reverend became lost in his seasonal reverie and started rambling,' I said, relieved we weren't there. 'And after our experience in the graveyard, we should be grateful there weren't any malevolent spiritual presences requiring a Christmas exorcism... Oh, and talking of exorcisms, how did Muriel's performance go with her Banjolele?'

'Ah, she didn't do it,' said Jocasta, like I should know. 'Agnes told me Muriel was indisposed with a troublesome headache and sudden bout of vertigo. She must have asked the Reverend to speak with Mother Frobisher about us visiting today.'

I smiled to myself, 'Ah, I see; that's a shame after all her banjolele and ukulele preparations. I wonder what could have caused her troublesome headache?'

'Hmm, indeed,' grinned Jocasta. 'Now, don't be naughty, dear boy; one mustn't mock the afflicted. Let's hope this bracing cold air clears her head and puts a spring in her step.'

I hoped it would; I liked her.

We made our way down snowy lanes, turning onto what would be a rough dirt track had it not been covered in snow and ice; someone had left their footprints in the snow. Drystone walls created a barrier between the track and wild expanse of wind-swept, snow-covered fields dotted with mature trees, their branches groaning under the weight of the snow. Tucked away in this rural haven, among ramshackle barns and old farm buildings, was a row of honey-coloured stone cottages oozing character and rustic charm.

'Agnes told me some of these farm buildings date back to the 17th century,' said Winston, his breath dancing in the icy air. 'They look like something from a country scene by John Constable. I can imagine them filled with hay and bathed in golden sunshine on a lazy summer's day, with birds twittering and insects buzzing in the background. The air tinged with the smell of wildflowers, honeysuckle, blackthorn, and freshly cut summer straw.'

I could picture that in my mind; I'd been there back in the day, and it wasn't as romantic as it sounds! However, some of the stone buildings had certainly seen better days!

To the front of the cottages were enclosed gardens and tucked in a corner, shaded by some gnarled trees, was a row of privy middens with battered wooden doors. I wouldn't fancy having to visit them in this freezing weather or being caught short in the middle of the night. In the snow, I could just make out a footpath that ran to a farm at the back of the cottages and countryside beyond. In the distance, I spotted a snow-covered bench next to an icy stream. The stream snaked its way through the fields carrying ice crystals, the ice making the stream look like it was hemmed with silver. The cold air was tinged with the smell of silage and the muffled sound of farm animals.

We walked up the irregular snow-covered path, and Jocasta knocked firmly on the oak Dutch-style door; a bright bunch of holly hung above it, covered in masses of bright red berries. We were surprised to be greeted by Muriel, who smelt delightful and looked resplendent in a purple wool skirt suit, pearls, and gold jewellery, with not a hair out of place. The only allowance she'd made to practicality was her black, fur-lined snow boots.

'Morning,' she said, all bright and breezy. 'I'm pleased you've managed to locate the cottages; they're not the easiest to find. I must have given you good directions. I've only just arrived myself and removed several layers,' she smiled playfully. 'Including my hat and coat. Do come in. You must all be frozen; I know I am - mother is eager to meet you. I've been telling her about your interior design work up at the Hall.'

'Who is it?' Shouted mother impatiently. 'Hurry up and shut the door; you're letting in all the cold air. I'm chilled to the bone; I can't seem to get warm these days. I'm sure this winter will be the death of me; I swear it's getting colder, like the Highlands of Scotland.'

We stepped through the front door and straight into the cosy lounge with its thick stone walls. Behind the front door were some uneven stone steps leading up to the first-floor bedrooms. The room had a slightly sweet scent, delicate like butter; it felt welcoming with cream-coloured walls, a low beamed ceiling, an inglenook fireplace containing a cast-iron range and a blazing fire. Every surface was covered in nick-nacks and colourful Christmas Cards. A small Christmas tree sat on a quaint pine dining table surrounded by four spindle-back chairs; a pine door led to a small scullery.

Mother was a tiny figure, sat almost on top of the raging fire, wrapped in several wool blankets. We could see strands of her white hair peeping out from the wool shawl covering her head while her hands were covered with fingerless wool gloves. Muriel took our coats and hung them on hooks attached to the back of the front door. She did the introductions, then headed to the scullery to make some tea, 'Mother, I've brought you some of Mintie Clinch's Christmas cake,' she shouted from the scullery. 'We can have it with our tea.'

'Oh, that's kind of you. Of course, I used to make my own,' shouted Mother. 'I find everything such an effort these days, the spirits willing, but I'm afraid my body isn't... Mintie seems to be doing well with that tearoom of hers. But I hope she's put more spice and brandy in her cake. I was disappointed with the one I had last year; it was a bit dry and bland. I like my cake full of flavour and very sweet; otherwise, I can't see the point in it.'

'Mintie says she's changed the recipe, so you'll have to tell me what you think, and I'll let her know,' shouted Muriel from the scullery. 'She's always trying to tempt Donald with her sumptuous delights and exotic teas. Mind you, the church ladies are just as bad,' she sighed despairingly. 'It's like they're all trying to curry favour with him... I can't think why.'

I don't know if it was the mention of cake, but Jocasta jumped to her feet and went to help. I sensed she wanted to talk to Muriel about her life as a vicar's wife and her feelings of unfulfillment.

Next to the scullery was the old dairy, still adorned with old meat hooks and bursting with what Jocasta described as 'old world charm', which made me smile. Trust me, back in the day, there was nothing charming about dairy farming; it was hard manual labour and probably still is today.

When Muriel and Jocasta returned, Muriel looked like she'd been crying. But after everyone had their tea and Christmas cake, she brightened as we exchanged pleasantries almost sat on top of each other in the cosy room. Mother laughed as she talked about the events at the carol concert, which she'd found highly amusing, and then reminisced about her time at the Hall before we finally moved on to the reason for our visit.

'Does The Sisters of Listan mean anything to you?' Asked Winston raising his voice so Mother could hear him.

Mother's mouth fell open as she stared at him, surprised, 'After all these years, why do you ask about the sisters?' She bellowed, fidgeting in her chair.

Winston glanced at the three of us, 'I came across the name in the old church land registry records. I wondered who they were.'

Mother finished her Christmas cake, took a slurp of her tea, and stirred in another spoonful of sugar. 'You're going way back; I've not heard the sisters mentioned for many years.' She shivered as a chill ran through her.

'So, you have heard of them?' I asked.

'What did he say?' Asked Mother turning to Muriel. 'You'll have to speak up. I'm a bit deaf.'

'That you have heard of them,' Muriel shouted, mouthing the words.

Mother nodded, 'Yes, they were well known in these parts at one time, but as I say, it was a long time ago,' she crossed herself. 'My mother, God rest her, knew them, and I remember them visiting our house when I was a girl... From what I recall, they did a lot of good here in the village; they ran an apothecary and were doctor, nurse, and midwife to many of the folks who lived here at the time; I was delivered by one of them. Folks in the village grew to rely on them; like today, they couldn't afford fancy doctors and medicines.

'Why did they call them The Sisters of Listan?' Asked Florence, raising her voice. 'Were they a holy order?'

Mother shook her head and waved her hand, 'Everyone was religious back in their day, well, they claimed to be. The church was the hub of the community, the centre of everything, far more than it is today; everyone went to church. Life was simple, and I'm sure folks were much happier; I know I was,' she sighed longingly. 'Most folks around here made their living off the land, the sisters included. Many in the village hadn't had much if any, schooling; few could read and write, but the sisters could. They helped the illiterate, even teaching some of them to read and write.'

Mother glanced at Florence taking another slurp of tea. 'Now, to answer your question, they weren't part of a nunnery, holy order, or anything like that, but sisters by birth. There were four of them, all named after flowers, Marigold, Poppy, Lily, and Rose. Marigold was the eldest and most experienced healer and midwife; she was the matriarch of the family. The Listan family had made their living off the land for generations – they farmed the land near the Hall. All the sisters were married and had families; they were close and lived together as a tiny community. And although they were married, they were always known as The Sisters of Listan.'

'Did people think of them as witches?' Asked Jocasta raising her voice so mother could hear her.

Mother nodded and smiled, 'Aye, some did, but I'll come on to that. You're talking about different times, so it depends on what you mean by witches?' She laughed. 'If you're talking about women flying around on broomsticks and wearing pointed hats, then no. But if you mean someone who understood the land, nature, and perhaps some things which were unexplained, then I'd say yes. As I've said, folks weren't educated; they perceived things differently, and some thought of them as witches simply because they didn't know any better. The sisters had medicinal knowledge of plants, herbs, animals, and insects; they had a book of cures and treatments passed down the female family line. Each generation adding new discoveries to it.'

'Written records,' said Jocasta intrigued; I could see the cogs turning in her head. 'I don't suppose you know what happened to them?'

Mother took a deep breath shaking her head, 'No, I've no idea; it was a long time ago - why do you ask?'

'That's a shame,' said Jocasta thoughtfully. 'I was thinking what their book or books might have taught us. So much esoteric knowledge has been lost over the years. Did the sisters live where Rothery Hall is now?'

Mother shrugged, slurping her tea, 'I'd say they lived somewhere in the vicinity. They must have done; my mother told me they were thrown off the land when the Rothery family acquired it, but they weren't the only ones forced to leave,' she shook her head. 'It would have been devastating for folks; people relied on the land to survive. They lost everything, their home and livelihood, with no one to turn to for help and recompense.'

'Do you know if the sisters owned the land?' Asked Winston.

'Ah, that's the big question,' said Mother shaking her head again. 'As I've said, the Listan's had been on that land for centuries, probably before records began. As attempts were made to take the land, several people claimed to own parts of it, the Listan's included, and they were particularly stubborn in their defence of it. Remember, they had the advantage of being able to read and write - for several years, they succeeded in protecting the land for themselves and others.'

'Hmm, I see,' said Winston. 'I couldn't find any land ownership records, only their name.'

Mother shook her head knowingly, 'No, you wouldn't; it's my understanding no written record of the dispute exists; the records conveniently disappeared... Now, although the Listan's and others had been on the land for years, ultimately, they couldn't prove their ownership of it. They didn't stand a chance against the wealthy, educated, and unscrupulous - it's an age-old story of injustice.

You visit any of the villages around here, and folks of my generation will tell you a similar tale. Those who couldn't read or write were easily taken advantage of by those seeking to build their fortunes. However, the Listan's didn't fall into that category. My mother always said Marigold Listen was as sharp as a knife and that she'd cut herself if she weren't careful. She had all the best characteristics of a wise woman - she was a devoted wife, homemaker, generous as a neighbour and teacher, and an excellent mother to her children. The Listan's fought hard and held on till the very end.'

'Hmm, I see,' said Winston reflectively, rubbing his chin. 'We know that Montague Rothery was given the land to build the Hall by his father, Bernard. Do you know if it was Bernard Rothery who threw the Listan's off the land?'

'Ah, well, this is where it gets underhand and messy. Just when it looked like the Listan's might win their claim to the land, things suddenly took a turn, and the four sisters were accused of witchcraft.'

Jocasta's ear pricked up, 'Witchcraft? Do you know who made the accusation?'

Mother shook her head, 'I've no idea; no one did. But anyone could have made it, even a child. The sisters had little chance of getting any redress for the accusation, nor the abuse and suffering they went on to endure because of it.'

'No,' said Winston sadly. 'Their situation wouldn't have been helped by the witchcraft act of 1736, which stated someone couldn't be incriminated for accusing someone of being a witch. To make matters worse, local magistrates interpreted the act differently, and we know Bernard Rothery was a magistrate.' He glanced at the three of us, putting the pieces together in his head. 'Do you know what year the sisters were thrown off the land? We know Montague Rothery moved into the Hall in 1854.'

'Ah yes, dear Master Montague,' said Mother with a broad smile. 'He and Elspeth, his wife, were lovely people. Like his father, Montague was also a magistrate, but he always showed compassion. As I told you, I was one of the first to work at the Hall when they moved there in 1854; I watched the house being built. Everyone in the village was excited, hoping it would bring much-needed work to the area, which it did. I left my position shortly after I married, but I enjoyed working there. But in terms of the land, the sisters were eventually forced out in the late 1840s when they were arrested on charges of witchcraft. They were the last ones to go.'

Mother finished her tea, 'Ah, I needed that... Now, as the years passed, Montague Rothery developed the estate, buying up the land surrounding the Hall and beyond; the estate became huge, and he allowed folks to become tenants on his land; he built these farm cottages and several others,' she smiled. 'Master Montague was a good man and well respected by everyone who knew him, as was his son Edmund and his wife Violet,' she shook her head. 'But the Rothery family have had more than their fair share of tragedy up at the Hall - misery hangs over that place.'

'So, we understand. But what happened to the Listan's?' I asked, fearing the worse.

Mother's mouth tightened, and she shook her head, 'It was a nasty business, shocking. Following the accusations of witchcraft, the four sisters were given the maximum penalty for witchcraft of a year's imprisonment by the then magistrate, Bernard Rothery,' she shook her head again and sighed. 'It's hard to believe that such a man was the father of Master Montague; the two men couldn't have been more different.

At the time, it was the talk of the village, folks who the sisters had helped and should have known better turned their backs on them. Views were divided; it turned neighbour against neighbour. My mother was a big supporter of the sisters and wouldn't hear a bad word about them, nor would she have anything to do with the villagers who'd spoken against them. And she never forgave the church, believing they should have intervened to protect the sisters who lost everything they had. Mind you, the villagers, in their foolish ignorance, also lost out. With the four sisters behind bars, they had no one to turn to for medicine, medical help, a midwife, or help with their reading and writing.

'Hmm, as you say, tragic but highly convenient for Bernard Rothery,' said Winston reflectively, finishing his tea. 'In terms of the land ownership, it sounds like he'd found the loophole he needed to finally get the Listan's off the land by using the accusation of witchcraft. You see, the law of 1736 assumed that there were no actual witches, that no one had real magic power and that those claiming such powers were cheaters, extorting money from unsuspecting people, making it a crime.'

'Oh, the sisters never claimed to be witches, and they certainly didn't take money from folks,' said Mother. 'In fact, they vehemently denied the accusation. Even when put under great duress, they never confessed to the accusations of practising witchcraft. But their protests fell on deaf ears; people didn't seem to want to hear the truth.'

Winston nodded, 'Yes, I can imagine. The political elite frequently invoked the Witchcraft Act in the early 19th century to root out ignorance, superstition, criminality, and insurrection among the general populace. Some also used it to their advantage; personal influence carried more weight in those days, far more than it does today.'

'Have you any idea what date the sisters were arrested?' Asked Florence. 'Would it have been around this time of year?'

Mother thought for a moment pulling at the strings of her memories, 'Hmm, I can't be sure - I think it was in the late summer; I was very young,' she moved her blankets to one side, stood up slowly and began putting more logs on the fire. 'But Christmas time has certainly been tragic for the Rothery family.'

Once she'd finished putting the logs on the fire, she rubbed her gloved hands together and sat down heavily, grabbing the iron poker and began prodding the fire. 'What I do know is that once the Listan's were arrested, tragedy followed them. The four sisters were imprisoned at East Sutton Park Prison near Maidstone. Their families ended up at Tonbridge Workhouse; there was nowhere else for them to go. Folks in the village didn't want to be associated with them; they worried what people would think and say - concerned the sisters' misfortune might affect them; it was shameful. And those who were sympathetic didn't have anything to offer them; they could barely support themselves.'

Mother took her handkerchief from her pocket and wiped her eyes, 'It's silly, I know, but even after all these years, it still upsets me to talk about it. You must excuse me; I find as I get older, I have no control over my emotions... Now, where was I?'

'You were talking about prison and the workhouse,' I said.

'Oh, yes. You must remember that workhouses and prisons were highly unpleasant places, even worse than today, and bound by hard labour. This was when the first tragedy happened; while in prison, Rose died in childbirth - on Christmas Day of all days...'

'Christmas day!' Exclaimed Jocasta, glancing at the three of us; we were all thinking the same thing.

Mother nodded, 'Yes, she was heavily pregnant with her second child when they were sentenced; her child also died. But it gets worse - when her husband found out, he hung himself in the workhouse. They said he was inconsolable, that his heart was broken. And it didn't stop there; months later, Poppy died in prison from tuberculosis.'

Silence...

'What happened to Marigold and Lily?' Asked Jocasta uneasily.

Mother dabbed her eyes, 'Oh, they survived prison and were eventually forced to join the rest of their families at the workhouse. Remember, they'd lost everything and had no chance of finding any employment - beyond that; I've no idea - they never returned to the village; in those days, few left the workhouse alive.'

This was true; I had first-hand experience in workhouses. Mother's news was a lot to take in; the room took on a sombre tone...

'Mind you, Bernard Rothery suffered,' continued Mother. 'Not long after Rose died, he was taken ill; he had terrible rheumatic gout, along with heart and breathing problems. They said he was in agony and became housebound; poor health plagued him for the rest of his days. Of course, some thought he deserved it after what he'd done to the Listan's. Some said he'd been cursed by them, not that I believe in such things, but who could have blamed them?'

Who, indeed, I thought. I could see the others were thinking the same.

'What a tragic story,' said Muriel dabbing her eyes. 'History is full of intolerable cruelty, and this happened right here on our doorstep,' she hesitated. 'I know I shouldn't say this, being married to a vicar, but sometimes I struggle with God and the bible. If God is so loving, why is there so much hate, deceit, and cruelty in life? If I try to talk to Donald about it, we just end up arguing.'

'Hmm, it's a question many ask,' said Winston. 'Particularly in times of misery and darkness, history is full of that. Many sceptics and atheists claim God is cruel. The Bible is full of suffering, punishment, and judgment, but it's also full of compassion and joy. I'm sure it's a question we'll keep asking ourselves and probably never answer. Perhaps it's something we, as humans, are not meant to answer or understand.'

'Yes, the human condition takes a lot of understanding,' declared Jocasta finishing her tea and eyeing the last slice of Christmas cake. 'History is full of great acts of kindness, but also acts of great evil. I suppose it all goes back to Adam and Eve and the creation myth; that provided the basis for the doctrines of the fall of man and original sin.'

It was all getting rather profound; after the things I'd witnessed as a time-travelling ghost, it was a question I'd asked myself many times, but I had no answers; I think you could go mad thinking about it. I cleared my throat, wanting to move on, 'Do you know if any of the Listan family survived?' I asked. 'Could any of their children's descendants live in this area?'

Mother shrugged wistfully, 'Hmm, I must say I've never given it any thought, but I suppose it's a possibility, although I'm not aware of anybody,' she looked at Muriel narrowing her eyes. 'What about you?'

Muriel shook her head, 'Oh, don't ask me; I've no idea; I wasn't even aware of the Listan sisters, let alone their tragic tale,' she glanced at the window. 'Oh, look, it's snowing again,' she stood up to check on the weather... 'It's settling, and the sky looks full of it; I think we'd better make a move. I need to get back to the vicarage; we're expecting some of the church ladies and volunteers for a little pre-Christmas gathering. We do it every year as a sort of thank you. I've left Mrs Gunnerson getting everything ready; Miss Duckworth and Miss Prothero are helping her,' Muriel groaned despairingly, shaking her head again.

'We'll probably never hear the end of the saga of Miss Prothero's hat. She does pride herself on her statement hats, although sometimes I fear for the bird population with her elaborate feathered creations.'

Jocasta moved to the window and glanced at the sky, 'Yes, you're right, the weather does look ominous, and that biting wind is getting up again; we're having quite a winter,' she shivered and glanced at her wristwatch, patting her wrist. 'Goodness, just look at the time. We'd better get back to the Hall and report to Agnes and Clementine.'

Mother pulled her blankets around her, looking at us puzzled, 'Tell me, what do The Sisters of Listan have to do with you redecorating the Hall?'

Hmm, good question, I thought.

'Oh, err... well... we always like to know the history of a place when we're working,' said Jocasta, thinking on her feet. 'It's essential with grand houses. We must deeply probe the essence of not just the house but the history of the whole area; somehow, it then filters through into the chosen colour scheme and soft furnishings.'

Even I was impressed with that answer!

Chapter 10

The others had not long retired; I lay on my huge four-poster bed in the dark with the curtains open, staring out of the rattling windows at the night sky, reflecting on our day. Outside, another blizzard raged, the falling snow dancing in a frenetic waltz as the gusting wind howled and screamed erratically. The bare trees swayed in a dramatic ballet as the wind whipped their branches in every direction. In the bleak sky, the austere moon and twinkling stars played a game of hide and seek among the inky-edged clouds; the clouds seemed to be winning, silently taking over the brooding night sky.

I could barely remember walking back to the Hall from Mother Frobisher's cottage. The four of us were too engrossed discussing the tragic demise of The Sisters of Listan, trying to pull together the strands of our mystery; we barely noticed the freezing weather and sparkling winter scene around us.

Following the accusation of witchcraft, The Listan Sisters lost their land and livelihood, finding themselves abandoned in the cruellest of circumstances. We believe they somehow managed to instigate Bernard Rothery's slow demise making sure he suffered along the way, followed by the tragic misfortunes of the Rothery family here at the Hall. We were convinced they sought revenge using dark magic. After all, it was human nature to seek justice and retribution, and in our experience, some turned to magic to do that.

It was snowing heavily by the time we returned to the comfort of the house; the others were freezing and exhausted, retiring to their rooms with hot cups of tea to rest before dinner, with Winston saying tea warmed, cooled, cheered, and calmed all at the same time. In terms of rest, Jocasta declared that, like a top athlete, she needed to keep her chakras in tip-top condition to maintain communication with the spiritual highway and celestial planes, reminding us that all consciousness resided in the Astral Plane.

Dinner became an elaborate affair, so I excused myself. Ethel seized the opportunity to practice her festive gastronomy, delivering a feast of several courses and numerous dishes, all accompanied by decadent sauces and specially chosen wines. Jocasta described it as a nice little meal! When I glanced in the kitchen, Ethel looked to have used every utensil, pot, pan, and dish in the house. I was pleased I wasn't doing the washing up!

During dinner, Agnes and Clementine announced they were expecting several guests from the village for lunch on Christmas Day; the Reverend, Muriel, and Miss Duckworth among them. They planned to perform a selection of Christmas carols for their guests, so following dinner, they moved to the grand piano to practice their operatic Christmas repertoire.

Ethel didn't take a break, spending the evening in the kitchen delicately piping icing onto a Christmas cake to create an intricate snow scene. After finishing that, she prepared her forcemeat stuffing for the Christmas turkey, soaked her ham, trimmed the Brussels sprouts, and made some fondant fancies and more mince pies; she was so organised!

Winston and Florence returned to the study to scrutinise some family records they'd discovered. In their hunt, they found evidence that Edmund had been consulting alchemists, mystics, shamans, and soothsayers, looking at pagan rituals and beliefs, ancient cults, and magic in his desperation to find a cure for Thomas. It looked like he'd been meddling with things he didn't understand, convinced a treatment was out there; it set alarm bells ringing.

On closer inspection, Jocasta wasn't persuaded; she didn't believe Edmund's actions were linked to the mystery hanging over the Hall and Rothery family. Had that been the case, she felt sure she would have had an immediate presentiment when we arrived at the house leading to an eventuation! I hoped she was right. She reminded us that the curse was linked to Bernard Rothery and instigated before Edmund was born.

While Winston and Florence were in the study, I was with Jocasta in her room; we re-examined the music box, diary, and pocket watch; we sensed their energy as we brought the three innocuous-looking items together.

'These are most definitely connected to the Listan's curse,' mused Jocasta assuredly, although she looked bewildered. 'But how could the Listan's send these items to different generations of the family from their grave? And these are expensive items; we know the Listan's had no money.'

I smiled reflectively, 'You're thinking logically, and as you know, logic and magic don't go together - reality and the balance of probabilities are never a factor. Magic works in mysterious ways, and as for the music box and diary, I guess they had to look the part and fit in with this grand house, which is why they needed to look expensive.'

I picked up the music box admiring the artistry; it was beautiful. In 1776 I'd seen similar things in Marie Antoinette's private chambers when I was at the Palace of Versailles. She was vivacious, outgoing, and bold, a social butterfly who loved gambling, partying, beautiful things, and extravagant fashions. I liked her, but that's another story.

'These may not even be physical items but enchantments – if we can break the spell or curse, they may just vanish into the ether; we've seen that happen before.'

I put the music box down and picked up the pocket watch; it gave me a ghostly tingle in a way I couldn't explain; I'd never experienced anything like it before. Since we'd brought the three items together, I'd noticed the hands on the watch had begun spinning anticlockwise.

'Oh, do be careful with that,' implored Jocasta, her blue eyes sparkling nervously as she tried to calm a sudden stirring in her chakras. 'I fear we may have activated something - Mr Biddercombe from The

Society for Psychical Research in London had a strange experience with an enchanted timepiece that started spinning backwards. He claims he ended up in the remote Darhad valley of Outer Mongolia, just south of Siberia.'

I looked at Jocasta dumbfounded, unable to believe my ears, 'Did you just say Outer Mongolia!'

She nodded nonchalantly, 'Yes, he was missing for several years and returned a changed man speaking in strange tongues. He wrote a thesis based on his experiences. It was published in several of the psychic journals, and there are copies in the society's library and at the Psychic Institutes in New York, Rome, Paris, and Milan,' she shook her head and folded her arms, looking severe. 'Now, he won't go near a clock or timepiece and is guided by the sun.'

'The sun?' I asked doubtfully, pulling a face.

Jocasta nodded, sensing my cynicism.

'Hmm, I see - fascinating. And what did Mr Biddercombe conclude with his thesis?'

Jocasta lifted her shoulders in a half shrug, and her face fell into an expression of disappointment, 'Oh, the usual - that further research was required, it was all very inconclusive,' she shook her head, and her brows drew together. 'I don't think Professor Wimble was impressed. I saw him writing copious notes as he read Mr Biddercombe's thesis in the society's library; he was there all day, which is never a good sign.'

As a time-travelling ghost, I knew Outer Mongolia and looked at Jocasta with raised eyebrows and a hint of scepticism, 'I can't say I'm surprised. Where was Mr Biddercombe when this happened, Russia?'

Jocasta's eyebrows shot to the top of her head, 'Good heavens, no, he was in Aberystwyth. He was working on a psychic investigation at Aberystwyth Castle with three of the society's noted patrons. Baroness Fortescue, Countess Podmore, and Lady Bantry; they all adore Professor Wimble,' she bobbed her head knowingly, clasping her hands together. 'Like most castles, it has a long and chequered history. Mr Biddercombe was trying to contact the Welsh prince Llywelyn the Great from 1221; he believes him to be a forgotten mystic known for his marbles.'

'Marbles!'... I was lost for words. I knew the nomadic Darhad tribe, and part of me was intrigued; they spent most of their time travelling and were completely self-sufficient, but that was another story, one we didn't have time for now.

I looked at the pocket watch sensing its magic, but I didn't feel we'd activated anything; however, to be on the safe side, and much to Jocasta's relief, I moved it away from the music box and diary and the hands stopped spinning. 'This watch must hold a specific spell, or do you think it's holding onto a moment in time?'

Jocasta shook her head, still looking bewildered, taking a deep breath, 'I've no idea, but it's certainly holding onto something. Clocks and watches are unpredictable things where enchantments are concerned; they can hold onto magic for eternity. Time has its own flow, yet somehow magic can distort it - In my experience, whenever magic is involved, nothing happens by chance,' she pursed her lips, moving them from side to side and held her chin in her hand. 'I think these items link to their recipients and must act as anchors to the haunting of this place. That said, it's not the house that's cursed but the land it's built on.'

I hadn't given that much thought, but Jocasta was right, 'Yes, of course, that makes perfect sense. To the Listan's, it will always be their land,' I picked up the diary flicking through its blank manilla pages, hoping for a eureka moment; I knew the pages held hidden text; we just needed to reveal it. 'You know, I doubt we could destroy these items even if we tried. The symbol here is the clue.

We need to deal with the source of the magic; that's the only way to break the curse on this place, and I suspect we'll need these three items to do it.'

Jocasta agreed and spent the rest of the evening consulting her crystal while munching her way through a packet of digestive biscuits. She didn't make any progress blaming it on troublesome elementals affecting her vibrations and core chakras. She considered contacting Titus, her spirit control, or going into a trance but decided against it. Jocasta was stoic, but I think she was weary from the weather and all the effort and stamina required to walk up and down narrow country lanes in the snow and ice; it wasn't easy. Communing with spirits was physically demanding and draining; it required intense concentration and even more stamina. I felt sure we would need Titus to help us find the source of the magic and symbol. I hoped he'd be in a good mood; I may have mentioned - he's a terrible diva!

I was given Edmund's room; every day and night since I'd been here, I sensed his presence; it was intense and not easy to describe, but it felt insidious; it shouted at me; I tried not to focus on it for long – it was too unbearable. I felt his sadness and pain as if his torment had been absorbed into the walls of the room, pressing in from all sides. I hoped he could find peace, yet I feared none of the Rothery family would ever be at peace, Agnes and Clementine included, particularly at this time of year, at Christmas. We needed to end whatever held past generations of the family here at the Hall and kept Bernard in torment at his grave.

No matter how heinous his crimes and guilt, I felt he'd paid his debt, as had the innocent and unwitting members of the Rothery family. We couldn't undo Bernard's cruel deceit and thoughtless greed, nor could we change what happened to Montague, Elspeth, Edmund, and Violet. But we had to find a way to free them from the plight of the Listan's curse. I didn't know if it would be possible, but I wanted them to find peace and be together again.

Likewise, The Sisters of Listan needed to let go of the hate in their hearts and thirst for revenge. No one could blame them for seeking retribution, I knew that better than anyone, but after all this time, they needed to lay it to rest; otherwise, they would never be able to move on and would remain in the Twilight Zone. They'd unwittingly trapped themselves in a cycle of eternal misery by cursing the Rothery family.

Every Christmas, something watched over this house and Bernard's grave, as the ghosts of the Rothery family were forced to return here to live out their past pain; I wondered if the Listan's were watching. Did it give them satisfaction to observe the Rothery's anguish and suffering? I sensed it didn't and only served to remind them of their own unfortunate plight and misery.

My thoughts drifted to Mother Frobisher and what she told us; I felt sure we were missing something. She said the sisters were well known and respected in the village until the accusation of witchcraft. The sisters knew the medicinal properties of plants, herbs, and insects, and were good people using their education, knowledge, and nature to help others. Mother never mentioned them practising any forms of magic or witchcraft, and while that troubled me, it also gave me hope.

Of course, the definition of witchcraft changes; many things in your modern world would have been seen as witchcraft in the past. That said, using powerful magic to curse someone or something requires esoteric knowledge, special skills from those well versed in the dark arts of the occult. And there was something else, how could the sisters have used dark magic from prison? Magic requires all the tools of the trade. And where did such powerful magic come from? It's hardly something the Listan's were known for... No, something wasn't right.

The grandfather clock in the hall had just chimed to indicate fifteen minutes past midnight... The noises started as I lay on my bed, listening to the final chime. I heard a sound like a long gasp followed by whispers - troubled, incoherent ramblings coming from the walls. The murmurs quickly turned to more sinister and despondent sounds. The ghosts of Rothery Hall were back, making their presence known.

The whispers turned to groans, banging, sobbing, and a child crying - an inconsolable child, that was the most disturbing, a sound you couldn't ignore; it tugged at the heartstrings, triggering the human fight or flight responses and feelings of distress. Like before, the noises seemed to come from everywhere in the house, echoing and getting louder with sounds of anguish and misery.

The commotion seemed loudest on the landing, where we all gathered, the others in their night attire, all of us strangely drawn to the same place. Agnes and Clementine looked terrified, not that Jocasta, Florence, and Winston looked much better.

We were startled when Ethel appeared in a full-length cream wool dressing gown. Her face covered in a thick layer of cold cream, and her hair full of kirby grips topped with a white hairnet tied at the front in a perfect bow; she carried a heavy bible. I wondered if she intended to use it as a weapon. She looked a ghostly site; however, I felt sure she'd frighten any ghosts away; she certainly gave the five of us a nasty shock.

'Whatever is happening?' She asked nervously with a shiver pulling her dressing gown closer to her. 'Goodness, it's freezing here, like the arctic.'

'It's – it's the ghosts,' said Agnes in a whimper, clinging to Clementine, her sharp eyes rolling as her face contorted.

Somewhere in the house, a door slammed shut with a loud bang; we all jumped, then silence...

I glanced along the landing, desperately trying to pinpoint the location of our ghosts, 'Ladies, are the house hauntings normally like this?'

Ethel looked at Agnes and Clementine, who both seemed lost and incoherent, 'It's hard to say,' she spluttered, taking a deep breath, putting her hand on the wall to steady herself. 'But it seems louder tonight and more – and more fraught.'

'Hmm, I fear there's no rest for the wicked,' muttered Jocasta, her eyes swirling in every direction as her breath danced in the cold air; she seemed to be gazing into the distance.

We all looked at her questioningly.

'By that,' she continued, 'I mean for whoever cursed this house and the Rothery family.'

'What should we do?' Asked Agnes hurriedly, clinging onto Clementine and Ethel like her life depended on it; all colour drained from her face.

Jocasta put her finger to her mouth, 'Shhh,' she whispered sharply. 'I feel a presence here on the landing,' she did a 360-degree turn, carefully glancing around her, narrowing her eyes like she was looking for someone in a crowd.

We all stepped back nervously as we heard a sigh, a long, weary sigh filled with raw emotions.

'Did you hear that?' asked Jocasta stiffly, sniffing the air, her eyes sparkling with anticipation.

We all looked at each other and nodded apprehensively.

She sniffed loudly, 'Ah yes, just as I suspected, I can smell ectoplasm; it's strong by these windows.'

We heard someone taking a long deep breath. In the blink of an eye, a dark shadow flickered across the landing; Ethel dropped her bible with a loud thud and put her hand over her mouth, trying not to scream, clinging onto Agnes.

The air felt heavy and took on a peculiar earthy aroma; unlike anything I'd smelled before, I couldn't describe it. There was a whisper, the words 'annus horribilis' echoed softly across the landing, followed by the sound of a man sobbing. Outside, the wind raged, rattling the glass in the windows. The moon peeped from behind a ragged cloud, its light cutting through the inky darkness. The house creaked...

The lights flickered and buzzed before going out. Agnes, Clementine, and Ethel gasped as they huddled together fearfully, holding their breath. In the falling snow, the moonlight cast eerie shadows across the landing and onto the family portraits, their sombre faces staring at us disapprovingly.

We could hear the steady tick-tock of the stately grandfather clock downstairs in the hall, like the beating heart of the house. The glass in the windows had misted in the cold night air; something unseen wrote the name Edmund on one of the panes of misted glass. Then we heard a faint muffled voice saying, 'Pull yourself together, man,' followed by the distant sound of someone banging a fist on the wall.

'Edmund, is that you?' Asked Jocasta firmly, holding out her hands. 'Please don't be afraid; we want to help you.'

Silence...

The door to what had been Violet's room began vibrating and shaking rapidly like it might explode...

***

Violet took a monogrammed handkerchief from her pocket and dabbed her eyes; tears seemed to overwhelm her most days; how many tears had she shed - how many more did she have? That she couldn't answer other than to say, far more than she'd ever imagined possible.

Unconsciously she rubbed her hands until they were red and blistered. She sighed wearily, looking out of the window at the eerie night sky and falling snow. The wind blew the snow in ghostly swirls as it danced across the gardens, forming deep drifts. She dreaded the cold weather and winter months; it filled her with foreboding and fear. She dabbed at her eyes again, full of self-loathing. Violet despised herself for being so needy, wishing she could be strong and not so weak and feeble.

A shiver ran through her; she pulled her beautiful, French embroidered wool shawl around her shoulders, admiring it for a moment. Violet trembled and sighed, consumed with the gnawing emptiness she'd had since Thomas died. Her thoughts turned to the women in the village, like her, many had lost a child through childbirth or sickness; she knew their pain and suffering. Rich or poor, it was universal. She glanced around her room; Rothery Hall was a place she had loved, but it had become her prison, a gilded cage full of unbearable pain.

As much as she tried to think of happier memories and keep them at the forefront of her mind, she couldn't. Her mind was on a loop and consumed with misery, repeatedly returning to the same painful thoughts. Thomas becoming ill, his suffering and her feelings of helplessness and despair. She glanced at the large portrait above the fireplace, a treasured painting of her and Thomas painted in the house gardens during the glorious summer of 1900.

What was that?... Violet listened hard; she was sure she could hear someone sobbing; it sounded distant, far away... It stopped; perhaps she'd imagined it; tears ran down her cheeks, but she made no effort to stop them. It was almost the first anniversary of Thomas's death, a time of sadness and remembrance, not celebrations and parties. Violet could never enjoy any festivities; she would never celebrate Christmas. She doubted she would ever be able to smile again, let alone have any joy in her life...

***

The door to Violet's room stopped shaking.

Silence...

In the darkness, everyone breathed.

'Give me a moment,' I said and dashed to my room, not giving the others chance to say anything or protest.

I returned with an oil lamp; the flickering light helped to cut through the murky darkness. Ghostly hauntings aside, electricity was unreliable at the best of times in grand houses, and most of the rooms in this house seemed to have oil lamps on standby.

'Good idea, dear boy,' said Jocasta, still sniffing the air, trying to centre her vibrations.

'Right, follow me,' I said, trying to sound like I knew what I was doing. We all tentatively moved to the door of Violet's room and huddled together...

'Shall I open it?' I whispered.

They all looked at each other, their hearts thumping.

'Of course,' said Jocasta impatiently, pushing up her dressing gown sleeves like she was getting ready for a fight. 'We've no time to lose and must strike while the iron's hot, important clues could be waiting for us, even a presentiment.'

In the semidarkness, I slowly turned the handle, and just as I was about to open the door, the door to the nursery began to shake and rattle. We could also hear the rhythmic sound of the rocking chair moving backwards and forwards...

***

Elspeth Rothery sat in her white night clothes, tightly wrapped in a thick wool blanket, rocking backwards and forwards in the nursery rocking chair, trying to compose herself. She'd no idea how long she'd been sitting there, losing all sense of time. Elspeth wiped away her tears, but as fast as she did, more came. Apart from the rhythmic creak of the chair, the house seemed so still and quiet.

She glanced around the beautiful nursery, thinking it felt out of place in the house and a cruel reminder of her misfortune. Their home seemed so lifeless; Elspeth didn't remember the Hall ever feeling so quiet and empty.

She closed her eyes tightly, wanting to shout, scream, and cry simultaneously. Her hopes of being a mother had disappeared; the dreams she had of holding her boy and watching him grow were gone, shattered to pieces; the thought of it consumed her.

Now, she just wanted peace and quiet, to be left alone to grieve and come to terms with what had happened. Elspeth couldn't imagine a day when she would ever heal and find tranquillity. Montague told her they would recover and be stronger but said it would take time, not that she could think about the future.

Elspeth closed her eyes again, shaking her head violently, trying to snap herself out of her misery and focus on something else. She couldn't imagine ever feeling content with life, and herself, let alone smile again. She could hear the steady tick-tock of the grandfather clock in the hall and concentrated on its melodic rhythm, taking comfort from its familiarity.

She dug deep, trying to summon her resolve. More tears rolled down her face. She let out a long sigh, trying to move her thoughts to the future, hoping and praying the new year would be better. Elspeth never imagined she'd be happy to see the end of 1856; after all, it had been a year full of hope, joy, and happiness. Yet it had all come to this, nothing but unbearable grief and misery.

She stopped rocking and stood up slowly, pulling her blanket around her and moved to the window. A single star shone brightly in the night sky like a beacon; it was snowing heavily, the snow settling on everything it touched, forming deep drifts across the gardens. Elspeth trembled, pulling her blanket closer to her; her vision swam; she rubbed her head and put a hand on the wall to steady herself. Over the past week, she'd started having dizzy spells, something she'd never had before. She put it down to weakness caused by childbirth. It was a strange kind of dizziness; she felt like she was in a dark, spinning tunnel heading towards a bright light. It made her feel lightheaded and faint; she must remember to carry her smelling salts. She should probably eat something but had no appetite.

She glanced around the room. Something felt different, yet everything looked just as it always had. Why did she have a nagging feeling of unease? She thought of Montague, wondering where he was and what he was doing; she knew he grieved as much as she did. She heard a creek; her eyes moved to the rocking chair; it started rocking backwards and forwards...

***

We stood at the door to Violet's room; I had my hand on the door handle, 'What should we do?' I asked as the nursery door shook loudly and more disturbing whispers, moans, and the sound of a woman sobbing reverberated from the walls. The sound of the rocking chair becoming faster and louder, 'Should we split up?'

'Split up! Are you mad? We could all be murdered where we stand,' exclaimed Clementine; her voice trembled, and her eyes rolled as she started to panic; she looked like she might faint.

'Calm yourself, Clementine,' said Jocasta taking her hand and patting it firmly. 'Hold your breath and count to a hundred.'

'A hundred!' She exclaimed.

'Yes... err - no,' Jocasta sighed, shaking her head impatiently. 'What I meant to say was that you should count backwards from a hundred,' she glanced at me, sighing again, trying not to look irritated. 'Jasper, under the circumstances, I think it's better if we all stick together.'

I nodded, although, in these situations, there was rarely safety in numbers. I was about to open the door when we heard a door shaking and rattling violently downstairs...

***

Montague Rothery sat crumpled in his study; he could finally let his tears flow; it was the only room in the house he could guarantee he wouldn't be disturbed, the only place he felt safe to let his emotions and grief surface. It was something he had to do in private, away from prying eyes and loose tongues.

The servants never came into the study uninvited and had a strict timetable for cleaning and attending to the fire. Montague told them he didn't want to be disturbed and would be busy. They wouldn't bother him unless it were something unexpected or urgent. He knew the house staff were just as shocked and upset as he was; they were all mourning in their own way.

A heavy lump formed in his throat; he held his head in his hands for a long moment and sat taking deep breaths, trying to silence irrational thoughts and calm his bleeding heart, telling himself everything would be alright - it had to be. How would his darling wife ever recover? He would never forget the look on her beautiful face when he told her their child was... he couldn't bear to think of the word, let alone say it. The look on her face would haunt him forever; he felt so insignificant, helpless, and powerless.

He took his handkerchief from his jacket pocket and quickly wiped his eyes and nose, determined to be strong. Naturally, he was shocked and stunned by what had happened earlier, never realising how quickly excitement, expectation, and joy could turn to tragedy and grief. Powerful emotions coursed through him, the likes of which he'd never experienced nor wanted to experience again. Tortured feelings he didn't know anyone could feel, let alone be expected to endure. He'd discovered a whole new side of himself.

Montague's thoughts drifted to the poor wretches who ended up at the Tonbridge workhouse, wondering how any of them managed to survive due to their misfortune. Most came from the streets or slums, and many children were orphaned, having the worst possible start in life. He was trying hard to make radical reforms there using his own money. And here he and Elspeth were, able to give a child the best of everything, yet their child had been taken away from them before taking its first breath. It made no sense, and he felt outraged.

His mind went around in circles, asking the same questions, looking for reasons and answers, but he had none. Could it be their fault? Had they done something to cause the stillbirth? The lump returned to his throat. He glanced around the study, thinking how quiet and empty the house felt.

The wind howled outside, causing the snow to swirl in an ethereal dance, forming deep drifts across the gardens. Montague jumped as something tapped at the window - it was a gnarled tree branch covered in a blanket of snow; it would blossom in the spring. His thoughts turned to Elspeth, hoping she would do the same and be able to blossom too. He wondered how you could mend a broken heart – he had no answer but would try with every part of himself.

He looked around the study at the rows of leather-bound books perfectly lined up on the bookshelves. He shook his head; something felt different, yet everything looked the same. He had a strange feeling of déjà vu as he glanced at the fireplace and couldn't understand why the fires hadn't been lit or why he hadn't noticed it earlier, particularly given the freezing weather, not that he felt cold. The mantel clock had stopped at three o'clock, the time of the birth; Montague shuddered as a chill shot through him.

He rubbed his head as his vision swam; over the past week, he'd been getting strange headaches making him feel lightheaded. Montague felt like he was in a dark spinning tunnel heading towards a bright light; he couldn't explain it, wondering if he had eye strain or was developing a head cold.

Eyes wide, he glanced at the side table. It seemed to glow with a peculiar luminosity; he noticed a book. He wondered who could have put it there; no one other than Elspeth was allowed to touch his books; she often joked about it. Montague trembled as he stood up and moved to the table. He was surprised to see his pocket watch; without thinking, he felt his waistcoat pocket. 'How on earth did that get there?' He muttered to himself, picking up the watch and carefully putting it in his waistcoat pocket; it had belonged to his father; he gave it to him on his eighteenth birthday.

His attention turned to the leather-bound book; he'd never seen it before; on the cover, it said, 'My Diary 1861', the year his father died. It had a dark red mark or symbol above the words. He opened the book flicking through the pages; they were blank with no diary entries, or so he thought. As he skimmed through the pages, Montague blinked several times, trying to focus his eyes, unable to believe what he saw. As he ran his fingers across a page, an animated picture of his father appeared; he looked disturbed and troubled as if he was desperately trying to say something - something urgent... What was that? Montague glanced around the room; he could hear a noise – distant, far away; he stood motionless, listening hard... it sounded like a child crying in distress...

We all stood by the door to Violet's room as the house fell silent... The silence and stillness were deafening... None of us moved; we stood listening hard, waiting for the whispers, sobbing, and moaning to start up again... but they didn't.

I finally opened the door to Violet's room, and as my eyes adjusted to the darkness, I cautiously stepped inside with my oil lamp in hand; as I did, the lights in the house came back on with a buzz.

The room looked just as it should, with nothing to indicate a ghostly visitor or presence. Jocasta flicked on the light switch, illuminating the room, which, in a breath, helped ease the tension among the others; it went from critical to high alert. Uneasily we examined the room and found nothing out of the ordinary; everything was where it should be. Although Jocasta said she could smell ectoplasm by the windows. We then vigilantly made our way downstairs to the study, which, like Violet's room, looked untouched; it was just as Florence and Winston had left it earlier in the evening.

'Whatever is going on in this house?' Asked Ethel, her voice going up an octave as she tried to hide her fear and apprehension. She grabbed the little gold crucifix hanging around her neck, trying to seek some comfort from it. 'It goes from bad to worse. I don't normally agree with such things, and I can't believe I'm saying this, but do we need to ask the Reverend to come here and perform an exorcism?' She shuddered, taking her smelling salts from her dressing gown pocket, quickly unscrewing the top, inhaling, and wincing as she clutched her bible close to her and swallowed hard... 'I know I can't take much more of this. You never know what might happen from one moment to the next in this house. Are we to be possessed or taken in the night to the gates of hell for all eternity?' She took another sniff of her smelling salts, closed her eyes, and began silently praying to herself.

I could see from Agnes and Clementine's faces they were feeling the same, and although I thought Ethel was getting carried away, I couldn't blame her for feeling on edge. We always fear the unknown – me included.

'I doubt an exorcism would help,' said Florence calmly, pulling the strands of her thoughts together. 'Let's take a moment to look at what we know so far about this case.'

She had our full attention.

'Things seemed to have reached a dangerous turning point on Christmas Day when Rose Listan died in childbirth, also losing her child while in prison; I'm guessing she died at three o'clock. That event, date, and time are key; it secured the fate of the Rothery family and the subsequent events that have followed here in this house,' Florence paused as she stood by the fireplace pulling the evidence together in her mind. 'Add to that Rose's husband's suicide in the workhouse and the death of her sister, Poppy, in prison from tuberculosis and - well, you must agree you have a perfect storm for blame, hate, and a thirst for revenge. Given the circumstances, I'm sure we'd all have felt the same.'

Even Ethel had to agree with that synopsis.

Winston nodded reflectively with a shiver, 'Sadly, the history books are full of such tales. As the years pass, we forget about the many injustices of bygone days,' he glanced around the library. 'But not, in this case, someone doesn't want the occupants of this house to ever forget their misery and wants them to continue to suffer.'

The room took on a sombre tone, and although we were all innocent of the past crimes connected to the Rothery family, we suddenly felt a sense of responsibility.

'Yes - yes, you're right, and what happened was tragic,' agreed Agnes, trying to get her breath as she clung onto Clementine. 'But what can we do about it now? We can't undo the crimes of the past, nor what happened to The Sisters of Listan.'

'No, but we now know a lot more than we did,' interjected Jocasta trying her best to sound optimistic. 'Although we don't have all the pieces of the jigsaw just yet,' she rubbed her hand across her brow, pondering our next steps. 'I will need to contact Titus,' she glanced at the mantel clock and sighed, stifling a yawn, 'Look, it's late; we're all tired, and there's nothing we can do right now. Let's try and get some sleep, and we'll regroup in the morning, energised and ready to face the new day - we'll really put our backs into it.'

Agnes suggested Clementine and Ethel spend the night in her room; understandably, none of them wanted to be alone. The two women agreed, with the three of them clinging to each other as they nervously returned to Agnes's room, all on high alert. I hung back for a moment with Jocasta; she was lost in contemplation about the case. I was curious and wanted to ask her about something else...

'When we visited Mother Frobisher, and you were in the scullery with Muriel, I sensed Muriel had been crying. What was that all about?'

She smiled at me, the corners of her mouth pulling back, 'Oh, you do sense these things, dear boy. You have a heightened sensitivity to people's feelings - that's what makes you so special,' she paused, looking at me probingly. 'If you must know, I had a presentiment and felt I needed to set Muriel on a new path, or at least plant a seed, so I quickly read her palm,' Jocasta's face fell into a frown of disapproval. 'Although I don't approve or condone such things as palm readings. They're for the seaside, a cheap fairground attraction,' she shook her head contemptuously. 'But I felt there was no other way. You see, at the moment, Muriel is lost and unfulfilled.'

I nodded, knowing she was right, 'Yes, that's true; Muriel isn't an earth-bound sort of person. She needs to be able to spread her wings and fly.'

'Oh absolutely, I told her she had to take a risk, that I could see her using her dance qualifications, skills, and talents to open a dancing school. I said she would start small in the Village Hall, but it would quickly lead to bigger and better things,' Jocasta's eyes sparkled brightly; she looked energised and pleased with herself. 'I felt deep in my base chakra that she would be much happier and find a sense of fulfilment she hasn't had for many years. In fact, when we returned here to the Hall, I saw it quite clearly in my crystal,' she smiled dreamily, looking pleased with herself.

I didn't know if it was just me, but I could see a flaw with this idea and plan, 'Hmm, I see, and what about the Reverend? Where does he fit into all this career planning and happily ever after? Life is full of unexpected twists and turns and is never quite as we expect it to be.'

Jocasta's eyebrows rose, and her expression dulled, 'Ah yes – you make an important point. As always, you've hit the nail on the head,' I could see she'd thought about it. 'I must confess I'm not sure what will happen to the marriage, but whatever the outcome, I think the Reverend will be fine,' she hesitated, biting her lip. 'Of course, should their marriage fail, it will cause quite a scandal in the village, but I'm sure no one will blame him,' Jocasta stiffened as her eyebrows knotted together with disapproval, and she started finger-wagging. 'When they should. It takes two to make a marriage work and fail; no one is ever entirely blameless.'

She exhaled loudly and put her finger away, 'Anyway, I'm sure if that should happen, Miss Duckworth and the church ladies will rally around and look after the Reverend. They'll be fussing around him like mother hens,' she pressed her hands to her cheeks as she reflected on her advice and beliefs. 'I know it won't be easy, but if Muriel dares to take another path, I feel in the long run, they will both be happier. Sometimes the only way you can find yourself is by being alone. There's no point in staying in a loveless marriage - after all, we only have one life,' she hesitated, pondering their future. 'Who knows, it may even bring them closer together and energise their relationship, make them appreciate what they have... Oh dear, listen to me. I'm going all philosophical - but I do believe that... I blame the war.'

Now I was lost, 'The war!'

She bobbed her head slowly, 'Yes, dear boy. You see, many men and women lived in the moment; they had to make the most of every day, not knowing what the future might hold. I feel women made bad choices both during and after the war, sometimes out of desperation. I think that's what happened with Muriel... And let's be honest, she was never cut out to be a vicar's wife,' Jocasta moved to the window, watching the falling snow in the moonlight, her mind reflecting on the war years... '. The war changed everything; it gave women a chance for a new career, but after it ended, they were expected to give everything up and be happy and grateful to become homemakers again. Of course, there's nothing wrong with that, and many women were happy to do so.'

She heaved a sigh, still staring out of the window taking in the brooding night sky, 'Thinking about it now, not much has changed. Today, women are expected to conform, have few aspirations, marry, have a family and be content with a domestic life when they have so much more to offer,' she looked at me, her mouth set in a hard line. 'Ambition and a woman's career are funny things – full of sacrifices along the way - surely everyone deserves a chance in life,' Jocasta shook her head despairingly. 'Anyway, I digress. My point is that when Muriel married, there was a shortage of eligible men because of the war. Nearly one million young men were killed, which increased the gender gap. Many women never married, simply because they outnumbered the men.'

Jocasta rubbed her arms briskly and shuddered, remembering the horrors of war - her tone changed; it became sombre. 'So many young men were needlessly lost; it was a tragic time, one that I hope will never be repeated, yet I fear it will. As Winston says, man never seems to learn histories lessons; progress is so fragile.'

Chapter 11

The four of us were in the study. As I gazed out of the windows, I had to narrow my eyes due to the glare from the snow. Thankfully it had stopped snowing, the morning sky had turned an icy azure blue, and the cool sun sat low on the horizon. Its translucent buttery glow highlighted everything, picking out the undulating landscape, making the colours of the midwinter scene bolder and brighter. The snow reflected the colour of the sky, revealing blues, violets, and even crimson; everything had a new sharpness and clarity.

The shiny green foliage of the spiky holly leaves stood out while the red berries sparkled like rubies against the crisp whiteness of the snow. Hungry blackbirds sheltered among the snow-covered conifer trees foraging for food. They plucked away at the juicy berries of the holly, much to the annoyance of the territorial robin redbreast, which lost its cheery whistle trying to chase the blackbirds away; it was a losing battle.

We had a restless night apart from Jocasta, who said she'd slept like a log due to the bracing country air; it had left her feeling energised and raring to go, helped along by her three-course breakfast with all the trimmings! She'd brought her Gladstone bag into the study and was getting ready to consult her crystal as Ethel knocked on the door and walked in with a tray of tea; she smelt of lavender wood polish and had an immaculate linen tea towel draped over one arm. She looked tired, grey, and weary; everything seemed an effort. Her appearance wasn't helped by her pale, well-scrubbed face, severely scaped back hair, sombre black jumper, skirt, and pristine grey apron.

Jocasta stroked her chin, surreptitiously studying her for a moment... 'How are you bearing up, Ethel?' She asked, trying to sound bright and breezy. 'Did you manage to get any sleep? I know Agnes and Clementine struggled; they are both quite worn out. Although when we left them, they were heading to the piano to rehearse their Christmas repertoire for tomorrow's Christmas day celebrations here at the Hall.'

Ethel tried to hide her frustration but bristled and tutted loudly, 'Yes, so they keep saying. All I can say is thank goodness I'm an early riser. As you know, we decided to sleep in the same room, supposedly to protect each other from whatever haunts this place,' she shuddered and gave a cautionary shake of the head. 'I still think we should ask the Reverend to perform an urgent exorcism – if we don't, I'm sure we'll be tempting fate - heaven only knows what might happen to us all; we might not see in the new year.' She took a deep breath, trying to steady herself and put the tray on a side table, carefully arranging the cups and saucers, 'And if they were awake all night, I wonder how they account for all their blood-curdling snoring with their gargling and squawking. As soon as one of them stopped, the other started, it...' she hesitated and raised her eyebrows, forcing a nervous smile. 'I was going to say it was loud enough to wake the dead.'

Jocasta grimaced and nodded, 'Hmm, I can see that would have been annoying. I must admit I wouldn't want to live with someone who snores. I imagine it could lead to more than just disrupted sleep and cause conflicts and feelings of resentment,' she chewed on her lip. 'I'm sure it would affect my chakras and connection to the Astral Plane. At times I even find Cassiel's purring distracting to my vibrations.'

Ethel swallowed hard, looking blank, 'Cassiel?' She asked meekly.

Jocasta nodded, 'Yes, he's my pet cat, black, of course. He's named after the archangel and guardian of Capricorn, my star sign. I find cats can be very spiritually minded; that's why they have nine lives.'

Ethel's mouth fell open, and she slowly bobbed her head, trying to be polite. She quickly distracted herself by putting out some silver teaspoons. 'The snoring reminded me of when I started in service with the wealthy Featherswallow family at their country estate in Stourton, Wiltshire. I used to share a room with a girl called Esme Cannon – she had a primal snore, like a bull in rutting season. I didn't think anything could sound worse until last night,' Ethel smiled to herself, rubbing an imaginary mark from a teaspoon with her tea towel. 'Isn't it funny the things you remember? I hadn't thought about Esme in years; she was a tiny little thing but full of energy. I wonder what happened to her?' She shook her head, still smiling. 'Esme was a character and used to do impressions of people - she was good at it.'

She exhaled loudly, lost in her memories. 'It was a long time ago, years before the war; we were so young and full of life and - hope... Anyway, I can't stand here chatting; there's work to be done - Christmas in this house won't happen on its own. If you need anything else, I'll be in the kitchen doing some kneading; it's bread day - I might make some Chelsea buns.'

I could see Jocasta's mouth-watering, 'Oh, they're one of my favourites,' she said dreamily, hunching her shoulders and crinkling her eyes. 'I do like a nice juicy currant.'

Ethel nodded, pulling her mouth to one side, and left in a fragrant flurry of lavender wood polish, closing the door behind her.

Just before breakfast, Florence had managed to telephone Effie Evander. She lived in remote Knoydart; it was only accessible by boat and sat between Loch Nevis and Loch Hourn on the west coast of the Scottish Highlands; I was amazed she had a telephone. Florence said that despite being an accomplished witch, Effie liked all the modern conveniences, and due to her love of oats and a high-fibre diet, a toilet with a satisfying flush! Apparently, she was obsessed with plumbing... Scotland was famous for its witches and remote covens; some have existed since the bronze age.

Effie was the principal of the ancient Knoydart Witches' Fellowship. Of course, Florence was a member and contacted her to pick her brains about our mysterious symbol. Ever since we'd discovered it in the music box and on the cover of the diary, Florence had been trying to reach her, but the phone lines had been down in Scotland due to the bad weather.

Effie told Florence she had the definitive book of symbols in the fellowship's extensive library and would send it over. She said the book listed all known symbols, along with their affiliations and other minor bits of trivia. Effie instructed Florence to use the ancient Knoydart calling spell, and she'd make sure the book was prepared and ready for thaumaturgy travel.

Florence had been sitting at the study desk for some time frowning; she was lost in thought about various spells, particularly the Knoydart calling spell, wanting to ensure she uttered the right words in the correct order. When she finally began speaking, she stood with her arms dancing in the air like she was conducting an orchestra summoning unseen forces, holding them taut, drawing them in tighter before she cast the spell. I wasn't an expert in Latin, but I could make out some of the words as she closed her eyes and spoke, although, to be honest, most of it sounded like mumbo jumbo to me.

'Monjo luba anuado, seratne agantia. Antiquae sophiae sorores, vos supplico bibliothecariumque nostrum, ut mihi mittat encyclopedia symbolorum magicorum cum originibus suis, Larena supra duta.' Florence opened her eyes and glanced around the study, briskly brushing her hands together, and nodded, looking pleased with herself. 'Yes, I think that should do it; we'll just have to wait and see what happens.'

I wasn't sure I liked the sound of that, it sounded rather vague, but while we waited, I stood gazing out of the window, admiring the winter scene. Winston studied various books on the bookshelves while Jocasta sorted out her crystal and centred her chakras. Florence sat drumming her fingers on the desk, patiently waiting, hoping she'd executed the spell correctly.

We were lost in our own little worlds, I don't know why, but I was thinking about a messy case involving the first Sultan of Zanzibar back in 1870. He had an untimely death due to overindulgence in sensual pleasures and stimulants, but that's another story. I was brought back into the moment when an exotic-looking bird tapped at one of the study windows. I did a double take because I'd never seen a bird like it. It was about the size of a kestrel and had a shimmering aura like a rare opal; it was every colour of the rainbow.

'Ah,' said Florence, looking relieved as she stood and moved to the window. 'I think this must be my delivery.'

We all watched as she opened the window, and the bird spoke to her with a warm Scottish burr, 'Delivery for Florence Dearden.'

Florence smiled with delight, 'Yes, that's me,' she fluttered conspiratorially. 'Please come in.'

The bird spread its wings, 'I don't mind if I do, lassie. It's bitter out here; I could do with a warming wee dram; I can't stay long.'

In a blaze of shimmering colour, the bird flew into the room, settled on the desk, and immediately and amazingly morphed into an ancient leather-bound book the size of an encyclopaedia; the book had an ornate carved gold clasp. Florence closed the window with a shiver and moved back to the desk, taking a deep breath, 'Well, this is it. I must say you can't beat Effie Evander's magic; that bird delivery spell never fails to impress me. Although she must have changed it because she normally uses a shimmering Eurasian Eagle Owl - they're such intelligent birds. Anyway, I knew she wouldn't let us down. That woman is a genius, a master at her craft.'

We had to agree!

We huddled around the desk as Florence uttered more words of magic, and the ornate gold clasp unlocked. She then opened the book; it looked well thumbed. As she did, there was an eerie whooshing sound, like she'd released something under pressure, and the fragrant smell of spices from faraway places assaulted our nostrils. Jocasta and Winston quickly stepped back, 'Don't be alarmed,' said Florence calmly, crackling with static electricity. 'Effie told me this is normal; the book is a living thing. Over time its magic builds, and the book must be opened to allow it to reset its energy levels in the meridian of supernatural spheres and the megacosm.'

Florence sat down at the desk, 'Now, I described the symbol to Effie, and she told me to look at page 136,' Florence started carefully turning the ancient parchment pages revealing all manner of age-old wonders. 'We need to be careful; we don't want to activate anything; this book is like a cauldron of magic; one wrong word or a misplaced finger, and anything could happen... Ah, here we are, page CXXXVI, 136, and look, there it is.'

Don't ask me how, but the page looked strangely alive, like the symbol was dancing and winking at us!

'Absolutely fascinating; what does it say?' Asked Jocasta eagerly, peering over Florence's shoulder as Winston put on his glasses.

Florence readout the heading, 'It says attribution Madrigal Fortune and The Union of Insight and Illumination, symbol registered in 1799.'

'Hmm, The Union of Insight and Illumination,' said Winston reflectively, curling his lip. 'I thought they were nothing more than folklore and legend. It was said to be a magical society dealing with religious philosophy and alternative realities. I'm amazed none of us has seen this symbol before.'

We all looked at him.

'You've heard of them?' Asked Florence, her eyebrows shooting to the top of her head with surprise.

He nodded, peering at page CXXXVI, 'Yes, not that I know much about them, other than what I've just said. Is there anything else?'

'Of course,' replied Florence defensively, quickly scanning the text. 'Hmm, it says The Union of Insight and Illumination was a secret order based in Canterbury here in Kent. It was active in the early part of the last century. The Union practised and taught occult magic and alchemy to both men and women. Madrigal Fortune was its leader and founder, developing her own curriculum, teaching occult rituals and spells; she also ran an apothecary - love potions were a speciality.'

'Do you think that was her real name?' I asked doubtfully.

Florence shook her head, 'It doesn't say, but I'm guessing it wasn't. Anyway, according to this, Madrigal claimed to have an ability to contact certain supernatural entities, known as the Exegesis-Elucinati, who she described as authorities on the order of all magic, including divination, astrology, incantations, alchemy, sorcery, spirit mediation, and necromancy. She alleged they existed in the hidden fissures of the Astral Plane.'

'Exegesis means critical explanation,' said Winston. 'It's a word often used when describing religious scripture.'

Why wasn't I surprised!

'I've never heard of such supernatural entities or these hidden fissures in the Astral Plane,' bristled Jocasta waving her hand dismissively with a sneer. 'I suspect this Madrigal and her society was nothing more than a piece of theatre or a fairground attraction - love potions indeed. I doubt it was anything of any significance and substance - her name says it all,' she shook her head, chewing on her lip as her eyes flashed a warning. 'Mind you, she was playing a dangerous game if she was dabbling with the occult. Even the most accomplished practitioners can come unstuck and get their fingers badly burned, sometimes with disastrous consequences. I've seen it happen on several occasions.'

Florence agreed and continued reading, 'Those who completed her full curriculum became known as 'Grand Perceptives'. They were able to join an inner group known as 'The Dome of Grand Perceptives', allowing them to further develop their knowledge and abilities in the dark arts.'

'Hmm, it all sounds most sinister,' mused Jocasta pursing her lips, finding herself thinking about past cases that defied all logic and reason. 'Once people learn there is more to the world than they expected, some will want to stay ignorant. In fact, they will be happy to do so. While others will want to know everything, whatever the costs to them and others.'

She shook her head, pulling together her thoughts. 'Hmm, I find it interesting they didn't describe themselves as witches or wizards - I wonder if they deliberately avoided the term 'witch' to evade problems with the law and a stint in a house of correction... However, it's fascinating, and there's far more information than I expected. Do go on while I pour the tea; we mustn't let it get cold.'

'Oh, the information in this book will be the tip of the iceberg,' replied Florence proudly. 'The Knoydart witches are known for their attention to detail; that's why they've survived for so long; they're always one step ahead of anyone else. Anyway, it goes on and says Madrigal used a Ritual Table; its top was engraved with our magical symbol and covered with a ceremonial white cloth. The symbol was used on talismans and when performing enchantments. It was also used to call on spirits,' she paused... 'Hmm, that's interesting.'

'What is it?' I asked impatiently, trying to look around her.

Florence gazed at Jocasta with a look of acknowledgement, 'It says she also used a stone and mirror for scrying.'

'Ah, just as I suspected,' replied Jocasta growing in stature as she handed Winston his tea. 'My crystal is never wrong. Is there anything else?'

'Hmm, unfortunately, there is,' said Florence with a warning in her tone. 'Just one other thing. When Madrigal used the symbol for enchantments, it was often drawn in blood, blood being a powerful thing associated with life, death, and pain - the blood adding power to the magic. As we know, blood spells are an ancient and dangerous form of magic. I suspect that's why the symbol we've found in the music box and on the diary has that familiar red-brown tone. I don't know why we didn't think about it sooner.'

Just what we needed, 'What about the pocket watch?' I asked.

Jocasta put down the teapot, 'Ah, good point, dear boy. I'm

pleased you've mentioned that I've been thinking the same thing. You see, I don't think the pocket watch was ever an enchanted gift to the family like the music box and diary. I believe it already belonged to Bernard Rothery. Madrigal or someone under her influence must have managed to put a hex on it. I'm sure the watch acts as a catalyst for the magic attached to the box and diary. Spells are most potent when linked to someone's personal possession; think of it like dark voodoo.'

I had more questions and was about to speak as Jocasta raised her hand.

'Dear boy, please don't ask me how the Listan's or Madrigal Fortune managed such time travelling magic because I've no idea - we'll probably never know, other than to say complex dark magic from the vaults of time is involved.'

Florence carefully closed the book and fastened the gold clasp by casting another spell, 'Well, it's a good question,' she said decidedly. 'I, for one, would certainly like to know how they did it, as would any witch worth her salt.'

Winston put down his tea and took the piece of paper with the symbol from his wallet, the one we found in the music box, putting it next to the red symbol on the 1861 diary; his face fell into a thoughtful frown. 'I'm confused; what does Madrigal Fortune and The Union of Insight and Illumination have to do with The Sisters of Listan? Do you think the sisters attended Madrigal's magical order?'

I shook my head; that didn't sound right to me, 'From what Mother Frobisher told us, I can't see that. I didn't get the impression the sisters had any interest in spells, magic, or involvement with the occult. Mother described them as a force for good, using their knowledge of plants and remedies for healing, not as a force for evil. Nothing we've found so far suggests otherwise,' I glanced at the beautiful music box and diary; they looked so innocent, no one would ever guess they were enchanted with dark magic. 'No, the Listan Sisters came unstuck, not because of their reputation as healers or witches, but because of their land. Their crime, if you can call it that, was claiming ownership of their land, fighting every step of the way to keep it until their voices became too loud, and they had to be silenced.'

'Jasper's right,' proffered Jocasta, carefully passing Florence her tea, trying not to spill any into the saucer. 'And thinking about the mystery that hangs over the Rothery family, this house, and the land, Madrigal must have used blood from the Listan sisters to seal her spell or curse. I believe the blood was from Marigold as the matriarch – we know she survived prison. I need to consult my crystal; I'm sure we're missing something,' her mouth tightened as her thoughts turned to something else. 'And where could that stone and mirror be?'

***

Florence had sent the book of symbols back to Effie Evander; the bird told her she could only keep it for a few hours as it drank a wee dram of fortifying Scottish whisky; the book was wanted at a Knoydart coven on the island of Haiti. Ethel brought in another tray of tea and some of her homemade shortbread biscuits, Christmas cake, and mince pies; she was covered in flour from her breadmaking, but her efforts had brought some colour to her cheeks. Agnes and Clementine were still at the piano rehearsing their Christmas repertoire, going through their octaves - it sounded painful. I did wonder if them having guests on Christmas Day was such a good idea, given we were heading into the unknown, but it was too late to turn back now.

Jocasta was engrossed in her crystal; she'd been absorbed with it for some time, centring her chakras, becoming at one with the Astral Plane and spiritual highway. However, she couldn't resist taking a break for tea, biscuits, and cakes; they were too distracting, not that Winston and Florence were any better where tea and cake were concerned!

Once they were fully replenished, Jocasta returned to her crystal. The three of us waited patiently; Winston busied himself writing up proceedings of our case in his trusty notebook, with Florence helping to verify his memory of events. My mind wandered to past cases. I lost track of time...

'Ah, at last, I think I've had an eventuation,' declared Jocasta scrunching up her face and breaking the silence. 'For some reason, the mystical networks are incredibly busy today. Christmas can be a busy time in the spirit world; the spirits are drawn back to their families, wanting to send them Christmas wishes and messages of love, joy, and goodwill. Anyway, I'm sure I've made a breakthrough.'

I hoped so; she had our full attention.

Jocasta stared into her crystal, her eyes burning into its sparkling core, 'I can see Marigold Listan; she met Madrigal Fortune in prison after Rose died. Like her, Madrigal had been imprisoned on charges of witchcraft, although Madrigal was also charged with extortion. Perhaps the charges of witchcraft gave them something in common, although the two women couldn't have been more different,' Jocasta slowly turned her crystal in her hands. 'Madrigal must have helped Marigold to place a far-reaching curse on Bernard Rothery using her knowledge of the occult and dark arts.'

'You can see all that in your crystal?' I asked doubtfully.

Jocasta nodded, still staring deep into her crystal, 'Yes, as clear as day. I can see that Bernard Rothery was also responsible for Madrigal's imprisonment. I suspect with all the injustices of the legal system and prison back in their day, Madrigal also wanted revenge. I doubt she would have taken much persuading to help the Listan sisters with their plight.'

I had to agree; many things could trigger a need for revenge. I knew once it took hold, it could consume people and eat them up until they lost all trace of themselves; I'd seen it happen many times. I looked at Jocasta, 'Yes, but we're talking about polar opposites. The Listan's worked for the greater good, while Madrigal was peddling and teaching evil, developing a cult seemingly for her own financial gain, power, and status.'

Winston took his pipe from his jacket pocket, shaking his head, 'It's all getting increasingly complicated.'

'Nonsense,' bristled Jocasta raising her head from her crystal. 'When has the spirit world ever been straightforward?'

Which was true!

'Now we have most of the facts; I need to contact Titus and pick his brains. As Miss Tilling always says, you can't make an omelette without breaking eggs.'

'Miss Tilling?' I asked, intrigued.

'Yes, she's famous in my village for her Seville orange marmalade. She always wins the Marmalade section at the Folkstone Summer Fete; she's become quite the local celebrity and is known as the marmalade queen; she says it's all in the zest,' Jocasta smiled to herself, looking quite satisfied. 'Anyway, I fear we're wasting time; it's Christmas Day tomorrow. I'm sure that's when we'll need to act. Otherwise, I fear we'll be too late, miss the moment and will have to return next Christmas. Titus will hopefully point us in the right direction so we can put this case and mystery to bed once and for all,' Jocasta stood up stiffly and put her hands on her hips, glancing around the room. 'Right, let's prepare for a séance and really put our backs into it.'

Preparing for a séance involved drawing the curtains to darken the room, although some light still peeped around their edges, and we had the warm glow of burnt orange hues from the fire. Jocasta told Agnes, Clementine, and Ethel we didn't want to be disturbed. Then while the three of us sat at a small table, she spent some time preparing herself in case she needed to go into a trance. This involved her dancing around the table doing random pirouettes while she hummed one of Titus's favourite songs. His current preference turned out to be the Eddie Cantor song Makin Whoopie! I didn't know if all of this was necessary, but it played to his ego. Watching Jocasta dancing around the table in her divided skirt and singing the song was comical, but none of us laughed; I dared not look at the others.

'Yes, I think that should do it,' she muttered, sitting down slowly, sounding breathless. 'Now, join hands and let your minds go blank; let it wander into the void of empty spaces between the parallel dimensions in the multiverse, centre on your core chakra, that spinning disk of energy keeping it open and fully aligned.'

As a time-travelling ghost, I didn't know if I had any 'chakras', but the four of us sat in silence in the semi-darkness, trying to let our minds go blank. The only sounds came from the crackling fire, the birds twittering outside in the snow, and the creaks of an old house.

Jocasta took a deep breath, closing her eyes, 'Titus, Titus, can you hear me, dear? Are you there?'

Silence...

'Titus, are you there?'

Silence...

Jocasta sighed wearily and forced a patient smile, 'Titus, are you there dear?' ... The windows rattled as the fire dipped, and a sigh of air pushed under the door as the curtains fluttered...

Jocasta stiffened as her eyes shot open, 'What do I want? ... Well, really dear, there's no need to be like that.' Jocasta glanced at the three of us apologetically and whispered, 'I think he's stressed; as you know, he has a very delicate nature.'

I didn't know why she always made excuses for his diva-like behaviour. We had this performance every time she contacted him.

Jocasta continued, 'Hmm, but now you mention it, Titus dear, there is a little matter I need your help with... You're too busy... You're helping D H Lawrence, the English writer, novelist, poet, and essayist, with his new book... What's that, dear?... His works include Sons and Lovers, The Rainbow, Women in Love, and Lady Chatterley's Lover... Yes dear, of course, we've heard of him; he had quite a reputation... His reputation took away from his considerable talents... You think he's the greatest imaginative novelist of his generation and has artistic integrity and moral seriousness... Yes dear, I'm sure you're right... What's that?... His next book, the one you're helping him with, will be a work of genius... The Greek philosopher Socrates thinks it could be the best book ever written....'

Jocasta sighed again, trying to build her resolve, 'Yes dear, I'm sure it will... Now Titus, we mustn't let D H Lawrence, as talented as he is, distract us - as always, time is the essence. I'm dealing with a curse, a blood curse... Yes dear, that's what I said, a blood curse... Now, please don't be like that dear... I know they're difficult to deal with... I'm looking for Marigold Listan and a Madrigal Fortune from the last century.'

The table started shaking violently; we had to hold tight to keep it on the floor, 'Titus, stop that at one... really dear... What's that?... Well, I think Madrigal Fortune was an occultist, but Marigold Listan was a healer who, while in prison, may have come under Madrigal's influence in tragic circumstances... You will need to check with the Bureau of Occult Witches, the Bureau of Wise Women, and the Bureau of Curses... I see. Can you do that now, dear? Oh, and I'm also looking for a scrying mirror and stone....'

The table started banging and shaking violently; Jocasta raised her voice, going red in the face, 'Titus, I won't tell you again, I won't put up with this sort of thing and your childish theatrics – really, it's most vexing... The dearly departed Madame Tromberg, the famous medium, is willing to act as my guide if you're getting bored and distracted with other things; in fact, she's most insistent...' Silence... 'Now dear, stop this sulking and let me quickly explain what's happening - we don't have all day... You have a headache; well, take something for it dear while I tell you what we know....'

Jocasta explained our findings. We then waited while Titus sorted out his headache and went to investigate and consult with various spiritual bureaus, trying to cut through all their red tape and bureaucracy. Luckily, he made it his business to be well connected and know all the elites....

I stood up and put more logs on the fire; it sprung back to life as it spat and crackled, casting a dancing amber glow into the heart of the room. Jocasta yawned loudly, which made Florence and Winston yawn, 'Oh, do excuse me, I don't know about you, but I'm ready for some lunch. I know that's not like me; it must be this cold weather.'

I didn't say anything as much as I was tempted!

Jocasta drummed her fingers on the table impatiently. 'I do hope Titus won't be much longer; my chakras are quite drained... Ah, speak of the devil... Yes dear, we're still all here patiently waiting... Yes, I know these things take time, and I'm most grateful for all your efforts. Have you had any luck?... You have - excellent... I need to check the music box where I'll find the mirror and stone in the form of a necklace. The blood curse partly comes from a type of magic used on the Necklace of Harmonia.'

'The Necklace of Harmonia!' Exclaimed Winston going ashen; Florence didn't look much better.

Jocasta nodded nervously, biting her lip, '... Yes dear, I'm still here... Of course, I'm listening... Yes, I promise we'll follow any instructions to the letter....'

Chapter 12

I pulled back the curtains, narrowing my eyes against the glare from the snow; the sky had turned from icy blue to a silver grey as heavy clouds gathered, and twirling snowflakes fluttered to the ground. The others stood up and walked around the room to stretch their legs; they looked preoccupied and worried, as was I. 'What is The Necklace of Harmonia?' I asked tentatively, sensing their unease; I knew it wouldn't be good news from their earlier reactions.

Winston rubbed his eyes as they adjusted to the light, 'Like Madrigal Fortune's Union of Insight and Illumination, I haven't heard it mentioned in years,' he said, shaking his head reflectively. 'Our cases turn up so many unexpected things. The necklace was a fabled object in Greek mythology,' he glanced uneasily at Jocasta and Florence. 'According to legend, it brought great misfortune to all its wearers or owners, who were primarily queens and princesses of the ill-fated House of Thebes.'

Florence shivered and moved towards the fire, 'If my memory serves me right, the myth has it that Hephaestus, the blacksmith of the Olympian gods, discovered his wife, Aphrodite, goddess of love, having an affair with Ares, the god of war. Aphrodite bore a daughter, Harmonia, with Ares; Harmonia was later betrothed to Cadmus of Thebes. Upon hearing of the royal engagement, Hephaestus presented Harmonia with an exquisite necklace as a wedding gift. The necklace was cursed to bring disaster to anyone who wore it.

'Yes, that's right,' continued Winston; as a historian, I could see he wanted to tell this tale. 'The necklace allowed any woman wearing it to remain eternally young and beautiful.'

'Hmm, vanity,' mused Jocasta looking dour. 'The narcissistic desire for eternal youth and beauty – those insecurities are as old as time itself,' she shook her head disapprovingly and started finger-wagging. 'Throughout history, gullible women have used lotions and potions containing all manner of dangers believing it would keep them beautiful. In extreme cases, the fear of ageing had desperate women resorting to any number of grotesque horrors to stay young, often ending in disaster - even madness.'

'Indeed,' agreed Winston raising his eyebrows and contorting his mouth. 'Thus, in Greek myths, the necklace became a much-coveted object amongst women of the House of Thebes. Although no detailed description of the necklace exists, it is mentioned in ancient Greek passages as being of beautifully wrought gold, in the shape of two serpents whose open mouths formed a clasp; the necklace was inlaid with precious jewels.'

Florence shuddered, rubbing her hands together in front of the fire, 'As the necklace passed down the generations, it continued to bring disaster to family descendants, who all suffered various personal tragedies. Ultimately, the necklace was entrusted to the Temple of Athena at Delphi to prevent further disaster amongst human wearers. However, the necklace was stolen during the Third Sacred War in 356 BC by the tyrant Phayllus, one of the Phocian leaders, who gave the necklace to his mistress, bringing more misery. After she wore the necklace, her son was seized with madness and set fire to the house, where she perished with all her worldly treasures. After the story of Phayllus's mistress, the cursed necklace vanished; no one knows what happened to it.'

'Hmm, well it sounds like Madrigal Fortune knew,' I replied grimly, looking at Jocasta, who was examining the music box, shaking it gently. Of course, it didn't rattle; if it had, I'm sure we'd have spotted it earlier.

'We're not looking for the Necklace of Harmonia,' she said pointedly. 'Titus used it as a comparison to describe the origins of

Madrigal's magic in the curse. She must have known about the necklace's power, which isn't unusual given its fame. Although I must admit, until today, I didn't believe it existed; I thought it was just another myth from ancient Greek religion,' Jocasta sat down heavily, putting the music box on the desk. 'You see, it's not the music box which is enchanted but the scrying necklace hidden inside it; I really should have known better,' she shook her head reflectively, annoyed with herself. 'I think I've greatly underestimated Madrigal Fortune's knowledge and occult abilities,' she sighed despairingly. 'I'm suddenly reminded of Miss Astrid, headmistress from the church school in my village. She wisely says, one's education isn't something you ever finish, and in terms of the spirit world, that's certainly true.'

I had to agree; the spirit world was an abyss, a place of light, darkness, and hidden dimensions often best avoided and left well alone; the more I knew about it, the less I wanted to know. You never knew what might be lurking there and waiting to pounce. 'Let me see the music box,' I said, taking it from the desk and moving to the window and light. I began scrutinising it using my ghostly intuition, examining the beautiful ornamentation of angels and the baby Jesus. I carefully checked the music box from every angle, looking for a hidden switch or button... 'Hmm, I wonder... Winston, pass me your pencil.'

He looked at me curiously but took his pencil from his jacket pocket and passed it to me, 'Have you found something?'

I held the box up to the light from the window, narrowing my eyes, 'I'm not sure; give me a moment; I've found a tiny indentation near the manger.' I moved back to the desk, closely followed by Winston and Florence. I took the pencil and gently pushed the point into the indentation, there was a satisfying click, and a secret drawer opened in the base of the music box.

'Dear boy, well done, but do be careful, said Jocasta nervously. 'We don't want to release anything else into this troubled house.'

I nodded in agreement and carefully pulled open the drawer revealing a chain necklace of tiny mirrors and polished stones; the stones were all carved with our symbol. The necklace arranged in a circle sitting on a bed of black silk.

Jocasta bent down, peering at the necklace for a long moment rubbing her chin... 'Well, there's no denying this is the work of Madrigal Fortune and her Union of Insight and Illumination. Her symbol is carved onto every polished stone - what trouble she went to for the sisters of Listan in their quest for revenge.'

'I don't think she did it for purely altruistic reasons,' I said stiffly. 'But her own desire and thirst for revenge - I wonder what happened to her?'

Winston put on his glasses to study the necklace, 'The Union of Insight and Illumination seemed to have been disbanded at some point, fading into folklore,' he said. 'Possibly when Madrigal was imprisoned. Those who dabbled with the occult often paid a high price with their own safety and mortality - Titus may know.'

Jocasta ran her finger along the top of the music box, careful not to touch the drawer holding the necklace; she suddenly jumped... 'Goodness, you gave me a shock, dear,' she said breathlessly. We all looked at her, 'It's Titus,' she whispered, putting her hand to her ear. 'What's that dear, Madrigal Fortune was trampled to death by a horse-drawn carriage in 1862... I see, how tragic... she rushed into the road to push a child out of the way... How brave of her, did the child survive?... It did... Titus, are you there?' ... Jocasta shook her head. 'No, he's gone, but at least he's paying attention.' She glanced at me, raising her eyebrows, 'Now you have your answer; it sounds like Madrigal wasn't all bad. But then again, people rarely are – in my experience, they're multidimensional, some with a propensity for good and others evil.'

Jocasta returned her attention to the music box and necklace. 'This looks like an innocent charm, the sort of thing you mind find at a country fair, yet it's powerful and holds mystical energy; I can sense it in my vibrations,' she stepped back to get a better look at the necklace standing next to Winston. 'Thankfully, it's dormant now, but it must become active at this time of year. Its magic, combined with the enchantments held in the pocket watch and diary, keep generations of the Rothery family in a loop of torment and misery.'

'And Bernard Rothery's gravestone,' I said pointedly. 'We mustn't forget that - it shares the same enchantment.' I patted the cover of the innocent-looking diary, 'And let's not forget the hidden text in this. Did Titus say anything about that?'

Jocasta picked up her crystal and carefully put it in her Gladstone bag, 'As a matter of fact, he did,' she replied knowingly. 'Titus thinks anything in the diary is only visible to its intended target, and I agree with him. Although I can't help feeling the book holds another secret or isn't quite what it appears to be.'

That sounded ominous, 'How do you mean?'

Jocasta shook her head thoughtfully, 'Oh, I don't know, at least not yet, but there is something,' she hesitated, pulling her mouth to one side, 'I'm sure there is something - something wrong about it. I may get a presentiment at some point which may lead to an eventuation.'

I sighed resignedly; it always felt like one step forward and another back, 'So, what now?'

Jocasta glanced at the mantel clock tapping her stomach, 'Food, dear boy, that's what. I simply can't do anything until we've had lunch; I'm quite worn out, and I need time to think about what Titus said; then we must make our plan for tomorrow,' she sniffed the air licking her lips. 'Yum, I'm sure I can smell ham roasting and,' she sniffed again. 'Roast potatoes, delicious; I hope there's some piquant mustard sauce for the ham.'

***

We'd endured another night of house hauntings; they were

getting worse; Clementine, Agnes, and Ethel had hardly slept. They were up early, spending the morning making their final Christmas preparations, which helped take their minds off despairing family ghosts. The four of us were up all night as we continued our investigation; we were now back in the study. Jocasta felt the study was an epicentre for spiritual activity and where we should base ourselves. However, she cautioned that we needed to be ready to move to any room in the house. She was uncertain how things would unfold over the coming hours, which didn't inspire confidence.

Clementine and Agnes's guests were a determined lot; despite the heavy snow, they'd braved the weather to attend the Christmas Day celebrations at the Hall. They were all suitably dressed for the freezing weather and occasion and had even brought indoor footwear, the ladies bringing heels to finish off their chic outfits. Under their many layers, they all wore their best finery, all grateful to get out of the cold and into the warmth of the house. The flames of the welcoming fires danced and blazed in the elegant fireplaces of the exquisitely presented reception rooms and huge entrance hall.

Clementine and Agnes were beautifully dressed in beaded cocktail dresses in heavy silk satin fabrics, Clementine in deep red and Agnes in moss green. They sparkled in diamonds, smelling delightful with perfect makeup and not a hair out of place as they floated elegantly from room to room. Even Ethel had made an effort in a dark blue, long-sleeved cocktail dress and tasteful jewellery. She had a less severe hairdo, and I spotted a hint of makeup, although I caught a whiff of lavender wood polish!

As they arrived, I counted twenty guests. Despite the inclement weather, they all sounded merry and full of the Christmas spirit, becoming more so as they began working their way through the brandy, whisky, sherry, and chilled champagne while reminiscing about Christmases past in the village.

Not that Muriel needed any excuse for a drink. She looked perfect and as polished as ever in a fitted gold silk dress with a draped detail from the shoulder; it emphasised her slim figure. However, I think she must have had several martinis before leaving the vicarage, because she hiccuped several times as she told everyone about her plans to open a dancing school in the village.

Everyone thought it was an excellent idea, with several guests demonstrating their dancing skills and how light they were on their feet. Although the Reverend didn't look amused and hovered nervously with a large brandy, hanging onto Muriel's every word in case she made a faux pas in polite company.

Miss Duckworth was onto her third sherry as she tickled the ivories of the grand piano, giving her rendition of God Rest Ye Merry Gentleman and Jingle Bells, with Agnes and Clementine chiming in with gusto, quickly going through their octaves.

The house smelt of roasting meats, herbs, sweet spices, and French perfumes. Ethel had spent all morning in the kitchen, rushed off her feet preparing the food, occasionally helped by Clementine and Agnes, although I'd call their role more supervisory!

Earlier Jocasta had briefed the three women about what might happen this afternoon while trying her best not to alarm them. Having a house full of guests was far from ideal, but Jocasta said 'needs must' and to keep the guests away from the rooms we knew were haunted. The mention of the word haunted made Ethel light-headed and rush for the smelling salts.

We hoped to break the curse on the Hall and Rothery family as we followed the instructions given to Jocasta by Titus. It was a massive leap of faith and journey into the unknown, even for the four of us, but more so for Clementine, Agnes, and poor Ethel. I'm sure they were nervous, but so far, they managed not to show it and were the perfect hostesses; the house was full of Christmas cheer and sparkle.

As we'd entered the study, we left the others full of Christmas merriment, happily making their way to the dining room for Christmas Dinner. The room was beautifully presented with boughs of holly, fresh flowers, and sparkling Christmas decorations. The dining table was covered in the finest French table linens with three silver candelabras, all glimmering from the dancing flames of the tall white candles. The candles help set off the elegant Minton, cobalt blue and gold patterned dinner service, serving dishes, tureens, sparkling Baccarat glasses, and polished silver cutlery. It looked perfect. Of course, we had to make our excuses and, without going into detail, told everyone we had prior commitments and would join them later.

I could tell Jocasta, Winston, and Florence were sorry to be missing the great feast, although I felt sure they'd make up for it later, that is, if we survived the afternoon and whatever lay ahead of us. Jocasta said it was essential we acted today; it had to be at three o'clock on Christmas Day. She was convinced there was no other way of ridding the house of the Rothery curse, not that she or any of us were sure it would work, the spirit world being notoriously dangerous and unpredictable.

Jocasta closed the study door, glanced at the mantel clock, and moved to the windows, 'Hmm, it's starting to snow again - I do like a white Christmas; everything looks so pure and still.' She shivered and drew the curtains, 'Right, time is of the essence; you all know the drill; please sit around the table and let your minds go blank; I need to contact Titus and see if he has any more information for us - let's hope he's ready to act.'

As we sat down, the windows suddenly rattled, the fire dipped as the temperature dropped in the room, *Be gone - be gone...*' Echoed around the room in a sinister hiss...

Jocasta stiffened; well, we all did, 'Hmm, it appears there are still watching eyes; I wonder if it's Madrigal Fortune,' she said, glancing around the room. 'We shouldn't be surprised, but we won't allow ourselves to be distracted.'

Jocasta spoke with a raised voice; I didn't know if she was talking to us or the watching eyes as she straightened her back, strengthening her steely resolve. We sat around the table and joined hands; Jocasta closed her eyes and took deep breaths centring her vibrations and chakras. She paused, looking at the mantel clock to check the time; it was almost three o'clock. We could hear peals of laughter coming from the dining room and the clinking of glasses as someone made a toast.

Jocasta cleared her throat, trying to ignore the intoxicating smells of food which permeated throughout the house, 'Right,' she said firmly. 'As I said, we mustn't allow ourselves to be distracted. Now focus and let your minds go blank,' she took another deep breath and looked up to the heavens... 'Titus, are you there, dear?'

The clock began to chime, indicating it was three o'clock... 'Ah, there you are, dear, and right on time... What's that?... Will this take long?' Jocasta sighed as her nostrils flared; she shook her head, clearly irritated. 'I've no idea,' she said sharply... 'You're asking because you have a lesson with Peter Carl Fabergé, the famous Russian Jeweller. He's teaching you how to make one of his priceless Fabergé eggs using precious metals, pearls, and rare gemstones... Yes, I know it's important to learn new skills, but really dear, now isn't the time; we're at a crucial point in our investigation. You need to focus; you can't allow yourself to be distracted for a second by trinkets and baubles.' Jocasta sighed hopelessly, rolling her eyes, feeling exasperated. 'Now,' she snapped, 'are you ready at your end?'... 'You are, excellent, then we have no time to lose, let us begin and do take care, dear, concentrate hard, and I hope you're right.'

Jocasta nodded to Florence, who stood up and began an elaborate calling spell waving her arms in the air, drawing on ancient magic, secret covens, and the winds of celestial time. Like all her spells, it had its own language, none of which I understood. Once she'd finished, she sat down looking exhausted, and we nervously waited; every groan and creak in the house became a potential threat...

We didn't have to wait long; from nowhere came a whooshing sound, like a bird flapping its wings, and the temperature dipped. The air rippled and twisted around us, taking on a hazy appearance like early morning mist; it had a strange petrichor smell; the past was about to play out before us. Slowly a court scene came into view. Four women stood in the dock, all sobbing, bar one who stood rigid, her face red with rage, filled with hatred and contempt.

'That must be the four Listan sisters,' whispered Florence, wrinkling her nose as she studied the scene. 'The severe-looking magistrate must be Bernard Rothery; he's passing his sentence... The red-faced woman must be Marigold; her expression says everything.'

As the four of us sat mesmerised, the scene changed to a grim women's prison and a woman in childbirth, then to another woman gasping for her last breath. The air rippled, and the scene changed to a gloomy-looking icy courtyard, the prison graveyard and three solitary graves; one was a child's, all had no name, 'Paupers' graves,' said Winston solemnly, putting on his glasses. 'They must belong to Rose, her child, and her sister Poppy; it must have been heartbreaking.'

The air twisted and rippled as the petrichor smell became stronger; next came the dreary walls of a workhouse. It was a place of cruelty and misery; I knew the workhouse routine well. Ragged men, women, and children were all separated but working; no one spoke other than the indoor staff, who were barking orders at each other and roughly pushing the inmates around. The scene moved to another solitary icy courtyard, the workhouse cemetery, and another unmarked grave, 'That must be the grave of Rose's husband,' said Jocasta sombrely, wiping a tear from her eye.

The air swam and rippled around us; we were still in the past but now here back at the house; a man stood on the landing looking out of the window at the night sky and moonlight; it was snowing, 'I bet that's Edmund,' muttered Florence. 'He looks broken, tortured – like a man only half alive.'

The scene changed. We were in Violet's room. She stood sobbing, looking at the large portrait of her and Thomas, the one painted in the colourful gardens here at the Hall. The two of them were playing with a little dog in glorious sunshine,' 'That must be Violet,' said Florence sadly. 'She looks even more broken than Edmund.'

The scene rippled; we were in the nursery. Elspeth sat in white night clothes, tightly wrapped in a thick wool blanket, rocking backwards and forwards in the nursery rocking chair, wiping away her tears, but as fast as she did, more came. 'She looks just like Violet - broken,' said Jocasta, her lip trembling.

The air continued to swim around us, and the scene changed to here in the study; a man sat at the desk sobbing, his tears flowed, 'This must be poor Montague,' said Florence taking a deep breath to steady her emotions. 'The Rothery family history is playing out before us.'

As we watched the tragic scenes unfold, I was so absorbed I lost track of time; Jocasta brought us back into the moment... 'What's that, dear?... Yes, of course, I'm still here... The time is nigh,' Jocasta quickly glanced around the study... 'Well, we're as ready as we'll ever be; I just hope you're right, and do stay focused,' Jocasta looked at Florence, who nodded to indicate she was ready. 'Now, try to stay calm - here we go...'

The study seemed to swirl for a moment; the windows rattled, shadows flickered across the room, the curtains swished dramatically, and the central ceiling light began to swing from side to side like a pendulum. The door flew open with a bang, and Miss Duckworth entered, looking like she'd seen a ghost; then, everything became strangely still, silence... None of us moved as we stared at her; she looked different like she was lost in a trance, unaware of us and her surroundings.

'Hmm, curiouser and curiouser,' said Jocasta in a whisper as she and Florence slowly stood up. Miss Duckworth moved towards the music box, pocket watch, and diary; they were all laid out on the desk as per the instructions from Titus. She immediately picked out the diary and opened it; as she did, it changed, becoming an old, ragged notebook; words danced off its pages, as did drawings of herbs, wildflowers, insects, and the familiar smells of nature, both good and bad.

'Ah, I knew it,' said Jocasta resolutely in a whisper. 'I sensed that diary wasn't right. That must be the sisters of Listan's book of cures, remedies, and magic, the one Mother Frobisher mentioned. It may hold the answer we need.'

'What is Miss Duckworth doing here?' I asked, quite bewildered, not taking my eyes off her.

Florence put out her arms, trying to sense the unseen forces around us, 'She must be related or connected to the sisters,' she said softly as she and Jocasta followed Miss Duckworth to the desk.

Jocasta stopped, putting her hand to her ear, 'What was that dear?' she asked in a low whisper... 'Ah, I see; I did wonder... Yes, you were right,' Jocasta turned to the three of us and whispered. 'Titus says Miss Duckworth is descended from Marigold Listan - Marigold was her great grandmother but died before Miss Duckworth was born; he says she's the only living descendant of the four sisters.'

'I did say there could be family descendants still living in the village,' I reminded everyone modestly.

Jocasta nodded, pursing her lips, 'Yes, you did, dear boy.' She patted my hand in reward like I was a pet dog. 'You can be so intuitive about such things.'

I looked at my hand then at Jocasta and whispered, 'So, what should we do?'

Jocasta put her finger to her mouth, Miss Duckworth took the diary, which was now a ragged book, and as she did, a faint outline of a man appeared; he was sitting in the desk chair; it was Montague. She didn't show any emotion or reaction and turned to leave.

I looked at Montague's shadowy figure as it faded away and then back at the others, 'What should we do?'

'Follow Miss Duckworth, of course,' said Jocasta sharply, already on her heels. 'We mustn't be distracted or lose sight of her for a second; we don't want to lose valuable clues which may lead to an important eventuation.'

We followed as Miss Duckworth quietly made her way through the hall, past the stately grandfather clock, up the stairs and onto the landing. As we did, we could hear raucous laughter coming from the dining room; a man was waxing lyrical about the forcemeat stuffing and gravy! Miss Duckworth stopped near the landing windows; we could see the faint outline of a man; he stood sobbing, 'That must be Edmund,' said Jocasta, still whispering.

We continued and followed as Miss Duckworth quickly made her way to Violet's room; as we entered, we could see a faint outline of a woman gazing at the portrait on the wall.

'What is Miss Duckworth doing?' I whispered in Jocasta's ear.

Jocasta shook her head, 'I'm not sure; it's like she's checking to make sure the curse on the family is still active and working.'

Miss Duckworth moved to the nursery; we could see the faint outline of a woman in the rocking chair, the chair rocked backwards and forwards.

Miss Duckworth turned, still oblivious to our presence; we followed as she made her way back downstairs to the study. Once there, she put the ragged book on the desk next to the pocket watch and music box. She took something from her pocket and pressed at the indentation opening the secret drawer which held the scrying necklace, expecting to find it, but it wasn't there. The fire suddenly spat and crackled, which made us jump.

Jocasta quickly steadied herself, taking a deep breath, 'Now let's see if this works,' she looked up to the heavens. 'I hope Titus is right,' she had the necklace and took it from her divided skirt pocket, promptly placing it around Miss Duckworth's neck. We all stepped back; I sensed the others were holding their breath.

Miss Duckworth stood motionless; we all did; at first, nothing happened, then the air buckled and shimmered like light reflecting off water, and slowly something ghostly began to appear by her side... an older lady in Victorian dress. Her shabby dress indicated she was from the working classes; tiredness and suffering were deeply etched into her features, she also brought with her a fetid smell. She looked confused as she cast her gaze on the motionless Miss Duckworth, the study, and the four of us... 'Where - where is this place, and what am I doing here?' She asked hesitantly, patting her shadowy self all over to see if she was real.

The study door opened, and Clementine walked in, 'Are there....' She stopped mid-sentence clutching her chest, steadying herself on the door.

Jocasta bristled and waved her in, 'Quickly, come in and close the door,' she snapped, heaving a sigh. 'Stay there, and don't move.'

I could see that wasn't going to work. As poor Clementine stood by the door open-mouthed, all colour drained from her face, and her knees began to buckle. I quickly closed the door, took her by the arms, and sat her down in a chair by the fire, telling her to take deep breaths hoping she could compose herself, but she fainted.

'Leave her,' said Jocasta flatly as she turned her attention back to the shimmering ghostly figure, 'You, I believe, are Marigold Listan?'

The woman hovered nervously, still taking in her surroundings; she nodded, looking perplexed and lost, 'Yes, how did you know?'

Jocasta moved in closer with one of her probing expressions, 'I'll come to that, but please don't be afraid; you're quite safe. I'm Jocasta Bradman, and you're at Rothery Hall in the year 1931. Our associate Titus brought you here at my request,' she turned and gestured to the three of us. 'These are my associates.'

Marigold's shoulders dropped slightly, 'Oh, is that his name?' she asked, lightening for a moment, giving a half-smile. 'He was most impatient, saying he had a class to attend - something to do with a Russian and some eggs. He insisted I came here; then I found I couldn't stop myself and felt compelled to come here,' her image fluttered, becoming hazy as she floated back, looking Miss Duckworth up and down. 'I feel a strange pull and connection to this woman,' she studied her. 'What ails her? And why is she so still? Does she have the horrors?'

'She's in a trance,' said Jocasta as she slowly circled the room. 'Actually, she's the one who called you here, although she doesn't know it.' Jocasta proceeded to tell Marigold about her connection to Miss Duckworth, what we knew about the Rothery family curse, and the tragic events surrounding her and her sister's demise, none of which Marigold denied. However, she looked bewildered and overwhelmed; it was a lot for her to take in... 'Marigold, it's time for all this to stop; no one can ever be at rest, including yourself, while the curse continues.'

Ghostly tears welled in Marigold's eyes as her image rippled before us, becoming stronger.

Jocasta stopped pacing, folding her arms across her chest. 'It needs to stop; surely you must see that yourself after all these years of suffering? Let Miss Duckworth release everyone from all this pain and anguish, including you and your sisters. It's time to put the past behind you, to spread your wings, to look to the future, to find some joy and have new adventures.'

Jocasta moved closer to Miss Duckworth, who seemed oblivious to what was happening around her. 'I assume Miss Duckworth is responsible for keeping the curse and misery of the Rothery family going? Not that she knows it.'

Marigold nodded, slowly dabbing her eyes as painful memories of the past flashed into her mind like a knife stabbing at her soul - the injustices, cruelty, suffering, pain, and torment. Yet among them were tender memories, moments of joy, love, family, and great friendships. She remembered her love of nature, the land, and the pleasure she gained from helping others; she didn't usually allow herself to think about such things keeping them locked away. She turned to Jocasta, overwhelmed, 'I believe it's her connection to my family that keeps the curse alive. Madrigal Fortune told me while ever our family and the Rothery line survived, so would the curse.'

Jocasta nodded slowly, curling her lip, 'I see,' she replied, gathering her thoughts as she moved to the desk. 'But Madrigal also told you how to stop the curse in case you ever changed your mind,' she patted the ragged book with its curled, faded, and torn pages tinged with yellow. 'I believe the answer lies in your family's book of cures and remedies.'

Marigold bobbed her head, still overwhelmed by memories of the past.

'What happened to you?' Asked Florence softly, moving in closer.

'How did you manage to survive and escape the horrors of the workhouse?'

Marigold shuddered; she hadn't thought about that period in her life for longer than she could remember. It was too overwhelming... 'It - it was the kindness of strangers, a Christian philanthropic family who somehow heard of our plight,' she dabbed at her eyes with her dress sleeves. 'Just when I'd lost all hope and thought we'd been forgotten and left to rot in the workhouse, my family and I... or what was left of my family were offered a place in service at an estate in the village of Chilmington Green, here in Kent.'

We could see she was drawing on her memories of that time, trying to maintain her dignity and composure and not feel overcome by the terrors and heartache of the past...

'With sheer determination and hard work, we managed to make a living and slowly rebuild what was left of our lives,' she wavered, looking tortured, reliving the tragic events of that time. It still felt so fresh and raw, like a wildfire destroying everything in its path. She shook her head mournfully, trying to shake the memories away, 'But things were never the same; we were changed forever, the past hung over us like a dark spectre, particularly me. I couldn't let it go... I was consumed with a need for justice and revenge for Rose, Poppy, and everything they lost – we lost,' her lips trembled as she wiped her ghostly eyes with her hand. 'The cruel injustices of the past still eat away at me like a plague, despite the passing of time.'

Marigold drifted to the window, hovering there for a long moment in silence, taking in the snowy scene outside. Her face remained expressionless; she looked adrift... '1931, you say? It's strange; I never thought I'd ever return to this place; I wanted to remember it how it was when,' she swallowed hard, 'when it was ours - how it's changed,' the scene brought more grief as memories bubbled back to the surface; she turned from the window, casting her gaze around the study. 'How grand it all is now. The things you can take if you have power, position, and money, never giving a moment's thought to the cost and suffering, it would bring to others.'

We stood in silence until a voice chimed by the fireplace, 'A good man built this house,' said Clementine firmly. She'd recovered from her fainting spell, regaining her composure. 'Montague Rothery was a good man, and so was his son Edmund,' she stood up stiffly and very much on the defensive. 'I don't condone for a second what Bernard did, such wickedness, but from what I've learned, Montague and Edmund were nothing like him,' she glanced at Jocasta and then back at Marigold. 'They've more than paid for the crimes and sins of the past.'

Jocasta moved to her side, 'Clementine's right, Marigold. It's time to stop this vendetta. I implore you to do it for yourself and your family, along with the innocent members of the Rothery line. Stop their suffering so everyone can move on in this world and,' Jocasta suddenly stopped talking, looking startled, and put her hand to her ear. 'Just one moment... What's that, dear... You've found Madrigal Fortune in the twilight zone and have her with you... She's watched the years of suffering at the Hall with regret and is ready to act at your end if required... Excellent work.' Jocasta grew in stature, turning to Marigold, looking like someone who held all the winning cards, 'So what's it to be? If you don't end this, I'm assured by Titus that Madrigal Fortune will - he can be very persuasive.'

Marigold dithered, looking confounded and lost again, recounting the heartache and pain from so long ago. What to do? Would she be betraying Rose and her husband, along with their lost child and, of course, Poppy? Then there were all the years of hardship, grief, and suffering for those left behind.

She looked at Jocasta begrudgingly for a long moment having an inner battle with herself... 'Yes – yes, you're right,' she muttered reticently. 'A big part of me doesn't want to let it go, but I know I must for everyone's sake, including my own.' She stood for a long moment as her inner battle continued. Eventually, she pushed her shoulders back and drifted to the ragged book on the desk.

She stared at it for a long moment like she was wavering and fighting with her conscience. Nothing could ever change the past, her loss, pain, and suffering, nor how she felt about the injustices and events of that time. Not a million apologies or attempts at recompense could ever repair the damage because it couldn't change what happened; those events were deeply engrained into her core for all eternity.

To cope with her grief, Marigold had tried to rewrite the past in her mind, but reality always found its way through. It was one of the reasons she delivered bunches of poisonous plants to Bernard Rothery's grave every Christmas. She wanted to show him she hadn't forgotten what he did and never would, ensuring he was still being held in torment to account for his sins. She looked up to the heavens like she was looking for a sign... Now was not the time to dwell on the past but to have the courage to move forward and let it go....

Finally, she began flicking through the curled pages of the ragged book, looking for something from long ago... 'Ah, here it is,' she muttered, staring at a page covered in mystical symbols, strange lines, and squiggles drawn in blood and presumably created by Madrigal Fortune. 'This page looks so innocent, almost like a child's drawing,' she said pensively as she tore the page from the book, quickly handing it to Miss Duckworth before she could change her mind.

Miss Duckworth was still in a trance and moved to the fireplace throwing the torn page on the fire. As the page burnt, turned to ash, and the smoke fluttered up the chimney, there was a sound like a long gasp. The air around us seemed to shudder and the room to tilt. No one moved; we stood nervously in silence, looking at the fire, hoping it would end years of misery...

As the fire burnt, the sad history of this house swirled around us on the ancient winds of time... First came poor Edmund, then Violet, then Elspeth, followed by Montague... Last was a spinning image of Bernard's grave, the place he was held in celestial torment... We stood motionless, not daring to move, watching the scenes play out before us in black and white until they faded away and back into the ether. Silence...

Marigold fluttered as she wiped more ghostly tears from her eyes. Had she done the right thing... Slowly, as we stood in silence, she began to change... Marigold looked lighter, younger, and suddenly unburdened by the terrible events of the past... I sensed that the house felt different - like it had surrendered to grace and was finally at peace...

Jocasta broke the silence, 'You've done the right thing, Marigold,' she said, offering a sympathetic smile. 'Eventually, we all must let go of the pain of yesteryear,' she cast her eyes to the heavens sensing celestial vibrations. 'Go now. You don't need to linger or ever return to this place or carry the encumbrances of the past. Go back to the Astral Plane and join your family; I know they're all there waiting for you. And what better time to be reunited than at Christmas - such a family time - I'm sure happier days lay ahead.'

Marigold's image rippled as her expression changed, her eyes narrowed, she looked distant like she was looking through the rolling mists of time trying to find something... 'Yes – yes, I can see them,' she said with surprise as her face broke into a beaming smile. 'Rose, Poppy, Lily,' she waved wildly with both hands calling out to them frantically, 'I'm over here - I'm here...' Gradually, her image faded away. As she did, the scrying necklace around Miss Duckworth's neck disappeared, and she came out of her trance. She glanced around the study, then at the five of us, looking quite lost. 'What – what am I doing in here?' She asked uneasily, looking at Clementine.

'It's a long story,' interjected Jocasta as she pulled back the curtains; it was still snowing, adding to the winter wonderland around us. 'I'll explain everything in detail, but first, I think we should join the others; they'll be wondering where you are, and I need some sustenance; my chakras are quite drained.'

Clementine agreed with a flutter, taking Miss Duckworth by the arm as she opened the study door to be greeted by raucous laughter coming from the drawing room. 'Just listen to that; it doesn't sound like we've been missed,' she trilled.

'You go ahead,' said Jocasta with a nod, 'and we'll join you in a moment.'

The four of us watched the two of them make their way to the drawing room, and once they were out of sight, I turned to Jocasta, 'Do you think we've really done it?'

Jocasta put out her hand, 'Oh, just a moment,' she moved her hand to her ear. 'What's that, Titus dear?... Madrigal says the curse is lifted, and she feels unburdened... Even Bernard Rothery can now transcend... Yes dear, I sensed that... Edmund, Violet, Elspeth, and Montague have moved on and are back together again... Yes, I'm sure they'll have much catching up to do,' Jocasta's face broke into a beaming smile... 'Oh, that is good to know and such a relief.' She turned to the three of us, wiping a tear from her eye, 'Titus says Edmund and Violet have been reunited with Thomas... What's that, dear?... You've never seen such rejoicing and happiness; it's brought a tear to your eye... Yes, I can imagine; I'm so pleased - it will be quite the celebration, with hearts bursting with joy... Thank you, dear, and yes, you take care, we'll speak soon... Yes, and merry Christmas to you; I know you need to get to your class with Mr Fabergé....'

Jocasta dabbed her eyes, taking a moment to compose herself, she was emotionally drained, and I wasn't surprised. Once she was ready, she took a deep breath, and we followed Florence and Winston, making our way toward the drawing room. As we did, I turned to her; I had a nagging question, 'Tell me, how did you know the answer we needed was in the diary or notebook?'

'Ah yes, of course, I haven't explained that have I - I had a cunning presentiment which led to an eventuation,' Jocasta said proudly. 'It was a calculated guess but also the most logical explanation. The sisters recorded all their cures and knowledge of nature and magic in the book, and I knew that diary wasn't right; it had the wrong aura. It will need to be returned to Miss Duckworth,' she smiled mischievously, hunching her shoulders. 'I suppose you could call it a family heirloom.'

The four of us entered the drawing room with its sparkling Christmas tree and roaring fire. Clementine and Agnes were at the piano, giving their operatic rendition of Hark the Herald Angels Sing; Miss Duckworth sat in an armchair near the fire draining her glass of sherry.

The Reverend sat opposite her asleep with an empty brandy glass in his hand; Muriel quickly topped up Miss Duckworth's sherry glass to the brim and then her own, 'Ah, there you are,' she said warmly, looking full of Christmas spirit – by that, I mean the alcoholic kind! 'I was beginning to think you must have left.' She hiccuped loudly and turned to a middle-aged couple. 'I was just telling Mr and Mrs Whitlock here from the Chemists that you're here redecorating the Hall.'

Jocasta smiled, acknowledging Mrs and Mrs Whitlock. 'Yes, we were, but following our deeply probing research, we decided the historic house is perfect just as it is,' she smiled sweetly. 'One must never mess with history and perfection.'

Muriel agreed with a flutter, 'Well, I did tell you I loved this place just as it is.'

Winston walked to the drinks cart to pour himself, Jocasta, and Florence a much-needed drink; they'd earned it. Jocasta was eyeing the large bowls of nibbles and boxes of chocolates.

I moved to one of the windows; it was still snowing, it looked quite magical. Of course, by magical, I mean in a good way. I glanced back into the grand drawing room and at the merry throng. I wondered how people would get home, but then I remembered Clementine said Mr Jenkin, the farrier, had offered to collect people from the Hall in his horse-drawn sleigh. We could only hope he'd paced himself with the mulled wine and Christmas cheer.

I supposed if people couldn't make it home, there was plenty of room for them to stay here at the Hall. I felt sure they'd all have a peaceful night, as would Clementine, Agnes, Ethel, and the past generations of the Rothery family, not just now but in the many Christmases to come. My ghostly intuition told me our work here was done.

A NOTE FROM THE AUTHOR

Thank you so much for reading The Christmas Ghosts of Rothery Hall. The Ghost from the Molly-House. I hope you've enjoyed it; it was great fun to research and write. For any new author, it's tough to become established, but it's motivating to know that people are reading this story, which has existed only in my head. If you have enjoyed the story, it would be fantastic if you could leave a brief review online to help other readers discover the book and series. If you have any thoughts on the story you'd like to share with me, you can find me on my website below: Amazon, Goodreads, Bookbub, Facebook, Twitter, and Instagram.

www.grahamepeaceauthor.com

ABOUT THE AUTHOR

Grahame Peace was born in Huddersfield in West Yorkshire, England, where he still lives. He writes humorous, paranormal, historical, fantasy/mystery, and fashion fiction. Grahame has several nursing qualifications, a degree in Health & Social Care and a master's degree in Innovation and Leadership. He worked for many years for the National Health Service in Mental Health Services before becoming a full-time writer. So, he knows about 'life' and the many challenges, ups and downs it can throw at people, which is why he writes books he hopes will entertain and offer some escapism.

His other interests in no particular order are, keeping fit, fighting off the ravages of time, the theatre, music, history, the cinema, good coffee, travelling, reading, cooking, oh, and the odd glass of white wine or anything that sparkles!

OTHER BOOKS IN THE GHOST FROM THE MOLLY-HOUSE SERIES

The Ghost from the Molly-House

Meet Jasper, a time-travelling ghost with a sense of humour in these eerie, historic, amusing paranormal mysteries. The Ghost from the Molly-House is a collection of four stories that will appeal to fans of antiquity, period detective novels, tales of haunted houses, cosy mysteries, fantasy, and all things that go bump in the night.

The first story is set in Haiti in 1933. While searching for some ancient stones, said to have mystical powers. Jasper finds himself helping MI6, who are looking for a missing agent, while investigating dark voodoo rituals, drug smuggling, and modern-day slavery.

The Fazakerley Incident is set in Wales in 1923 at a large country house and tells the story of a séance and a vengeful poltergeist.

The Castle Stewart Werewolf is set in Scotland in 2018, at a 15th-century Castle. The owners are convinced the curse of a werewolf may have returned.

The Pluckley Incident takes place in 1934 and involves a disturbed grave, symbols, possible devil worship, and the stealing of souls.

The Jasper Claxton Mysteries

Meet Jasper Claxton, a time-travelling ghost with a sense of humour in these eerie, historic, amusing, paranormal mysteries. The Jasper Claxton Mysteries is a collection of three stories that will appeal to fans of antiquity, period detective novels, tales of haunted houses, cosy mysteries, fantasy, and all things that go bump in the night.

The first story is set in Paris in 1900. Jasper works with a perfumier and spiritual medium to try and stop a sinister Brotherhood. Members of the Brotherhood are trying to become immortal and control the supernatural and natural order of things.

The second story is set in Venice, Italy, in 1934. Jasper finds himself working with MI6, who are investigating a research centre and sinister Artificial Intelligence.

The third story is set in England in 2018. Jasper is working with The Psychic Agency, a group of psychic investigators. The agency is called to the home of a wealthy businessman who's made his fortune from computer software and is a collector of ancient Egyptian artefacts. He's just gone through a messy divorce from his wife, who's a social media and reality TV star. He's convinced his home has been possessed by evil.

The Pluckley Psychic Historical Society

Meet Jasper, a time-travelling super-ghost with a sense of humour; can he help to solve a 400-year-old mystery? And can he stop a coven of ancient Celtic witches from returning? In these eerie, historic, amusing paranormal stories.

The Pluckley Psychic Historical Society is based in Pluckley, Kent, the most haunted village in England. Its founding members are the noted academic, historian, and Cambridge scholar Winston Hatherton, the white witch Florence Dearden, and the celebrated medium Jocasta Bradman. They are assisted by an 18th-century super-ghost called Jasper Claxton, although none of the society members knows Jasper is a ghost.

This is the third book in 'The Ghost from the Molly-House' series, and this book describes how the Psychic Historical Society was set up and goes back to the group's first two official cases in 1919, just after the end of the first world war. The first story, 'The Jewellery Box,' involves a 16th-century jewellery box made from precious metals, which is found buried in a garden and reveals a 400-year-old mystery.

The second story, 'The Book of Souls', is set in Huddersfield, England, at a place called Jubilee Tower or Castle Hill. The tower was built to commemorate the diamond jubilee of Queen Victoria and is on the site of ancient bronze and iron age settlements dating back 4000 years. An old book of spells is found, and once opened, it appears to have released something ominous.

The Mystery at Winterburn Manor

A grave covered in strange symbols in the grounds of a 17th century Manor, what could it mean?

Winterburn Manor is a 17th-century house and one of the oldest Manor houses in England. It has stood empty for over 25 years and is now owned by the famous watercolour artist Elspeth Potter. She has been painstakingly renovating the house for the past four years but has only recently moved into the property, living there alone.

All Elspeth knows about the house's history is that it was built for the wealthy Evesham family, most of whom are buried in the church graveyard in the grounds of the Manor. The last owner of the house was the famous author Edmund Williams, a specialist in world religions who wrote gruesome horror stories; he's also buried in the graveyard.

Elspeth doesn't believe in ghosts but finds it hard to explain what she hears and sees at the Manor. Strange symbols have been etched onto some of the wood-panelled walls, and objects and furniture move on their own during the night. The symbols have also been found on Edmund Williams's headstone; what could it all mean?

Elspeth is convinced that something evil is lurking at the Manor, and it's hiding a dark secret. She calls in The Psychic Agency, a group of psychic investigators, and the clock starts ticking as they try to unravel a decades-old mystery before they all become Winterburn Manor's next victims.

The Sirens' Call

It's the winter of 1938; war is looming in Europe. Jocasta Bradman, the celebrated spiritual medium, is taking a break in the Cornish town of Mousehole, England, a place with a long smuggling history. The town has been experiencing unusually severe storms; she finds a piece of driftwood on the beach and feels an immediate connection to an old Spanish Galleon lost at sea.

Jocasta feels something is lurking beyond the walls and beneath the surface of the town and sea. A mysterious religious brotherhood calling themselves The Dawn of the Invidian is running the Lizard Point Lighthouse. The isolated Bluebell Inn, which is never open to visitors, has a new secretive owner from Germany, and an agent from MI6 has arrived in the town; why is she here?

Jocasta calls in her associates from the famous Pluckley Psychic Historical Society to investigate. They join forces with the MI6 agent, and a race against time begins as they desperately search for clues to discover what is going on in the town and who or what is causing it. Little do they know this tiny fishing port holds far more mysteries and dangers than any of them has bargained for.

A Christmas Wish

A Christmas Wish, and the kindness of a stranger.

It's 1850, and Christmas is fast approaching in Victorian London. Miss Desdemona Ward has recently inherited a vast fortune, including a beautiful house in London's exclusive Belgravia Square, from Lady Agnus Maudsley, a relative she didn't know existed. Since moving into the house, Desdemona has heard strange noises and seen the ghost of a little girl asking for help. Feeling haunted by what she has seen and heard, she calls in a psychic investigator, Jasper Claxton, not knowing he's a time-travelling ghost.

Jasper brings one of his associates from the famous Pluckley Psychic Historical Society, Jocasta Bradman, a noted spiritual medium, back in time to 1850 to help him, and together, as the clock starts ticking, they begin their investigation. An investigation which takes them to the many slums of London and the Covent Garden Workhouse. Could a well-known story about Christmas also help them on their journey to solve this touching ghostly mystery?

Lady Fenella and The Fleet Diamonds.

Diamonds sparkle; they are bright, beautiful, and valuable, but could they hold mystical secrets?

It's 1937, and Lady Fenella Windsor Hawtrey, a beautiful, elegant, and fearless MI6 agent, is a guest at Christóbal Manor in Wiltshire, England, the fabulous home of the glamorous Countess of Fleet. Among the other guests are the Hollywood film star Rita Delphine, a Mahârâja, and Jasper Claxton, a time-travelling ghost.

The countess is famous for her lavish lifestyle, entertaining, and collection of magnificent jewels, in particular, a parure known as The Fleet Diamonds. The set includes a necklace containing a rare, priceless blue diamond, although legend claims the diamond is cursed. During a lavish soirée at her country house, the necklace is stolen.

The police are called in to investigate; at first, it looks like a carefully planned jewellery robbery. However, as the story hits the news and newspapers, the noted spiritual medium, Jocasta Bradman, sees something in her crystal ball and believes there may be something sinister attached to the disappearance of the necklace. She contacts Lady Fenella and Jasper, along with two of her colleagues from the famous Pluckley Psychic Historical Society. As they begin their investigation, they discover the blue diamond has a connection to a long-forgotten Indian deity and religion. They realise something is about to happen, something which they must try to stop.

The Mystery at Woodside Cottage

What haunts the centuries-old Woodside Cottage?

The year is 1937; following the death of his aunt, Oswald Fernsby has inherited her charming, isolated cottage. The cottage sits on the edge of Styants Wood, a dense ancient forest located within the Kent Downs and home to an Iron Age fort. It should be the ideal retreat, but Oswald soon discovers it's anything but; he had planned to live there but barely managed to stay there for one night.

Convinced a dangerous presence haunts the house, Oswald calls on the noted spiritual medium Jocasta Bradman to investigate. She enlists the help of her three associates from the famous Pluckley Psychic Historical Society. Their investigation leads them to Ightham Mote, a medieval moated manor house, and the work of the evil Witch Finder General, Matthew Hopkins, in the year 1645. They find themselves entering a world of ancient magic, folklore, superstition, and witches.

Printed in Great Britain
by Amazon

12006589R10142